ROMANCING MISS QUILL

Willful Winterbournes
Book One

Sandra Sookoo

DRAGONBLADE
PUBLISHING, INC.

ARE YOU SIGNED UP FOR DRAGONBLADE'S BLOG?

You'll get the latest news and information on exclusive giveaways, exclusive excerpts, coming releases, sales, free books, cover reveals and more.

Check out our complete list of authors, too!

No spam, no junk. That's a promise!

Sign Up Here

www.dragonbladepublishing.com

Dearest Reader;

Thank you for your support of a small press. At Dragonblade Publishing, we strive to bring you the highest quality Historical Romance from some of the best authors in the business. Without your support, there is no 'us', so we sincerely hope you adore these stories and find some new favorite authors along the way.

Happy Reading!

CEO, Dragonblade Publishing

Additional Dragonblade books by Author Sandra Sookoo

Willful Winterbournes Series
Romancing Miss Quill (Book 1)
Pursuing Mr. Mattingly (Book 2)
Courting Lady Yeardly (Book 3)
Teasing Miss Atherby (Book 4)

The Storme Brother Series
The Soul of a Storme (Book 1)
The Heart of a Storme (Book 2)
The Look of a Storme (Book 3)
A Storme's Christmas Legacy
A Storme's First Noelle (in the *Star of Light* anthology)
The Sting of a Storme (Book 4)
The Touch of a Storme (Book 5)
The Fury of a Storme (Book 6)
Much Ado About a Storme (in the *A Duke in Winter* anthology)

Dedication

For Penny Sue Elliott.
It takes a strong person to continue on after the death of a spouse.
It takes a stronger one to realize there is still a good life after that.
I hope when you are reunited with your beloved husband, you
can entertain him with stories of what happened next. I think he
would like that.

Dedication

Acknowledgements

Thanks to the following people who were willing to share embarrassing stories of their own romances from an older woman's perspective.

Ella Sheridan

Sandra F. Schehl

Molly Moody

Sherri Fulmer Moorer

Sharon Villone Doucett

Linda Dell

Belinda Wiley Wilson

Margaret Murray-Evans

Gloria Pastorino

Penny Elliott

Nicole Atkeson

Susan Burns

Angie Eads

Beth Trissel

CHAPTER ONE

May 1, 1819
London, England

"WELL, BUGGAR."

Arthur Charles Winterbourne, the current Earl of Ettesmere, frowned at the missive in his hand. It was from his mother—the dowager countess—and had originated at their country estate in Berkshire. Her spidery handwriting filled the few pages, front and back, as well as covered the margins. Obviously, she had much to say, for she'd taken herself off to the country shortly after his father had passed a few years back.

And it appeared she was now summoning him and his siblings there to keep her company.

With a sigh, he brought the letter over to one of the windows in the drawing room and tilted it to the sunshine. Then he began to read.

My dearest Arthur,
I hope this note finds you well...

Much of the next few paragraphs detailed her existence at Ettesmere Park and how her social calendar was lacking, for so many of her friends and acquaintances had passed on.

He skimmed that until he came to the gist of the letter.

I also suspect you've fallen into the habit of keeping yourself shut away from life and anything that smacks of enjoyment. That needs to cease, for though you aren't a young man any longer, you are still vital and have much love to give if only you'd quit being so stubborn.

Arthur paused to point his gaze to the heavens. Over the last few months, his mother had been adamant in her quest to see him matched a second time. It wasn't that he was willfully resistant to the idea; he merely maintained that lightning wouldn't strike twice. He'd had a wonderful marriage to the ideal woman, and to ask for another one seemed selfish and a tad pompous. No, it was best to leave romance and love to the younger set. He'd had his taste of it, and those memories would sustain him.

Regardless, I have found I'm rather lonely without your father. This house is so big and empty without my family to fill it. All too often, I'm remembering how the years used to be when you and your siblings were small, and you'd run through the halls with shouts and laughter. Everything is so silent, and there are remembrances of your father everywhere. It's becoming difficult to meet all those ghosts by myself, and now that I've lived here alone for years, I'm wanting my family to surround me again.

So, I'm proposing this: come to Berkshire for midsummer. I wish to throw a ball like we used to when your father was alive, and that time is the anniversary of our wedding. It would be nice to honor him. During that time, there will be a masquerade, perhaps a fete one day, and all the other exciting entertainments I can think of that will entice you to come. I have also written to Sophia and Gilbert. Your siblings are all as resistant to familial gatherings as you are, but I hope to convince them. It's been an age since you were all together. I've even penned a note to your cousin, Louisa. We haven't seen her in ever so long that she's a near-stranger by now.

"Oh, good God."

Arthur glanced outside at the bustling Mayfair streets full of midafternoon traffic. Mother wished for him and his family to uproot their existences and come to Berkshire. As if all of them didn't have anything else to do. His siblings—Sophia and Gilbert—led their own lives and over the years they'd grown apart. Much of that could be laid at his own doorstep. He was guilty of shutting himself away to deflect the worst of the grief, both from his father's loss and the death of his wife as well.

Yet, he understood what his parent was feeling. The loss of a spouse was a singularly desolate grief to bear. That pain never went away. One merely made room for it in one's life. The business of living was still there but it revolved around that loss. Perhaps that pain and emptiness wasn't quite so acute as it was when the death first occurred, but it was always there, reminding one of what was lost.

He sighed. "Perhaps Mother is right, though. We should all take time to honor their wedding vows each year, especially for her sake."

Yet, he balked at the thought of making the journey. It was a busy time in London, and though he didn't take part in the social scene, he did enjoy spending time at his club with his fellows and talking about events of the day or politics. Parliament was dull just now, but that couldn't be helped. When so many men blathered on the floor merely to hear themselves talk, of course nothing would become accomplished. And there was also the problem of his nearly-grown children. They required his attention, especially since they would be home from their respective schools for summer holiday soon.

How had time passed so quickly? He rubbed his free hand along the side of his face. It seemed like only yesterday when he'd courted his wife. Merely a blink of an eye since he'd rejoiced in the birth of his second child. And now, his sixteen-year-old daughter, Emily, would complete finishing school in two years. Then it would be her Come Out. He wasn't ready for all that entailed. Dear heavens, once that occurred, she would want marriage... *Argh!* Already, his chest was tight with worry. To say nothing that his son, John—three and twenty just this week—should begin training to assume the title of earl in the midst of him prowling London and charming his way through the eligible young ladies of the *ton*, learning how to be a man.

Just as I did at his age.

That in and of itself was a large worry. There was all too much scope for scandal. Perhaps the summer was as good a time as any to take them both away from Town—away from temptation—and spend this last little bit of time with them before they, too, were caught up in their own lives and drifted away.

The irony of that wasn't lost on him, for that was exactly how his mother felt, and what had no doubt prompted her letter.

"Ah, Ellen, I miss you," he whispered out the open window. His hand drifted to his chest where he wore her gold wedding band encrusted with seed pearls about his neck on a chord. It had been the first one he'd given her, before he was ever the earl, when he hadn't much coin of his own, but she'd thought the bauble wonderful.

Now, he wore it as a remembrance, so she would always be close.

She should have been here at his side, watching their children grow and find their way in the world, but a particularly aggressive disease of the lungs had taken her away five years before. No doubt she would have adored preparing for Emily's presentation into society. His daughter deserved everything that special time of her life would bring, but he wasn't good at any of those feminine fripperies. He would need to rely on his mother's guidance, and that would mean the dowager would have to return to London for the planning.

He suspected it was something she didn't wish to contemplate right now, and yes it was two years in the future, but still he fretted. Being shut away by grief shouldn't mar the rest of living that was ahead. How, then, to accomplish that without seeming the specter of doom and gloom?

Yes, death walked hand in hand with life, and it was a razor's edge to balance.

As he lost himself in the breezy, conversational letter once more, rustling fabric at the door alerted him to the arrival of a visitor. With a smile, he turned and nodded to his sister. She sailed into the room, a bright spot in a jonquil day dress lined at the hem with embroidered white daises. Her cloud of blonde hair was piled upon her head and held in place with tortoiseshell combs. In fact, all the members of his family had the same hair color—even his wife had been blonde. It was very much a Winterbourne hallmark. "Hullo, Sophia." His middle sibling usually paid him a visit a few times a month, for she lived nearby but her health wasn't as robust as it should be. Or so she claimed. He suspected it was merely an excuse to not leave the house, for she was a widow two times over.

Damned death had touched them all and left every Winterbourne with scars no one ever saw.

"Hullo, Arthur." She promptly dug into her reticule and brought forth a letter, which was no doubt identical to his. "I assume you received a missive from Mama?"

"I did indeed." He held up his own sheets of paper. "Do you plan to travel to Berkshire?"

"I'm undecided." When she dropped into a chair with its pink and gold brocade cushion, she tucked her feet beneath it. The delicate gilded legs of that piece of furniture winked in the afternoon sunlight. "Traveling is exhausting and quite taxing. Additionally, there is Hannah to consider."

"True." Arthur sat on a matching sofa. He rested an ankle on a knee and tossed his letter to the space beside him. "Though your daughter is twelve, no doubt she'll think of it as a grand adventure." The product of his sister's second marriage, the girl trended toward a more studious, quiet path than the hoyden her mother had been at that age. Or so he assumed. He'd not spent enough time with the girl to know for certain how her personality had grown as she had.

"Oh, I'm not certain. Hannah would much rather tuck herself away on her window seat and read than venture out, and when she does, she's very much immersed into nature."

He snorted. "Are you sure that's what she wants, or is it your desire?" Though his sister had been a bit wild in her youth, she'd mellowed after her first marriage, and when war took her husband's life, she'd been lost. Upon her second marriage, she'd thrown herself wholeheartedly into that match, and it was from him she'd learned the value of finding joy in the little things.

But now that death had taken so much from Sophia, she was like the rest of them: wishing to hide away, nurse her broken heart in peace, and keep those memories close.

"Perhaps a bit of both." When she lifted her gaze to his, sadness lingered in those green pools. "Mama wants us to spend the whole summer with her in Berkshire."

"So I read."

She loosed an exasperated sigh as she unfolded her letter. "You know what the first of July is, don't you?"

"As if I could forget." All teasing fell from his voice as he stared back at his sister with a frown. "The anniversary of Ellen's death, as well as the same for your second husband."

That had been a dark time for the Winterbourne family, and none of them had been expecting any of it. Five years ago, he had kept vigil at his wife's bedside as she took her last agonizing breaths while a mere three streets over, Sophia had been praying that her second husband would remain safe while he fought in Belgium. Unfortunately, he never came home from that theatre of war.

"I'd rather not be social during that time. It still affects me so."

"As it does me." But he'd had to be strong for his children and niece while Sophia had fallen completely apart. That's when she'd first been diagnosed with the condition of a weak heart, from which she'd never recovered. Instead, she didn't really live any longer; she merely existed as if waiting for death to claim her too. "The trip will be good for you, though."

"I remain unconvinced." Sudden fear jumped into her expression, gone when she turned her face away. "Perhaps the stress of traveling will cause me to expire suddenly as the doctor warned. How will Hannah cope or survive with losing both her parents?"

Arthur's heart squeezed painfully as if thrust into a vice. "Surely the prognosis isn't as grim as all that."

"Who can say?" She shrugged, but her eyes reflected profound sadness. "On the one hand, it would be nice to see Michael and James again, as well as Papa, but on the other hand, I feel I must hang on for Hannah's sake, even if it takes everything that I am to cling to this world." She crumpled the letter in her hands. "It requires an enormous amount of strength."

"Yes, it does," he answered in a soft voice, for he'd fought that struggle more times than he was willing to admit. "However, I'm not giving up and neither should you. If we go, it will be nice to see Louisa again. Mother is right. Neither of us have laid eyes on her since she was a girl. We have no idea how our cousin has fared over the years."

Louisa was a second cousin once removed of his father's. Due to odd circumstances that had taken her to America and the Continent, she'd more or less grown up without steadying influences in her life, which had meant she was often in residence at Ettesmere Park in those early years. Though she was a good decade Arthur's junior, she used to have the gayest laughter and the prettiest wheat-blonde hair. Though the Winterbourne blood ran through her veins, the reasons behind her separation were dim at best, and Arthur had been too deeply involved in his own life to inquire.

"Perhaps." Sophia gave herself a tiny shake and once more focused on him. "I suppose for Hannah's sake—as well as Mama's—we should go."

"Indeed." For long moments, Arthur gazed at his sister. A longing to try and knit the family bond back into place grew in his chest, for life was far too uncertain to have those threads unravel. "What of you, Sophia? Should we go for *your* sake? You haven't been joyful for a long time, and going back to the park might give you a new perspective."

"No, I certainly haven't been that, and if I'm being honest, I'm bored. Life is somewhat dull without anything to look forward to."

For the first time in a long while, she was opening up to him, and he could scarcely breathe lest the fragile bubble break. "Will you marry again?" His sister was always happiest when she was a wife.

"Perhaps." She was silent for the space of a few heartbeats. "If the right man comes along, and if I have the courage to give away my heart again, knowing it will be broken, perhaps I would."

That was always the risk, and one he felt all too keenly. "Have you made it known you are searching?"

"Only to a few close friends, but I wasn't actively looking when my other husbands came calling. Our meetings were accidents, and they were glorious." She shrugged. "Perhaps fate will take a hand again if such a thing is in my future."

"I wish you luck." His sister was the type of person who needed someone in her life; she craved the closeness, the bond only marriage brought. How she continued to give out her heart in the face of risk, how she'd managed to survive the loss of two husbands was beyond him, for he couldn't contemplate doing all of that again. "By the by, have you heard from Gilbert lately? I suspect he's been ignoring me."

"No. He has been silent for me too." She frowned. "Once he returned home from India, he retired to the Berkshire property. I had one letter from him letting me know he was still alive but haven't had any word since."

"How odd." Arthur shook his head. Gilbert was his youngest sibling, and his life had been quite tempestuous. Even more so after he'd married. "He won't return to London to be with his wife?"

"Who can say? He's always been tight-lipped about his affairs, and since life moves so fast, I haven't had the time to ask."

"We must do better about renewing our relationships." He once more took up the letter from his mother. After skimming through it, he blew out a breath. "It's all too easy to lose people, and the regret is worse than grief."

"True." Sophia nodded. "What of you, Arthur? Do *you* wish to marry again? You're still quite an attractive man."

"Well, I'm not ancient, so there's that." He shot her a grin, glad when she giggled like she'd done in their childhood. "It's a difficult question. I was desperately in love the first time with Ellen. How selfish would it be to ask for the same a second time?" Besides that, how could he give another woman his heart when it belonged to Ellen? It was something he couldn't wrap his head around.

"Oh, Arthur." Her expression softened, made her beautiful and eased away some of the grief she struggled with. "It's not selfish, and there are no rules on how many times someone can fall in love. After all, I did it twice and perhaps wish for one more time before I expire." Her smile faltered. "It's rather wonderful to have someone special in your life, and love is remarkable when it's right."

That's what he'd had with Ellen. How could another love be that as well? It was too much to think about. "Yes, well, I'm not sure it would be fair to her memory."

Sophia uttered a huff of frustration. "Ellen wouldn't want you lonely or grief-stricken. She was such a happy person."

A grin sneaked across his face. "I *do* miss that. Her laugh, especially."

"I miss being wrapped in the safety of a man's arms. Oh, and I adored pillow talk. It was such a marvelous way of being closer to my husbands."

"True, but does that mean I should take a risk and have my

heart bruised?"

"Only you can say." A mischievous expression took possession of her face and her eyes sparkled. "Additionally, the distinct lack of intercourse that sends one flying grows unbearable at times. It's a good reason to consider marrying again."

"Sophia!" Heat rushed up the back of his neck and into his ears. Thankfully, he was spared from answering by the arrival of his daughter, Emily. "Hullo, poppet!" Arthur sprang to his feet and caught her up into his arms when she hurtled across the floor.

"Papa!" The girl hugged him around the neck. "I'm so glad to be home."

His heart constricted. Dressed as she was in pale pink muslin with a dainty flower bedecked bonnet sitting atop her blonde hair, she had the exact look as her mother had when he'd met her. "I just had a letter from your grandmother. She wants all of us to join her in Berkshire for the summer. What say you?"

When he thought she would balk, she vaguely nodded as she collapsed into the chair next to Sophia's. "It sounds like a great lark and in the country, I won't need to be quite as proper and prim as in London. And the air is stifling here once it grows sweltering."

"Good points, except for the proper deportment."

Sophia laughed. "You are absolutely right, my girl." She patted Emily's gloved hand. "Besides, we will all be back in London soon enough, so we might as well take this boon while we can." He didn't quite trust the twinkle in her eye as she regarded his daughter. "Furthermore, I'm trying to convince your father to court a woman again."

"Oh, yes, Papa! Do." Emily nodded as she removed the bonnet and let it drop to the floor. Interest and yearning lined her face. "It would be good for you."

Arthur rolled his eyes. "I'm not yet convinced."

"Pish-posh." Emily waved a hand in dismissal. "Mama implored you before she died to marry again and find happiness."

When an ache set up in his heart, he pressed a hand over that organ. "How can I without your mother?" He slowly shook his head. "Perhaps courtship and romance are best left to your generation."

She exchanged an exasperated glance with Sophia. "So, you will slowly dissolve into a doddering old fool well before your time because grief is easier than living?"

"I think, rather, it's a fear of doing all of that over again to the same results, and I've sadly been out of practice for far too many years." At least it was an honest assessment.

"You won't know until you try, Papa. Perhaps that is what's waiting for you in Berkshire this summer." She sprang up from her chair. "Now, if you'll agree, I wish for tea. Then we can all gossip before I examine my wardrobe and give it a refresh in preparation of leaving."

"Of course." Arthur watched her as she bounded across the drawing room to yank on the bell pull that would summon the butler. But the worry that had taken up residence in his chest didn't lessen. Though he fretted over his mother, his sister, and his daughter, he also wondered about himself.

Was remaining at the current status quo so very bad? Why did everyone believe a man needed romance in his life to feel complete?

CHAPTER TWO

June 10, 1819
Near Wokingham Village
Berkshire County, England

Miss Julianna Quill blew out a breath as she peered through her telescope at the darkened skies. By squinting one eye, the brass tube—much like the spy glasses sailors used while on the seas—brought the heavens into closer focus and allowed her to see things she never could with just the naked eye.

"Oh, you gorgeous things," she whispered to the heavens in general as the twinkling stars came into view. "Look at you shining so brightly and bravely."

There was nothing more in life that she enjoyed quite as much as star gazing, charting those stars, and perhaps discovering a new heavenly body. Everything paled in comparison, and oftentimes, Julianna dreamed of being among those stars. Imagine a world so advanced that it could send people into the heavens. What would that even feel like?

Slowly, carefully, she eased her telescope to the left until she found the North Star. It was always a favorite and made her feel comforted whenever loneliness crept upon her. All around, the nighttime buzz of insects provided a soothing backdrop. The scurry of nocturnal animals blended into those sounds, for there on Otis Hill—one of the highest points in the village—she pretended she had the whole of the sky to herself, and no one existed to tell her she was an aberration or a freak of a woman.

A soft wuffle from the overweight beagle at her feet meant agreement with her thoughts. She glanced down at her faithful companion of six years—Regent. He'd come by his name for obvious reasons, the least of which was a penchant for eating whatever he could find and considering himself oh-too-charming to female dogs.

"As if tending a man's house or letting him get off his jollies or bearing his children is the only future for a woman in these times," she whispered to the dog.

He woofed and rolled to his feet with his tail wagging joyfully.

"Yes, well, it matters not that I'm considered shoved to the back of the shelf and too old to bear children besides." Yes, seven and thirty was well past the first and even second blushes of youth. And yes, perhaps her chances had slipped by when she wasn't looking—or had her head buried in ancient star charts and tomes about astronomy that dated back to DaVinci's day, but that was also beside the point. Marriage and childrearing couldn't hold a candle to the wonders found within the heavens.

Though, to be fair, the stars couldn't offer physical comfort like the feel of a man's arms around her or give her heart a little thump or thrill as she'd heard other women talk about when referring to their suitors. And it certainly didn't matter that she'd attained this advanced age without ever having been kissed by a man. It merely hadn't occurred to her until much too late that she should probably think about letting someone—anyone—court her, but the pool of interesting or moderately attractive men in and around Wokingham was woefully small. The war had taken so many lives, and the ones who remained had mostly decided to try and find their fortunes in London and other places beyond.

Who could blame them? Berkshire County didn't offer much if one didn't wish to earn a living in a trade.

When the dog offered no further conversation, Julianna returned to watching the skies. The night was unseasonably warm, but she couldn't pass over the opportunity to observe the stars tonight, for there was a possibility that the anomaly she'd spied for the past four nights would return, and she fervently hoped it was a new comet that no one had seen or named before.

Or, it could also be merely a large cluster of tiny stars or even the fact that her lens wasn't powerful enough to properly identify what it was she'd seen.

"Buggar," she whispered to Regent. "Just once, I would like to have my work amount to something wonderful. That would teach those pompous arses of the Astronomical Society of London that women are capable of watching the heavens and understanding them as men are. We're even intelligent enough to understand what we're seeing."

Granted, that notable institution hadn't formally announced their organization to the world—it certainly would happen by the first of the year—but they maintained a building at Burlington House in Piccadilly, and she'd been there enough times trying to gain admittance in order to speak on the couple of subjects in which she was quite the expert, but every time those "gentlemen" turned her away, often asking of her, "What can a woman possibly know?"

Regent whined.

Julianna smiled as she tracked the progress of what looked more and more like a comet. Oh, to have it named after her! What an accomplishment that would be, and it would make the naysayers' mouths snap shut. "I'm going to succeed in this, Regent. Just you watch, and once that happens, I'm going to march into Burlington House with a glass of champagne, and I intend to toast my hard-won success without their support. They can eat their hearts out with jealousy after that for all I care."

Oh, yes, she had dreams, and they floated as high as the stars she currently watched. A life that was the same and expected of women in England was certainly not for her, and there was nothing wrong with that.

Except... it *would* be sweeter if she had someone to share that happiness with. As much as each little twinkling speck in the midnight velvet sky seemed to call to her, whisper to her to explore further, she wouldn't mind having endearments breathed into her ear under cover of that same night by a man who didn't think her odd or a societal reject.

A sigh escaped her and once more she glanced at her beagle. "Too much more thinking along these lines and I'll grow maudlin. It's too difficult to pull myself out of ennui once it descends, so I must ignore what I don't have and rejoice in what I do."

Regent woofed with acknowledgement. His wildly wagging tail thumped against her shin. Then he whined and rolled over onto his back with his chunky legs in the air.

"Surely you're not bored already? We've only been out here for an hour." Julianna lowered the telescope in order to contemplate her dog on the tattered quilt she'd spread out on the ground. When he made the sound again, she giggled. "Well, too bad, Your Royal Highness. I'm not quite done with my charting for the night. Find something to entertain yourself. Within reason, of course."

As if he'd been waiting for permission, Regent squirmed to his feet and with a bark sailed down the hill. Soon, his white and brown form disappeared into the inky darkness, but his joyful barking echoed on the summer's air.

"Silly dog." Her father had gifted her with the creature six years before. Regent had been abandoned as a pup, and her father had thought the dog might give her the company she craved since her brother had died. He would act as protection during her late-night rambles to watch the stars, for her father could no longer accompany her now that his mind was slowly slipping away from him. "At least I can work with no distractions." Perhaps Regent would find a burrow of rabbits to bedevil. That might tire him out, so he'd sleep through the night.

Plopping down onto the quilt, Julianna drew forth a note-book and pencil from the basket she'd brought with her. After lighting a single candle in a brass holder, she scribbled down the trajectory of the comet as well as the coordinates of where she'd found it tonight. Then she set about recording some of the more interesting stars as well as the constellations and planets that had been visible during her observational period.

An hour, perhaps two—she often lost track of the time when surrounded by the stars—a young lady climbed Otis Hill. Regent was cradled in her arms like a chubby baby. He happily licked the girl's cheek and neck, and if her giggles were any indication, she didn't mind in the slightest.

With a sigh, Julianna closed her notebook. She quickly stuffed it and the pencil into her basket and then blew out the candle. "I apologize if Regent has bothered you. He really is a rogue at the best of times."

"Oh, he's adorable and charming." Her voice was as melodi-ous as that of a princess in a fairy story, and the blonde ringlets that escaped from beneath her smart little bonnet were quite fetching, but she couldn't have been older than perhaps seven-teen. "He, ah, interrupted a clandestine meeting, which was probably a good thing, for the young man was quite a good kisser." She giggled again, but the dark concealed a probable blush. "Thank goodness for this little lad, else I'd been quite carried away."

Julianna kept her own counsel. Far too many starry-eyed maidens had found themselves in dire straits after such clandes-tine meetings with handsome young men. "Is that why you're out so late by yourself?" Over the years, she'd come to know quite a few residents of the village, yet this pretty miss had escaped her notice.

"Yes." The girl released a squirming Regent. Once on the quilt, he darted over to Julianna's location and slumped into her lap as if he'd been exhausted by his adventures. "I had to sneak out of my room by way of my window, for my father is quite vigilant. To say nothing of everyone else that's underfoot in the house."

"Ah." How interesting. That was something Julianna had never thought to do when she was this girl's age, though she could just imagine the heady freedom.

The girl came forward. She settled onto the quilt as if it was entirely natural to do so in a stranger's company and without invitation. "Honestly, I thought being in Berkshire would be dull, but some of the young men in the village are quite striking and entertaining." After a sigh, a startled expression crossed her pretty face. "Oh, but don't tell my father. He'd act cross and disappointed, for I'm to be a proper young miss ready to enter society in two years."

Julianna snickered at that. It was wonderfully refreshing to meet a young lady who didn't care she was outspoken. "Following the rules of a society who doesn't know a woman is alive outside their sworn 'duties' that are also laid down by that same society is certainly a prison sentence of sorts." She waved a hand. "I rather like people who skirt propriety."

"Oh, good!" The worry cleared from the girl's face.

"As a matter of curiosity, who *is* your father?" Perhaps he was a merchant who thought to use his daughter to attract a bigger fish through marriage.

"The Earl of Ettesmere. The whole family arrived in Berkshire to take up residence at Ettesmere Park for the summer at the request of my grandmother."

"I see." But she really didn't. None of those words made sense. "I'm afraid I don't know your father personally. I've only heard the title in passing, which means you've travelled a few miles to reach Otis Hill." As much as she championed independence in today's youth—women especially—it was reckless and foolish to be so far away from home in the dead of night.

"Oh, good." The relief in the girl's voice was evident. She leaned forward to stroke Regent's sleek head. "My father would only worry and then he would forbid me from taking another such outing."

"Frankly, so would I, but only if you continue to do so at night. I'm as safe as they come, but there are other people about under cover of darkness that are not." It was important she understand this concept. "In any event, your father is only looking out for you, I suspect. And furthermore, I'll wager you're his only daughter, correct?" She was certainly pampered and probably a tad spoiled, especially if she were a lady.

"I suppose he is, but he doesn't seem to agree that I want to try my wings beyond his reach."

At the last second, Julianna stifled a snicker. "All of that will come in its own time frame." In a way, she envied the young lady, for life—and her privilege—would take her much farther than she'd ever been able to go. "What is your name?"

"Lady Emily Winterbourne, but please, just call me Emily."

"It's all quite pretty. Much better than Miss Julianna Quill." The name made imaginings of a luxurious life, one full of parties and fine clothes, dance through her mind.

"But Quill is so fascinating!" The lady crept a bit closer, and she scratched Regent behind his ears with gusto. To which the dog fawned and began to drool.

Shameless animal. "You think so? I've thought it unique and oftentimes dull."

"Pish-posh, Miss Quill." In the starlight, Emily's eyes sparkled, and a grin curved her lips. "It sounds mysterious and clever. I like it." Then she offered a pout as Regent slipped from Julianna's lap in ecstasy. "You don't think I ought to be meeting young men at night?"

"I do not."

"What about in the daytime?" Hope clung to her tones.

Julianna couldn't help but laugh. "Since you're the daughter of an earl, if it were up to me, I'd agree to the scheme only if you took a sibling or a maid. You really don't want to ruin your life before it has a chance to begin." At least if the earl ever discovered this conversation, she had done her due diligence in pursuing his daughter to talk adjacent to proper. "I don't believe in clipping anyone's wings, for the world is large and interesting. Just be careful, be smart, and be discreet."

"That's much different advice than what my mother would have given, I think." A wistful note had crept into her voice. "Mama was forever saying what a lady should and shouldn't do. By those standards, I came to believe a lady will never have any fun at all."

"How adorable are you?" It might be nice to have this breath of fresh air come to visit occasionally. "But you speak as if your mother were dead. Is that the case?"

"Yes. Five years ago. I had just turned twelve." Her voice caught. "That's when I needed her the most, but I'll never again hear her voice or her advice."

"My profound condolences." Because it felt natural, Julianna reached out her hand and caught up the girl's fingers in hers. She squeezed. "I well know what that pain feels like, for I lost my mother long ago as well. Such a death leaves a hole."

"Yes." The young lady clung to her hand as she sniffed. "Oh, I apologize, Miss Quill, for burdening you with all of my blather. I miss Mama and I've found you easy to talk to, so thank you. I'm glad I found you tonight."

"Actually, I'm glad you did too." It was just what she'd needed to keep the ennui and envy away. She laid her telescope in the basket. "Perhaps another night you can join me here on Otis Hill. I often come to star gaze. I'm a self-taught astronomer, you see."

"How lovely!" The younger woman tipped her head back to contemplate the heavens as her hand slipped from Julianna's. "It's so pretty up there, almost as if the sky is strewn with wishes that haven't yet come true."

"Yes, indeed. It's a good way of looking at it." Julianna, too, contemplated the night. "It sounds silly, perhaps, for a woman of my advanced age, but I choose a bright star each night before I go home, and I make a wish."

Emily regarded her with interest. "Have they come true?"

"Some." She nodded. "Others, unfortunately, have gone astray in the nether, I'm afraid. I often wonder why those wishes never came to fruition, but then the thought pops out of my mind, for who can pine for something they don't know about when there are so many other interesting things to learn about?"

Oh, please don't let me sound like a ninny in front of this girl.

"I'm going to think over your words later. You're a very insightful person, Miss Quill."

"Thank you." She stroked a hand down Regent's side. "Well, it's late and you should probably go home. I shall escort you back, merely for my own peace of mind."

"That's largely unnecessary but I'll appreciate the company." Emily grinned. She was quite a pretty little thing.

Which of her parents did she favor?

Before she could speak, the lady rushed onward. "Are you attached, Miss Quill? You're out here alone, the same as me, and you're rather old, so I assume you are not."

Nothing like an unintentional slap in the face to make one aware of one's circumstances. But she took no offense, for every word of the statement was true. "No, I am not attached. I have let life pass me by while pursuing my own interests. You always think you have more time to get 'round to doing everything expected, but then, it's gone in a blink, and you either have goals met or unfulfilled dreams." She met the younger woman's gaze. "Just make certain you have no regrets either way."

For long moments, they were both silent. Then, Emily drew in a breath and let it ease slowly out. "Do you have regrets?"

Julianna offered a small, tight smile. "Not necessarily. I'm quite pleased with what I've done with my life. However, there is always the hope I can have… more if I wanted. Right now, more than anything I want to discover a previously unnamed comet, for then scholars in London will have no choice but to take me seriously."

Emily nodded. "I shall ponder those words, for I suspect you're quite clever and wise."

"If you'll rouse the lazy beagle, we'll head toward Ettesmere Park." It was at least a three mile walk there, and would be a three mile walk back for her, but she wasn't afraid of the darkness or anything that lurked therein, for who would think to molest a woman of no means and well past her prime? And she couldn't, in good conscience, let the girl wander around unattended after discovering who she was.

Emily nudged Regent to his feet. She took the leather lead Julianna handed her and proceeded to tie it to his collar. "I hope you find that comet, Miss Quill. It's truly interesting what you're doing."

"Perhaps I'll introduce you to star gazing soon." She took up her basket and then gathered the quilt into her arms. As they headed down the hill, she sighed. In a different life, she might have had a daughter. "What shall we talk about on the journey?"

Two and a half hours later, she stepped into the cottage she shared with her father just as the longcase clock in the parlor chimed half past the two o'clock hour. Her father was dozing in his favorite chair with a book spread open and abandoned on his lap.

"Ah, Papa, you didn't have to wait up for me." After letting Regent off the lead and depositing her things on a table, she moved to her father's side and gently shook him awake. "Time to retire upstairs."

He blinked at her with slightly rheumy eyes. "You were out late, girl. Meeting with a rogue?"

"Hardly." She couldn't help but chuckle. "Though I did have company tonight when a lady returned Regent to me."

Her father struggled to his feet. "One of these days, you will have to get 'round to snaring a man."

"I think it's rather too late for me in that endeavor." But she smiled. It was a conversation they often had on his more lucid days. "All I have are stars now."

"Then best make a wish on one, girl. No time like the present." He patted her cheek with a gnarled hand. Back in his heyday, he'd been a bricklayer and one of the best. "You are never too old. Remember that."

"I will." She followed him up the narrow wooden stairs and saw him into his room before she gained her own with Regent trailing behind.

Moving directly to the window, she glanced out and easily found a bright star, and fresh on the heels of a pleasant conversation with Lady Emily, she sighed as she worked the first button on her dress from its hole. *If there is anyone listening, I wouldn't be averse to something miraculous happening in my life.*

It would, at least, help pass the time and keep the loneliness at bay. But then she laughed at herself for being foolish and pulled the curtains closed.

CHAPTER THREE

June 12, 1819

T HOUGH ARTHUR AND his family had been in the Berkshire countryside for a few days, the bucolic vistas and clean air hadn't settled his nerves or lifted his doldrums as he'd hoped. In fact, removing everyone to Ettesmere Park had added an element of unease to his life, for as he sat at the breakfast table finishing that meal, his daughter had inadvertently introduced another layer of worry.

"Oh, by the by, Papa, I met a lovely woman day before yesterday by the name of Miss Quill. Her dog had run away from her. I found the dear thing and brought him back to her."

He paused his fork halfway between his plate and his mouth with a mound of golden scrambled eggs atop it. "I beg your pardon, but when did you venture out two days ago? I wasn't aware you'd left the manor."

A dainty blush stained her youthful cheeks, and she dropped her gaze to her plate while everyone at the table looked on. "Oh, I, uh had wished for some air and wanted a walk. So, I betook myself off sometime during the late afternoon."

"Yet you were with us for tea." The timeline didn't make sense.

"Right, this is true, but I left after that. It was still afternoonish."

"I see." Yet he really didn't. Once he'd resumed eating, he stared at his daughter.

His precious, innocent, daughter who was only seventeen. Surely, she hadn't gotten up to mischief already. And if she had, where the devil had she learned such behavior? Her mother had been everything proper, the perfect embodiment of what a woman of the *ton* should be. Hadn't she worked tirelessly to instill those values into Emily?

"One more question before I let the matter drop." When she met his gaze, he asked, "Please tell me you didn't have an assignation."

She snorted with apparent amusement or affront; it was diffi-cult to tell. "Really, Papa. I should think you'd know me better than that." As Emily pushed her plate away, she sighed. "I did not. I simply wished to take a walk and enjoy the countryside you keep lauding as a cure-all for whatever is ailing all of us."

That much was perhaps true. He had rather hoped this time away from Town—and pervasive memories—would give them all a different outlook.

"Very well." Arthur nodded with a quick glance at his moth-er, who shrugged. "Perhaps your grandmother could steer you into the direction of a few proper social meetings with people of your same age and class."

"Of course, dear," the dowager was quick to respond. The rings on her fingers winked in the morning sunlight. She bestowed a smile on Emily before moving her attention to John. "I know for a fact there are a few beauties who reside on neighboring estates. If you'd like, I shall offer invitations to their families for my Midsummer Ball."

To his credit, John hemmed and hawed, nearly choked on a swallow of tea as his face turned bright red. "That would be much appreciated, Grandmama. As of late, I've had rotten luck in the romance arena."

"Don't rush it, dear. These things often take time." She

flashed an amused glance at Arthur. "I've received word that Gilbert's wife should arrive at the park within the next couple of weeks."

"It'll be good to see her again." He frowned, for his brother was already in residence here but had apparently taken himself off for hunting in a neighboring county and would return in a week. "I'm sure Gilbert is anxious to be reunited with her."

"One would hope." But there was worry in his mother's expression. "Regardless, it would behoove you to perhaps keep an open mind in the same vein as your son, Ettesmere. You're not growing any younger, and you're a man who needs a woman in his life."

Not this again. Truly, his mother was like a dog with a bone. "I believe I've managed to struggle through these last several years well enough."

"You forget, my boy, I've known you longer than anyone at this table, and I know when you're lying."

"I'm not in the market to wed again." Why did everyone assume being single was a horrible fate? Granted, loneliness sneaked in at times, but still...

"Pish posh." She shook her head. A grin of victory curved her lips. "Never fear. I've sent invitations to many ladies. I'm certain you'll have a nice crop from which you can choose a new countess. You've far too much life left in you to knock about this world by yourself."

"I have John and Emily. I'm hardly alone."

"But Papa," his daughter inserted, "We're away at school most of the time. You're rattling around the townhouse all by yourself with nothing but servants to keep you company. Why shouldn't you wish to marry again?"

Damnation, this was rapidly growing out of hand. "Then you have all decided to wage a campaign against me until I'm matched? Regardless of what I want?" A sliver of panic wormed its way into his chest. "I loved your mother very much. Perhaps I still do. Why would I want to mar that?"

"As much as you adored Ellen—we did too—there is nothing wrong with wanting that same thing with a different woman." When his mother shrugged, mischief twinkled in her eyes. "Who knows? If she's young enough, you could have more children."

"Good God." A few gasps circled about the table, and to his mortification, heat climbed the back of his neck. "Babies at my age?"

Oddly enough, his son laughed as if that were the funniest thing he'd heard all year. "You act as if you're a doddering, stooped lord with a limp and missing half your teeth." He took a large bite of toast, and with his mouth full, continued, "I must say, the idea of having baby siblings intrigues me. I've always wondered what it would be like to have a brother."

"And they would be so darling," Emily added, which made things deuced uncomfortable to him, especially while his sister and mother looked on with obvious delight. "If that is indeed the case, having young children about is a good test for any man I might marry. Should the gentleman not show an inclination toward them, I'll strike him from my list of possible candidates."

Arthur tugged on his suddenly too-tight cravat. Though he and Ellen had wished for more children, fate hadn't deigned to fulfil those hopes. "I've had rather enough of this conversation. If you will all excuse me?" That sliver of panic grew into a tightening of his chest and the inability to properly breathe. Why couldn't his family understand that courting another woman felt wrong and an affront to his dead wife's memory? What he'd had with Ellen had been special—life changing. How did they think it could ever happen again with someone else? "I intend to walk the acreage, perhaps visit with a few tenants, and if there is time, take a meeting with my estate manager at some point. All activities that do not include finding a match I do *not* want."

Sophia shook her head. Understanding and sorrow warred for dominance in her eyes. "Perhaps you can do some soul searching while you're out there, Arthur. I truly believe that we are not meant to go through life alone when there is no need." Her smile

held a sad edge. "Our days on this mortal coil are precious. If you
have the chance to find happiness again, please promise me you'll
try and hold onto it."

As every pair of eyes at the table stared at him, he swallowed
heavily. "I shall consider it. Until then, I would ask that you all
respect my wishes."

Then he fled the room like the coward he suspected he was.

MEETINGS WITH THE tenants had been pleasant enough, as had
accidentally running into his estate manager at one of the taverns
in Wokingham village. It seemed all his investments and property
were performing as expected and would even turn an impressive
profit after the harvest. That was excellent news, and he intended
to pass along the largesse to his staff and tenants. Without those
people in his life, his title would mean very little. Already they
were content with his management and ownership; he wished to
keep them that way. When a man had responsibilities, he should
take them seriously.

Next time he visited, he would bring John with him. The boy
needed to learn the important values that came along with having
a title.

By the time afternoon arrived, his spirits had been buoyed.
Though it had proved a warm day, he reveled in the opportunity
to enjoy the sunshine and the fresh air as he walked the public
road that would eventually lead to the lane upon which the
manor sat.

When the excited barking of a dog reached his ears, Arthur
came to a stop. Looking about for the source of the noise, he
soon found it. A rather rotund brown-and-white beagle burst
from the trees at one side of the road. His brown ears flapped as
he ran, apparently overjoyed at his freedom, with his tongue
lolling from his mouth and his stumpy legs pumping for all they

were worth.

As soon as the canine caught sight of him, he changed direction and bolted over to Arthur's location. With an excited series of yips and barks, the dog danced about his dusty boots, stamping his paws upon them in an effort to gain notice.

"Ah, and who might you be?" He leaned down, picked the heavy animal up into his arms and then chuckled while the exuberant dog licked his face and chin. "Whoever you are, you certainly don't know a stranger." Despite the large belly, the dog was surprisingly muscled.

"Regent! Where the devil are you this time?" Though the hail and question were some way off, there was no mistaking the exasperation in the dulcet tones. "I'm growing weary of chasing your miserable hide all over creation."

"What sort of name is that?" Arthur snorted with laughter as he regarded the dog in his hold. "Ah, you must be named after Prinny, and if so, what a jolly joke indeed." He peered into the soulful brown eyes of the canine and grinned. "I believe your mistress is on the hunt, and from the sounds of it, she's not best pleased."

The beagle woofed with pleasure as he wriggled. This was no lightweight dog. He bussed Arthur's cheek with his nose.

"I mean it, Regent. Show yourself this instant. I don't have time for this nonsense." Seconds later, the owner of said voice broke from the trees and marched over the grass to the road. She held a willow basket in one hand and a leather lead in the other. A bonnet swung from its tied ribbons in the crooked elbow of one arm. When she saw Arthur and the dog in his arms, she sighed. "Oh, botheration."

"Good afternoon." He offered what he hoped was a welcoming grin. "I assume you're the owner of this rapscallion?"

"I am, unfortunately." She glared at the beagle and then rested her gaze on Arthur. The blue pools of those eyes had him unexpectedly arrested. "He has a nasty habit of squirming away just when I'm about to tie the lead to his collar."

"Such is a dog's existence, I'm afraid. Always searching for the next break of freedom." Though the burden in his arms grew heavier by the minute, he kept hold of the hound while looking over the woman with interest.

Of average height, she possessed a slender frame yet had enough curves to pique a man's desire. The dress of robin's egg blue suited her pale complexion and brought out another layer of color in her eyes. Curly black hair caught back in a loose chignon at the nape of her neck drew his regard to the elegant column of her throat, and as he came closer, the afternoon sunlight illuminated a sprinkling of freckles over her upper cheeks and nose. A tiny scar in the shape of a sideways V marred the smooth perfection of her forehead.

How mysterious. The need to know how she'd come by that scar took hold of his brain and wouldn't let go.

"Well, thank you for finding my dog. He's a handful at the best of times."

The sound of her voice wrenched him out of his thoughts. Arthur nodded, for he'd temporarily forgotten how to speak, apparently. "Are you from around the area?" Obviously, she must be. Otherwise, the dog wouldn't be so comfortable roaming.

"Yes. I live in a cottage not far from the village." She gestured with the hand that held the leather lead. "About a mile in that direction. Three from Ettesmere Park the opposite way."

"I see." He hefted the dog more comfortably in his hold.

She shifted her weight from foot to foot. "By the by, I'm Miss Quill. Usually, I recognize everyone from the village, but your face isn't known to me."

"Ah." Arthur glanced between her and the dog. "Oh! You're *that* Miss Quill." The woman his daughter had told him about at breakfast.

She blinked a few times in rapid succession. "Are there women with my name here in the village?"

"What?" That made no sense. Then he realized what she had asked. He forced a laugh. It sounded rusty even to his own ears.

Had it been so long since he'd done it? "Uh, no. Of course not."

Confusion filled her expression. "Then how do you know me?"

Heat crept up the back of his neck. As introductions went, he was certainly cocking this one up. "My daughter apparently met you two days ago."

"Oh." Her perfectly balanced lips formed an equally perfect "O", and he couldn't stop staring at those rose-colored pieces of flesh.

What the hell was wrong with him? Where had his manners gone? He knew better than to appear so vulgar in mixed company. After clearing his throat, he asked, "So then you've met my daughter?"

"Yes, I actually did. Lady Emily is quite a charming young lady." She quirked a finely arched eyebrow. "Did she mention when we met to you?"

Was the woman daft that she couldn't remember? "Sometime in the late afternoon. Beyond tea but before evening." What difference did it make?

"Right. That is quite true." Her expression cleared. "We *did* meet at that time." She smiled while the fat beagle writhed in his arms. "I found her lovely."

"She is that. I appreciate your acknowledgement." His reality suddenly came crashing back around him. He was an earl and a widower with a daughter who he suspected of sneaking out of the house. Why this stranger was corroborating her story was beyond him, but he would discover the why later. "Er, I should give you back your dog." And quickly, for the corpulent beagle had broken wind and produced a malodorous cloud that had the power to make his eyes water. He moved beyond the lingering odor and came closer to Miss Quill.

"Thank you again for curbing his escape." She took the wriggling bundle from his arms. Barely, their hands brushed, but a tendril of heat curled up to his elbow. The scent of apricot and vanilla and some sort of flower wafted to his nose to banish the foul smell. "He's a ridiculous animal, but I adore him. He's my constant company on the days when my father's illness becomes trying."

"I'm sorry to hear that your father is ailing." Arthur didn't wish to leave her company so soon. There was something about her that invited confidences, but why? Did Emily feel the same when she'd met this woman? "What does he suffer from?"

"His mind is fading. Some days are better than others, and on the days he's not lucid, he can turn angry and belligerent." In that one moment, she appeared vulnerable and afraid before those things vanished under happiness when the beagle licked her cheek. "You wouldn't need to welcome me back if you wouldn't run away, Regent." After another lick, she giggled.

The sound was surprising and captivating. Then guilt crept in to tighten his chest. He was still in love with his wife, wasn't he? Finding a connection or a tiny bit of interest in someone else felt entirely too wrong.

"I'm sorry to hear that." He resisted the urge to tug on his cravat. "What do you do to pass the time? Surely you don't spend all of it at home with your father?" She was well past youthful blooms. "Is there a Mr. Quill?"

A sharp stab of *something* went through him that he shoved away as soon as it made its presence known. He wasn't jealous; he barely knew her. What she did in her personal life was no business of his.

She chuckled. Amusement danced in her eyes. "The only Mr. Quill is my father. I have long ago missed my chances to marry, I'm afraid."

"Why? I mean, you're an attractive woman. Surely, you've had suitors." Then he berated himself for being rude. Why the deuce was he acting as if he hadn't a brain in his head?

A blush stained her cheeks. "I have not, actually. My time has been committed to one thing only over the years—the study of astronomy."

"How fascinating." And he meant it. Beyond that, he was

once more hooked on every word this woman said.

"I think so." She smiled, set the dog onto the ground, and then firmly and with efficient movements, she tied the lead to the beagle's collar. When she stood, she met Arthur's gaze. "Well, I should go. I still need to visit the market and then return to my father. He'll want tea soon, and the heavens will fall if I don't serve it to him on time."

An unexpected laugh escaped him. "That sounds like my mother. Ever since my father died, she has maintained a rigid schedule, perhaps as a way of coping with his loss." Yet he'd not discovered anything of import about her other than she was unattached. "Shall I see you again?"

Another giggle left her throat. When Regent strained at the lead, she stumbled to the side a few steps. "I know astronomy, my lord, not divination. The future remains a mystery to me."

He shivered even though it was a hot day. "Perhaps you're right."

She winked as she settled her bonnet upon her head and tied the navy ribbons beneath her chin. "However, each night I'm at Otis Hill to scan the heavens and chart the stars. If you are of a mind, come over for some company or a lesson regarding the skies."

How intriguing! "Is that an invitation, Miss Quill?"

"Only you can decide that, Lord Ettesmere." Then she wrapped a portion of the lead around her hand. "Have a pleasant afternoon." She continued on her way down the public road toward the village proper.

Arthur stared after her for a long time, not quite certain what had happened, yet he felt different somehow for the knowing of her.

Eventually, he returned to Ettesmere Park and entered the drawing room where the bulk of his family had gathered. When his gaze alighted on Emily, he grinned.

"As luck would have it, I had cause to meet Miss Quill this afternoon in the road." When she appeared startled, he decided to let her twist in the wind and addressed his mother instead. "She apparently lives not far from the village and takes care of her ailing father. Do you know of her or her family?"

"Not that I can remember. Is she of the *ton*?"

"Not that I could discern. She offered up no title or a relative who held one."

"Why do you wish to know?" Curiosity lit her face.

"No reason." He shrugged and hoped to God it appeared meeting her was merely a random occurrence.

Sophia's eyes widened. "Did you find her interesting?"

Not that they would ever know. "It was a fleeting meeting, Sister. Her dog had broken away. I gave him back to her. Then it was over." Except there had been so much more to it than that.

But his sibling would not drop it. "You're allowed to be attracted to a woman again, Arthur."

"Of course I am, but that's not what this was."

She cocked an eyebrow. "But if you were, we would understand."

He blew out a breath of frustration. "Leave it, Sophia. It was a polite meeting on a public road. Nothing more, and as I told you this morning, I have no intention of courting another woman."

If that were true, why, then, could he not easily evict Miss Quill, her freckles, and her pudgy beagle from his mind?

CHAPTER FOUR

June 13, 1819

JULIANNA KEPT AN eye on her father as he sat on a wooden chair in their garden at the back of the cottage. Often, when the weather was fair and his mind was lucid, he would pass the time there, where her mother's few rose bushes still produced fat, fragrant blooms while the bees and butterflies visited the other flowers and herbs that grew with wild abandon nearby. And during those days, he liked to watch the world go by until it was time for tea.

Though the scene was as idyllic as it always was, she couldn't help but wonder when her father would take his next turn, and once that happened, would his mind be able to bounce back. After all, the man was five and sixty. Truly, it wasn't all that old, but for whatever reason, his brain had decided to betray him, and frankly, it left her cold with worry many nights.

At the moment, there was nothing she could do about it, so she shoved the anxiety aside in an effort to enjoy the time she had with him now. "Are you comfortable, Papa? Do you need anything?"

"No, no." He waved a hand and then lifted his faded gaze to hers. "Just sit with me a while. It seems an age since we last spoke when you weren't haring off to chart the stars."

Julianna nodded. As soon as she sat on the first step, Regent bounded out of the cottage, zoomed past her as he flew down the remaining steps, and then fairly launched himself into the garden where he promptly ferreted out a rabbit and gave chase. "That dog will land into trouble once more before too long."

Would Lord Ettesmere be nearby to catch him?

She'd thought of little else since that chance meeting yesterday with the earl. He'd certainly been an attractive man in an older, distinguished sort of way with silver threaded through his fashionably arranged blond hair and heavy silvering at the temples. Even now, remembering the deep tenor of his voice sent tingles shivering down her spine. To say nothing of the fact it had been the first time in her life she'd met a member of the Quality, with the exception of chatting with his daughter.

"Papa?"

"Hmm?"

"Do you know of the Earl of Ettesmere? Is he a decent, fair man?" Her father had always been a man of few words, which had allowed him to observe everyone in the village and points beyond. It was a great way to know the measure of anyone.

"Of course I do." He didn't take his focus off the fat beagle as the dog rolled about with abandon in the dirt. "I worked for him once. Helped build a few of the outbuildings on Ettesmere Park land." Slowly, he nodded. Perhaps the memories were strong for him. "Beautiful acreage, that. Used to be a hedge maze there. One Christmas, the earl invited the families of all the tradesmen and villagers up to the Park for games and food. It was all quite grand." A grin tugged at his lips. "The countess was a taking little thing. Delicate and ethereal with loads of blonde hair."

Julianna chuckled. It was nice that her father could pull that from the murk that his mind sometimes was. "Dearest Papa, that man has passed on, for several years, I believe. His son holds the title. Arthur, I think he said his name was." The Christian name was proper enough, but the surname of Winterbourne conjured images of ancestral lines and stories of proud family members doing courageous things throughout the generations.

"Ah." Her father lifted a hand and patted her shoulder. "Arthur was a good lad. Haven't met him as a man. He once came around to lend a hand while we were working on the buildings. Said his father told him to go make something of himself that had nothing to do with the title."

How fascinating. "Was he of assistance to you?"

A bark of laughter escaped him. "Not at first. But once he'd watched us work, and after laying a line of truly hideous bricks, he came into his own." His grin widened. "One day, though, the fool boy lost a signet ring he'd been recently given. We feared it was embedded in the mortar, and it was a great joke between us all, but that young man probably had a dressing down from his father that night."

"Poor thing. I wonder if he remembers that day." What had Arthur been like as a young man? For that matter, did he have siblings? If so, what sort of relationships did he enjoy between them? Then she berated herself for a silly widgeon. He moved in different circles than she; chances were high they would never see each other again, despite her odd attempt at appearing flirtatious in his presence yesterday. "Suffice it to say, the earl is a grown man now."

An image of him jumped into her mind's eye. Broad shoulders had been highlighted by the sapphire jacket of superfine while a plain brown waistcoat had drawn her gaze to his midsection that didn't show a paunch or belly rounded by excess consumption. He'd worn buff-colored breeches yesterday that had hugged his lean legs, and the dusty boots he'd chosen had the appearance of being a favorite pair. Perhaps he wore them every day if he walked the acreage. Since yesterday had been sunny, she'd been able to discern fine lines that crinkled at the corners of his eyes when he'd grinned. Laugh lines framed his sensual mouth, but she'd rather had the impression he didn't do that often any longer.

Mild heat slapped at Julianna's cheeks. Oh, he was handsome

in an understated way, and from all accounts, he wasn't one of those men who was conscious of his looks. *And I have no business thinking lingering thoughts about him or his form.*

Not privy to her mental perusal of the earl, her father continued. "I recall his wife died years ago. That's a real shame." Then he glanced at her, and his expression was quite sly. "Good for you, though. If he's a widower, you should aim your cap for him."

"Oh, stop." Her blush intensified. "The earl is well beyond my reach, even if I wanted a man in my life." She shook her head. For the first time in her life, Julianna was glad she hadn't the first clue of how to attract a man. They would only be a distraction. "Besides, I'm well past the age that anything like that matters. I have more important plans."

Her father snorted. "Do you think people in this day and age incapable of having desire or romance once they're past a certain age?" A trace of censure had crept into his tone. "What rubbish is that, girl? Just because you're long past your Come Out years and you've wasted your youth playing companion to me doesn't mean a brace." He snapped his gnarled fingers. "Men and women have been coming together for more years than you and I have been alive. Age is only an excuse if you wish it to be."

"All that is well and good, but I would never assume to think a man with a title and I would suit. What do I know about that sort of life?" Nothing, that's what. She was the daughter of a bricklayer with her head in the stars.

"You're an intelligent woman, Julianna. And your mother raised you to observe proper manners, everything a lady would need to know." His grin faded as he contemplated Regent in the garden once more. "She was connected to that world."

"I know." Her mother had been a second cousin of a viscount, and though she'd had a couple of Seasons in London, she'd fallen in love with a bricklayer in the village when her family had visited the Berkshire countryside for a house party. "But she chose you over that life."

He huffed. "I was never worthy of her." When he cast a glance her way, his grin was sad at the corners. "Could have done much better."

"Stop such talk, Papa." Julianna reached over and clasped his hand. "She was deeply in love with you, and you with her. It was a love match worthy of the ages, and a good example of what a union should be."

"She wanted you to know the same."

"Sometimes, fate has other plans. The sooner we square with that, the happier our lives will be." She squeezed his fingers. "I am quite content with my lot." At least the overwhelming urge to marry and reproduce had faded. When she was a younger woman, that call of nature had nearly driven her mad, but as the years went by and a match wasn't in the offing, she'd moved on and the feelings had become all but forgotten. "I have the stars now and am on the verge of claiming one of those heavenly bodies as mine."

"That damned comet." He shook his head. "The stars consumed your brother. Now they've hooked you."

"But it's such a wonderful world beyond the one we walk, Papa." Julianna tipped her head up. It was one of those rare days when the faded moon had dared to be seen in the daylight in the attempt to chase the sun. "Can you imagine what stories those stars have to tell?" She smiled, for in the skies, the possibilities were endless. "I'm monitoring a comet, this is true."

"The same one Ned saw that one time?"

"I think so." Her throat crowded unexpectedly with unshed tears. The hole that her brother had left in her life upon his death hadn't healed. On the verge of becoming maudlin, she traced the outline of her brother's pocket watch in a pocket she'd sewn into her dress. "I, uh, haven't seen it in the intervening years from when he wrote about it in his notebook, so it could be. Or perhaps it's a different one altogether. I only know it's been visible through my telescope for four nights in succession, and its tail is magnificent."

Dear Ned. You would have adored this comet. But he'd expired too young, and those handful of years made her miss him more acutely now.

Her father sighed. "He would have been proud of you for continuing his work."

"I hope so." If it wasn't for him, she wouldn't have studied astronomy, and now she was on the threshold of making a discovery that would challenge the pompous men in London.

And that would be the start of a brand-new life for her.

For long moments, her father remained silent. Julianna didn't mind. She watched Regent's antics as he barked at a chipmunk and then chased yet another rabbit through the vegetation. When her father spoke again, he was no longer in the present.

"Your mother wants to a take a trip to London. Wants to show me some of her favorite sites. Think I'll do it for our wedding anniversary this year."

Part of her heart mourned for the loss taking place right before her eyes. "I'm sure she would have liked that, Papa, but you know she's been gone a while." Her mother had died before the trip happened. Many a night Julianna had overheard her parents talking and planning that trip when they'd thought she was abed. Rapidly blinking away the tears forming in her eyes, she stood. "Why don't we come inside? It's almost time for tea."

"Not until I talk to your mother." He shook his head. "We often talk out here in the quiet. Of late, she's been calling to me."

"Oh, Papa." She rested a hand on his shoulder. "Don't go just yet. You're all I have left."

"I promised her I wouldn't until you're settled." He laid a hand atop hers as he held her gaze. "You need to marry, my girl. Find someone to look after you once I'm gone. Not going to have your looks forever."

She laughed despite the sad subject matter. "I'll be fine." But knots of worry pulled in her belly. "Let me prepare your tea."

﹥﹥﹥﹥﹤﹤﹤﹤

No sooner had she gotten her father settled in his favorite chair with a book after tea than a quiet knock sounded on the front door. Once she'd pulled the wooden panel open, a child stood there with a small ivory envelope in his hand.

"I was told to deliver this to Miss Quill. Is that you?" The tow-haired boy in farmer's clothing held out the missive.

"Yes, but who is it from?" She gingerly took the envelope from him.

"Don't know, miss. Someone just gave me a shilling and told me to deliver it here." Then he touched the brim of his slouch-style cap and was off.

"How strange." As she stood in the door frame, Julianna broke the seal that told her nothing about the origin of the missive. Inside, a single scrap of paper waited with a line of bold handwriting across the surface.

If you know Berkshire as well as you assume, meet me atop Barker's Hill at sunset. If the heavens are clear this evening, we can make a wish upon the North Star.

She glanced toward the lane, but the messenger boy had vanished. Surely the Earl of Ettesmere hadn't sent it. Such a forward move wasn't his style, at least not what she'd gleaned of him from that quick meeting. He was more the retiring sort instead of overtly flirtatious. "The question remains: should I do as the note says merely to discover who sent it?"

If she were to ask her father, he would give her a resounding affirmation. Yet if her mother were alive, what would she caution? No doubt she'd tell her that proper ladies didn't go about by themselves—the same advice Julianna herself had attempted to impart to Lady Emily two days ago. She grinned as she closed the door. Thankfully, she hadn't been raised within the bounds of society and no one would gossip about the odd woman with her head in the stars if she once more went abroad that night.

Such was a boon to being undesired and unwanted. There was a certain freedom in being an odd student of knowledge. Reading the note once more, she tucked it and the envelope into her pocket for safe keeping. If it had indeed been sent by the earl, she had enough curiosity to wonder what it might mean, for he hadn't acted enamored of her when they'd met on the public road. And no man in her history had ever lost his mind to passion over her. In that she was safe enough.

She smoothed a hand down the front of her dress of sprigged muslin in a pale periwinkle hue. This would have to suffice for she didn't own that many outfits. She'd never worried over her appearance before, and she wouldn't start now. Regardless of who had sent that note, if they took exception to her outward trappings, she didn't need to tarry with them in the first place.

Regardless, she had the comet to track and stars to chart. Work was paramount, and she would forge her own path through life just as she'd done all along. Still, a queer little thrill shot down her spine, for nothing so intriguing had occurred in a very long time indeed.

I can meet whatever challenges await.

JUST AS THE sun set over the area, Julianna climbed Barker's Hill. It wasn't as prominent a spot as her favored one on Otis Hill, but this one was tucked further away into the darkened night amidst forest and rolling countryside. At this vantage point, the lights from Wokingham village faded to almost specks. It was certainly an idyllic location and in the right setting could prove romantic, though she had no expectations for that.

"Who goes there?" The masculine inquiry, tinged with worry, halted her steps.

A shadow rose up from a fallen tree where it had rested, and for the space of a few terrifying heartbeats, she stood frozen to the spot as her pulse ricocheted wildly. Had she made a horrendous error in judgment coming out here without a way of defending herself? But Regent—her ever-present guard dog—let out a baying howl. He then shot forward to greet the newcomer with apparent relish.

"Get off, you crazy hound. I am not your long-lost best friend," the man said, and there could be no mistaking whose tone that was.

Then Julianna squinted in the inky darkness, and her breath released in a sigh. "Lord Ettesmere?" She pressed her lips together to keep from laughing as Regent kept standing on his back legs and pawing at the tops of the earl's boots.

"Miss Quill?" When he came forward, she almost sagged so great was her relief. Since the moon was waning and would pass into a new moon in a couple of days, there wasn't enough illumination for her to see his face from that distance. "What the devil are you doing here?"

Well, that was an unexpected reaction. "I, uh, received a note…"

"So did I." He didn't sound happy about it.

"I see." A stab of cold disappointment went through her chest. Her one pseudo-foray into dealings with a member of the opposite sex, and this was what she'd found? "If you'd rather I depart in the hopes someone else might come by, I'd be happy to relocate to my usual hill." If her voice was rather chilly, she couldn't help it.

"What? No." He shook his head. "No, of course not. I was merely taken aback by the fact that someone unknown to me and apparently you is writing notes of assignation."

She stared. *"You* didn't write the note?"

"I did not." Then he shrugged and came forward, tripping once over Regent who'd decided to loll in adoration at the earl's feet. As he performed a few odd steps and hops in an effort to remain upright, Julianna bit the inside of her cheek.

"Regent, behave yourself." She tapped her free hand against

her upper thigh. "Come here." With a huff, the beagle obeyed the command. Julianna stooped and took hold of his leather collar. "I apologize for the dog, Your Lordship."

The canine in question whined his unhappiness.

Both she and the earl laughed.

"Think nothing of it." He held out a hand. "Allow me to carry your basket. As you can see, there's not much in the way of scenery up here, but there is a rotting, fallen tree that's rather comfortable for sitting. The least I can do is see you settled."

"Thank you." In the process of handing over the willow basket, her hand brushed his. Despite the gloves they both wore, tendrils of heat emanated up her arm from the point of contact. "As for scenery, you are very much mistaken. You only need to look up to find yourself ushered into a whole new world, even more lavish than anything society can provide."

She assumed since she'd never set foot into lauded halls or lavishly appointed drawing rooms.

"Do you know, I've never had cause to contemplate the heavens as you must." He led her over to the fallen tree and set her basket on the soft, springy grass. "But I can already see you have the right of it." Then, before she could answer, he quickly shed his jacket—a bright bottle green superfine this time—and spread it over the tree. "And for such a theatre, one must have a comfortable seat." He waved her toward his jacket. "I didn't wish for you to soil your skirts with dirt or lichen."

"Oh! What a lovely gesture." A queer sort of fluttering had taken up residence in her heart. "Thank you." When Regent made an attempt to jump onto the tree, she laughed and gently nudged him out of the way. "But your jacket will be the worse for wear—"

"I won't hear another word about it, Miss Quill." He remained standing until she'd settled upon that garment. Regent, thrilled to be a part of it, upended her basket before barking and wagging his tail while the earl seated himself beside her on the fallen tree. There was enough space between them to fit two other people. "So, what now? We've been summoned to this hill. Shall we both return home?"

And put an end to what was turning out to be the most glorious night of her life? "We could do what the writer suggested." She couldn't help looking him over. In his shirtsleeves and dark brown waistcoat and breeches, he was every inch the country gentleman. Was there anything more attractive and tempting than a man in such a state of undress?

"Such as?" He frowned, and when he stirred, the faint scent of bay rum and lime assailed her nose. It was quite a heavenly smell.

"We could make a wish on the North Star."

"I'm afraid I don't know where that is, truth to tell."

"How fortuitous for you that I do, Your Lordship." She allowed a small smile as she looked away to stare at the darkened skies strewn with stars. "Shall we have an impromptu astronomy lesson, then?"

CHAPTER FIVE

"**P**LEASE, BEFORE YOU start, I would like it if you called me Arthur," he was quick to insert while the fat beagle whined at his feet. "Something about the isolated darkness beneath the stars lends itself to a certain intimacy not found within proper forms of address."

God, I'm the world's biggest nodcock. That makes it sound like this meeting is for more than it should be.

Though what exactly it was, he couldn't begin to say. Nothing like this had ever happened to him before, and he'd certainly never received anonymous notes. Had she done this but hadn't owned up to it?

The shock in her eyes as she looked at him denied culpability. He relaxed by increments. "We're barely acquainted, haven't been formally introduced, yet you wish for me to refer to you by your Christian name?"

"Yes?" The sensation of tumbling assailed him. Three days ago, he knew exactly who he was and what he'd wanted from his life. He'd been well-versed with his past and had looked forward to watching his children grow into their adult lives. And now? Well, now he was sitting on a fallen tree with a veritable stranger, asking her for a familiarity only given to a select few.

What the devil is wrong with me?

For long moments, Miss Quill regarded him with skepticism.

Finally, she nodded. "Very well. Then you may call me Julianna."

He repeated the word over and over again in his mind. Each time, it sounded like music through a fairy pipe. "Hullo, Julianna."

"Hullo... Arthur." She turned her head and sent him a shy smile. "Would you like to learn about the North Star, or would you prefer to sit in silence?" With one hand, she tugged at the ribbons beneath her chin. Her plain bonnet tumbled from her head, bounced off the fallen tree, and then came to a rest on the ground at her feet.

Regent promptly pounced on it. He closed his jaws around the brim and took off with it down the hill.

Julianna sighed. "That is why I don't invest in pretty, dainty hats. They're a particular toothsome chew toy for the beagle."

"I'm sorry to hear that." No doubt she would look stunning in bonnets that weren't straw, headgear bedecked with ribbons and silk flowers. No, it wasn't that great of a loss, for it meant he had the luxury of seeing her hair, dark as a raven's wing, caught up in a similar loose chignon she'd worn yesterday. "One would think the dog too rotund to be very destructive."

She snorted. "That is the popular theory. However, Regent has enough energy, and he uses it well. Yet he remains overweight. Perhaps I doomed him as a pup when I gave him the name."

"Do you have other dogs from the litter?"

"No." She shook her head. "My father knew of someone whose dog had birthed puppies. He gave me one once they were weaned thinking it would be a companion for me now that he can't fill that role any longer." When her voice broke ever so slightly on that last word, Arthur was sucked into her pull.

"Oh?" He scooted a tad closer. "What is amiss? Has something occurred beyond what you've told me yesterday?" Though he'd never been acquainted with her father, and he certainly wasn't a tenant, he desperately wished to hear of her history.

"Not really." A sigh escaped her. She clasped her fingers in her lap. "I fear for the day when his mind completely leaves him. Recently, we've had more good days than bad." She shrugged. "In his prime, my father was strong, barrel-chested, an active man who laid bricks for a living. He was larger than life, and I thought he could do anything."

"That's how I thought about my father too. Yours must have quite a few stories to share."

"Oh, yes. However, it's been an age since he ruminated upon his past." Again, that tiny little wobble in her voice caught his attention and tugged at his chest. "I can't help but think he's too young to be afflicted with this."

"I agree, but diseases don't show prejudice." Despite their surroundings, despite his companion, despite the fact she prodded his curiosity, a swath of maudlin feeling swept over him. He trained his gaze to the darkened tree line. "Consumption took my wife well before her time. I... Though it's been five years since I lost her, I feel that loss so acutely on some days it's as if it were only yesterday."

Why the devil did he tell her that? They'd just met, for Jove's sake.

"You have my condolences, Lord... er, Arthur." When he thought she might lay a hand on his arm—it certainly hovered there in the air between them—she returned that appendage to her lap. Somewhere in the distance, the mournful baying of the beagle carried upon the air. Julianna gave him a smile, but it was tinged with sadness. "I imagine it's such a difficult thing to lose a spouse. Were you married long?"

"How can I judge what is long and what is short when I entered into that union for a lifetime?" When he glanced at her, his gaze alighted once more on that tiny scar on her forehead and his mind filled with questions. "Regardless, I had her in my life for twenty years. We wed when I was four and twenty; she but nineteen." He chuckled, but it sounded forced to his ears. "She was a Diamond that year, the toast of her Come Out Season."

"And you were utterly captivated."

"Absolutely. Ellen was… She was, well she was unlike anyone I'd ever met. Blonde, petite, proper—the perfect lady to become my eventual countess."

"I'm glad you had that." In the dim light from the stars and the waning moon, compassion pooled in her blue eyes. "It sounds like you truly enjoyed a romance of the ages."

"I did." His throat closed with unshed tears. Perhaps it he shouldn't still dote on a woman who'd left this mortal coil five years before, but he couldn't help it. When loved deeply, that grief never went away. "I've had to learn how to live around the grief. Though it pains me at times, I don't want to forget, and that sorrow helps to keep her memory alive, I think."

"Yet at the same time, you run the risk of being held prisoner by that grief." This time, she did fleetingly touch his sleeve. Perhaps he imagined it, but tendrils of heat ebbed up his arm to his elbow. "I'm sure the people in your life have told you there is still life ahead and that you should continue to live, put the past behind you."

"Yes." For long moments, he peered into Julianna's face. She was different from his wife in so many ways. Never would Ellen have considered coming out by herself in the dead of night merely to watch the stars. In fact, she would have been scandalized at the thought. "While I know deep down that advice is sound, how can I move forward without what I lost?"

And why the hell was he compelled to keep sharing the secrets of his heart with this veritable stranger? A woman who wasn't remotely connected to the *ton* and not even a part of the gentry?

Did it matter?

"You make the attempt every day. Starting over if you stumble." She shifted her position on the fallen tree, edged a tiny bit closer to him. "I would imagine you remember those you've lost, but don't cut off your nose to spite your face or close yourself off to new possibilities. Life, I think, is for enjoyment, for giving love. Why would you wish to deny that for yourself?"

"I don't know." For the first time since the discussion began, he had no answers.

A few days before her death, Ellen had made him promise if the chance for happiness, to love again, was offered, he would take it. Thus far in that he'd failed. Yet was this what she might have meant? Befriending this intriguing woman in an effort to discover where such a thing might lead?

Knowing his companion waited on an answer, he said, "You are wise, Julianna. I appreciate that."

She snorted with evident amusement. "I don't know about that. As your daughter was quick to remind me when we met, I'm quite advanced in years. Somehow, I've managed to forget everything I've told you in the pursuit of knowledge. If suitors were interested in me, I must have overlooked them, and now I'm sitting here in the dark with you, wondering if the choices I've made in my life were the right ones."

His eyebrows soared. "Emily was so uncouth as all of that?"

"She couldn't help it; that is the way of youth. They cannot fathom such an age gap and therefore think everyone beyond their set is ancient." When she giggled, the tinkling sound danced through the air and once more cemented his attention. "But it's true. I shall perhaps forever remain an old maid, forgotten and unwanted, except by the stars, and even then, I'm quite cognizant they are merely cold balls of cosmic debris who don't have feelings."

"You might claim those years, but you certainly don't look them." What the devil had prompted him to say such a nodcock thing?

"Thank you." She pasted her gaze on her hands resting in her lap. "I appreciate that."

How the deuce had this woman been overlooked by the men in Berkshire County? Were they all blind? For that matter, did they not want a woman who always went about with an eye on the stars? From the whole of his interactions with her, he'd discovered she was witty and intelligent. To say nothing of her form and looks. Yes, they had to be idiots of the first order.

And if he weren't careful, he'd become utterly enamored without basis. Hell, he'd courted Ellen for a year before he offered for her. Wasn't that how a man was supposed to conduct such things?

Stop it, Arthur! These thoughts are ridiculous. You feel nothing of the sort for this woman. There is nothing there of a romantic or even lustful nature. If anything, you are lonely.

When he would have given a rejoinder, too much time had passed, so he remained silent. Eventually, he tipped his gaze to the heavens. Stars sprinkled the dark velvet backdrop of the skies, some brighter than others.

"Would you enjoy a brief lesson regarding the North Star?" The dulcet sound of her voice was like the slide of silk over his skin.

"I would." Damn it all if awareness for this woman shuddered down his spine to lodge in his groin. Didn't feel lustful, eh? Perhaps that had been a lie. "Honestly, I've not given thought to the heavens before." Hell, seeing the stars while in London was an almost impossible task what with all the gaslights and other illumination and pollution.

Julianna moved closer to him, and began her lecture in a whispered voice, which meant he was obliged to lean toward her to hear properly. "The North Star or Pole Star is referred to in Latin as *stella illa quae polaris dicitur*. It means that star which is called polar. It is a star in the northern circumpolar constellation of Ursa Minor." Another round of tinkling laughter wrapped around him and held him as captive as her knowledge and use of Latin. "Everyone believes it's the brightest star in the heavens, but I have my doubts. In any event, the North Star holds nearly still while the entire northern sky moves around it."

"How is that possible? I assumed the stars were constantly moving."

"Because that particular star is located almost at the north celestial pole of the Earth and is the point around which the entire northern sky turns." She turned her head and found his gaze. Hers shone with excitement as she warmed to her subject. "The North Star marks the way due north, of course."

"Thus, the reason it's used as a guide or a marker of sorts for travelers."

"Exactly." Pleasure rang in her tones, and he grinned. "The North Star has played an important part in historical events."

"How so?" He'd apparently lost his mind, for during the course of her dissertation, he couldn't stop himself from watching her mouth. What would those two pieces of flesh feel like pressed against his?

"Well, for example, the so-called Star of Bethlehem or the Christian Star was recorded in the Nativity story in the Gospel of Matthew where the three wise kings from the East were inspired by the North Star to travel to Jerusalem." She shrugged. "The star allegedly led them to the Baby Jesus. I'm not convinced that is strictly true. Yes, those men probably saw *a* star, of course, but was it the *North* Star? More research is needed."

God, her passion and knowledge for astronomy was wonderful. Never had he been in the company of such an intelligent woman. The more she spoke, the more he wanted to learn about her. "I like how you don't accept things at face value or just because you've been told a thing is so. Independent thought is a rare trait these days."

"Thank you." When she grinned, Arthur leaned ever closer, as did she, until their heads were nearly together. So close that the warmth of her breath steamed his chin. The kiss he'd obsessed over was almost his... but at the last second, his courage failed, and he straightened with a rapidly beating heart.

Would kissing someone else mean he was betraying Ellen's memory?

A tiny little sigh escaped Julianna. Had she wanted that kiss as well? She tipped her head to consult the heavens. "Do you wish to hear more?"

"Yes, please." If she continued to talk, she would remain in his company a bit longer. No, this didn't feel like a courtship—at least not in his limited experience—but there was something about her that captivated him.

Why? Was he desperate or merely wishful hoping? *I do not need a romance.*

Another round of exuberant barking recalled his attention to the wayward beagle, who came closer with each utterance.

Julianna ignored it. From her basket, she withdrew a brass tube that resembled a spy glass sailors might use on board ships. Only this one was a tad longer and with a mechanism that apparently adjusted a lens inside. "This is a telescope. The lens isn't as powerful as I would like, but I have not the resources to replace it with a better model." She passed it to him, urged him to peer into it. "In antiquity, the North Star was not yet the closest naked-eye star to the celestial pole, and the entire constellation of Ursa Minor was used for navigation rather than any single star." She glanced at him as he looked through the glass, which brought a few of the stars into closer range.

"Good God, look how they seem to sparkle!" Never had he beheld such a sight.

"Sometimes they remind me of diamonds, as if a duchess had inadvertently spilled her box of jewels and they now decorate the heavens."

"There is so much one can see through this lens that wasn't visible before."

"Oh, yes. Eventually, because the Earth and the skies are ever-changing, the North Star moved close enough to the pole to be seen without a lens, even though still at a distance of several degrees. Numerous names referring to this characteristic as polar star have been in use since the medieval period. In Old English, it was known as *scip-steorra* or the ship star."

"Ah, and it has been used for navigation ever since." He trained his focus through the telescope upon the moon. A gasp escaped as he discerned shadows on the surface. "There is truly another world out there, one I had no idea existed, for I just assumed it... was."

"Now you know why the heavens fascinate me so." There was obvious affection in her voice. "The Bard wrote about the North Star, too. Shakespeare's sonnet 116 is an example of the symbolism of the North Star as a guiding principle. He says, 'love is the star to every wandering bark, whose worth's unknown, although his height be taken.'"

Slowly, Arthur lowered the telescope in order to look at his companion. "You're right. These things are said, and we hear them while watching plays at the opera, but I fear we don't really understand the words." He let that percolate in his mind before speaking again, and when he did, his words came out in a rush, so great was his excitement and intent to impress. "In fact, just a few months ago, I saw a play about Julius Caesar. There was a refusal to grant a pardon to which the actor said, 'I am as constant as the Northern Star. Of whose true-fixed and resting quality. There is no fellow in the firmament. The skies are painted with unnumbered sparks. They are all fire and every one doth shine, but there is but one in all doth hold his place...'"

"Very good observation." The obvious pleasure in her tones sent warmth sailing through his blood. "The North Star has been so constant that it's only natural it makes an appearance in every aspect of our lives."

"Why do people wish upon it?" Though the summer air was warm, the brass remained cool in his gloved hands.

"Quite possibly because it gives them hope, something positive to look forward to." When she smiled, his gaze dropped once more to her lips. "Everyone needs hope, Arthur. There is nothing wrong with wishing... as long as we are aware that change will only occur if *we* put forth the effort."

Was there a hidden meaning in her words? It was impossible to tell. "Perhaps." No, there was certainly not a courtship between them or even the potential of that, but he felt *something* for her, as insane as it sounded. There was a certain freedom in this, and no pressure to set up a nursery or do his duty toward his title. That had already been accomplished in his life. Did that mean he could enjoy her companionship without restriction or commitment?

It was interesting to think about.

"Since the North Star is ever so bright tonight, we should both send up a wish. After all, that anonymous note suggested the same."

Damn. He'd forgotten about the note as well as who might have sent it. Yet, panic welled within his chest. It was all too obvious their time together was coming to an end. "I would enjoy that." And to his surprise, he truly was.

"I'm glad to hear it." Once more, her hand drifted to his sleeve. When her fingers lightly rested upon it, he froze, suddenly breathless. "On the count of three, think of a wish but don't speak it aloud. It won't come true if you share it."

"Right," he finally said around a tight throat. "One…"

"Two…"

"Three…" He tipped his gaze to the bright, shining star, closed his eyes, and let go a wish into the heavens.

Send me a sign that I should move forward with my life, that it might be time to climb out of the shadows of grief and usher in the light again.

The slight pressure of her fingers on his arm recalled him back to the present. When he opened his eyes and regarded her, she smiled. "Did you make a wish?"

"Yes. Did you?"

"I did." The stars reflected in her eyes, and he wished it was full daylight so he could read the emotions therein. "Julianna?"

"Hmm?"

"Forgive the trespass."

"What?" Her expression crumpled into confusion. "I don't understand what—"

Arthur leaned into her personal space, stopped the flow of her words by briefly pressing his lips to hers in a fleeting kiss. Never since he'd lost Ellen had he felt the need to do so, and he hadn't.

So why now and with this woman he barely knew? Then sanity returned. Hot mortification poured into his chest and went up the back of his neck. Quickly, as if he were a green boy at university in danger of being found out, he edged away from her on the fallen tree. "I beg your pardon." Guilt slammed into him on the heels of embarrassment, followed by self-recrimination.

I shouldn't have done that.

Remarkably, Julianna giggled, and the genuine sound went straight through his chest. She touched a gloved finger to her lips. "There is no need for an apology, Arthur." Her eyes sparkled overly bright as she rested her hands in her lap. "It was rather pleasant." Then she trained her gaze on her lap, hiding her face from view. "Also, it was my first kiss," she admitted in a barely audible voice that had him leaning her way once more.

"What?" He gawked as if he hadn't been bred with manners. "But you're—"

She looked up with a darkly ached eyebrow. "Advanced in age?"

"I'm sorry. That wasn't well done of me." Damn, he must appear an idiot to her. "I'm merely shocked, for the men here must be blind." When the heat on the back of his neck intensified, he rushed to fill the silence as he shot to his feet. "This evening was lovely. Thank you for that."

"I thought it was too." She accepted the telescope from him as well as assistance in rising. "Uh... if you want to learn more about the stars, I'm usually at Otis Hill in the evenings. I could even show you the comet I've discovered."

A comet! The word was as fascinating as the woman who'd spoken it. Did he wish to further her acquaintance knowing that he had a visceral reaction to her? Barking from Regent hastened his thoughts. He rather thought he did... but for the companionship only. No more kissing. There was no need for a romance. Yet, he tugged at his suddenly too-tight cravat. "I shall certainly bear that in mind."

"Excellent." She put the telescope in her basket and then

lifted it off the ground. "Shall I escort you home, Arthur? I did the same for your daughter."

His eyebrows soared as surprise gripped him, but he was grateful she'd looked after Emily. "I shall be all right, but I'd be honored to escort you home." He offered her his arm crooked at the elbow.

"I would enjoy that." Julianna snagged his jacket from the fallen tree. "Thank you."

Arthur whistled for the beagle and set them into motion. "My pleasure."

The whole evening had been that, and perhaps he'd needed exactly that.

How very... odd.

CHAPTER SIX

June 14, 1819

J ULIANNA CROONED TO one of her hens as she slipped a hand
beneath the warm body to collect the two eggs resting on the
nest. "Thank you for your donation." She did the same to the
three other nests by rote while her mind wandered.

The Earl of Ettesmere had kissed her last night.

That thought circled round and round in her head like ponies
on a loop. At the age of seven and thirty, she had finally discovered what it felt like to be kissed. Then her eyebrows furrowed.
Actually, it had been all too quick and there hadn't been time to
really feel... anything.

How very disappointing.

"I assumed there would be, well, more," she told one of the
hens, who merely bobbed her head in answer.

But their discussion regarding the North Star as well as bits of
their personal history had been revealing as well as refreshing.
There was no doubt he was still affected by his wife's death, and
while she could certainly understand that, it was also a good
indication that nothing would come of their new acquaintance
other than perhaps friendship.

Not that she minded. He was interesting enough and had
seemed fascinated with her stars. There was something compel-

ling about the earl, that much was true, and in his company, she'd felt as if she could tell him anything without judgment. Yet the night had ended with an awkward goodbye at the start of the lane that led to her cottage as if he were suddenly uncomfortable in her presence, and then he'd vanished into the night.

"Good morning, Miss Quill."

The sound of the housekeeper's voice wrenched Julianna from her musings. She glanced up at the older lady who dropped by a few times a week to help with chores about the cottage and to give her a chance to have a break from watching over her father. "Hullo, Mrs. Draysley. I'm glad you came by."

"Of course, dear." The petite, gray-haired woman came through the garden gate. The handle of a market basket rested in the crook of one arm and in the other she carried an earthenware mug with a bouquet of wildflowers in it. "I thought you might appreciate a splash of cheerful color on your table."

"I do, indeed." Julianna straightened, told her chickens good-bye, and then led the way into the house. "Thank you for thinking of me."

"Flowers always cheer a person." Mrs. Draysley rested the mug on the table where meals were served. She looked Julianna over with a critical eye. "You have good color in your cheeks today, Miss Quill. What new has occurred?"

"Nothing, I can assure you." It wasn't necessarily a lie. Though she *had* met Arthur—twice—and he *had* briefly brushed his lips over hers, neither of those things were worthy of mention or gossip. "I'm still the same person I was the last time you saw me."

"Ah, that is too bad." The older woman tsked her tongue as she set down her basket. "I thought you might have found a suitor at last."

At last. That meant she'd been the subject of discussion at some point around someone's table or garden wall. Though she liked most of the women in the village, she could do without the rumor mill they caused to churn. Julianna stifled a huff of frustration. "I'm afraid not." However, here was the perfect chance to ask a question or two so she wouldn't feel so inexperienced. "By the by, how would one know if one *did* have a suitor? Do men announce that fact?"

Mrs. Draysley sent her an odd glance. "Not necessarily, but the honorable ones declare an intent. Otherwise, it's merely scandal and makes for fast women."

Well, *that* wasn't what she wanted to hear. Did that mean the earl wasn't an honorable man? She didn't have that feeling about him after the events of last night. If he'd had wicked things on his mind, he wouldn't have stopped at a barely-there kiss.

Right?

"Ah, thank you for clarifying. I've always wondered. You know, in the event I might someday stumble upon a suitor."

The other woman chuckled as if that were the funniest joke she'd heard all week. "One doesn't stumble upon a man who has an interest. If a man wants a woman, he'll give chase."

"And if he doesn't? Chase, I mean?"

She shrugged. "It could be he's afraid or shy or just a slow mover." Her gaze bore into Julianna's. "Are you certain there's nothing you'd like to share, dear?"

"I am." Julianna shook her head and hoped that the flush in her cheeks was attributed to the heat of the day. "Everything is how it's been the whole of my life. I have my stars, and that's perhaps enough."

Yet, that fact didn't bring her the comfort that it once did, all due to the arrival of Arthur. Oh, she still adored astronomy above everything, but some of her curiosity had shifted to the earl. It remained to be seen what—if anything—would come of their budding friendship.

"As long as you're happy, dear." The housekeeper bustled about the immediate area, setting things to rights. "Now, you run along. I'll look after Mr. Quill. There are a good several hours of cleaning and cooking ahead for the week. I might send your father down to the stream for a stint of bathing soon if he's of a mind."

"I appreciate all that you do." Her eyes prickled with tears. At times, everything grew so overwhelming, and with no one to talk to about her father's care, it began to take a toll. "I couldn't imagine doing this by myself." She'd already lost her mother and brother. The impending loss of her father was enough to make her wish to cower in her bed if she let down her guard enough.

"I well know what it's like to care for ailing loved ones." Mrs. Draysley patted Julianna's shoulder. "Life contains trials sure enough, but kindness blurs those sharp edges a bit."

"Yes, it does," she agreed with a whisper through a tight throat. "Thank you again."

An hour later, the housekeeper bustled into the tiny parlor where Julianna had sought refuge with a good book and a cup of tea. "This was just delivered for you, Miss Quill. I thought it odd since you rarely receive anything in the post." A familiar ivory envelope was clasped in her fingers.

"Oh?" Excitement coursed down her spine. Was the note from the anonymous source or from Arthur? Did it matter? This week had been the most interesting socially she'd ever spent. "Thank you." Swiftly standing, she plucked the envelope from the other woman's hand. "Perhaps it's word from a friend."

Mrs. Draysley gave her a quizzical glance but left with a frown and no comment, for they both knew Julianna didn't have many friends.

With shaking hands, she quickly opened the envelope, pulled out the scrap of paper, and then proceeded to read it.

In the village square, a fountain lies, but can you find the clue hidden therein?

"How intriguing!" She never knew there was a secret in the fountain, and she must have passed by it hundreds of times while in the village over the course of her life. Anticipation buzzed at the base of her spine, for she couldn't wait to explore.

Wanting to waste no time, she fairly pelted from the room

and up the stairs. Not having a large wardrobe, she donned the robin's egg blue dress, collected the matching bonnet since she had no intentions of taking Regent with her, and then came back downstairs.

She found her father on his chair in the garden. "Papa, I'm going into the village for a bit. Mrs. Draysley is looking after you today."

He waved a hand but didn't glance up from where Regent rolled about in the dirt. "Enjoy your time, girl. I'll be here when you return."

A half hour later, she entered the village square and walked straight to the fountain. No one lingered about the statuary. Equally, no one paid her attention. Julianna relaxed by increments as she moved closer to examine the stone. The fountain depicted a young woman in a peasant dress and apron pouring water from an urn while two lambs looked on. One stood nearby and the other sat at her feet. She supposed it was to represent the bucolic life of Wokingham, but otherwise, there was nothing special regarding the fountain. A shallow basin of barely moving water enclosed the sculpture. On days when the weather was sweltering, children would play in the pool, but today she was alone with the artwork.

With a frown, she walked about the fountain. The thin stream of water tinkled as it left the urn to splash into the basin, but the stone remained smooth if stained in a few places. There was nothing there to indicate an inscription or even a secret panel.

Why did the writer of the note say to come here if there was nothing to be found?

"Fancy meeting you here, Julianna."

Merciful heavens. Pleasure shivered down her spine at the sound of *his* voice, her name in those soft tones. Slowly, she turned about and then released an involuntary sigh of appreciation. Surely it was a sin for a man to look so handsome both day and night. A brown superfine jacket highlighted the breadth of his shoulders; the intricate knot of his cravat drew her attention to the sharp cut of his jaw. His waistcoat of bronze made her fingers itch to delve beneath merely so she could explore his form, but it was the buff-colored breeches he'd worn that made her throat dry. Lean, muscled thighs and calves on display enough to make a woman—her—swoon from the poetic beauty of him. "Hullo, Arthur."

How decadent it was to have been given leave to use his Christian name. Then she shook her head and firmly stuck her gaze on his face. *Honestly, Jules, you have no right to ogle the earl. It's practically scandalous. Have some respect for yourself.*

When he grinned and the delicate skin at the corners of his eyes crinkled, she bit her bottom lip to keep from making a sound. The only thing running through her mind was the fleeting feel of his lips against hers. Would he attempt to repeat the gesture? Would she let him? "Have you discovered anything of import?"

"Unfortunately, no." The words were a breathless affair, and she silently admonished herself for a silly widgeon. No doubt he had nothing of the sort on his mind. That kiss had been an aberration, brought about by an excess of emotion during a conversation in the dark. "Without a firm direction, I'm not certain what I'm supposed to be hunting for."

"I'll admit, that note sounded rather odd." He clasped his hands behind his back while he, too, examined the fountain.

"Then you received one too."

"I did."

"And you swear that you didn't send one to me." Would that she knew who the culprit was.

"I am nothing if not honest." He glanced at her. Amusement danced in those chocolate brown eyes. "Why would I go to the trouble of sending us both the same note?"

Julianna huffed. "I suppose you wouldn't." Then who'd sent the dratted missives and why? She contemplated the pool. There was nothing in the base of the statue that seemed out of place. In fact, no paint or other vandalism had occurred. Other than weather stains and the occasional smudge of dirt, the sculpture was as it had been every time she'd seen it. As unobtrusively as she could, she dabbed at the perspiration on her upper lip and temples, for the summer sun was quite warm. "I must say, that water is quite inviting."

The earl had finished his most recent perambulation around the pool. His grin remained in place. "Perhaps you should remove your boots and stockings then have a quick wade."

A gasp escaped her. She glanced from the basin to his face. His eyes beneath the brim of his top hat twinkled with mischief. And that glorious blond-silver hair fairly gleamed in the afternoon sunlight. "Not in broad daylight. Would you have me become the object of the local gossip mill?"

"Of course not." To her shock, Arthur winked. "Then you should return and try by moonlight, surely."

Her bottom jaw dropped. She stared at him as if she'd never seen him before. Was the earl... flirting? How preposterous. He wasn't that sort. Yet the uppermost question bouncing about her brain was wanting to know if he'd given any thought to that kiss like she had.

Of course he hasn't. Why should he? It means nothing.

Shoving the musings away, she shook her head. "If I could find the courage, perhaps, but I vastly prefer bathing in the little stream not far from my cottage. It's constantly moving, babbling, whispering, and there's a certain shallow pool just after it meanders into the trees..." Oh, *dear.* Heat infused her cheeks. That was entirely too much intimate information she'd divulged.

"Why, Miss Quill, never say you're an exhibitionist in your spare time." Surprise filled his expression. "I never would have thought that." He chuckled. "But then, a woman who has never been kissed must lead a secret life to some extent, hmm?"

Why, oh why did she have no experience with being in male company? Apparently, despite all the training on deportment and manners her mother had instilled in her, it had all fallen out of her head when presented with the conundrum of the earl.

"I… I am not. And no, I don't." Julianna ducked her head, for he kept staring at her with that quirk of his lips as if he found her quite entertaining. The warmth in her cheeks would soon consume her. "We, uh, don't possess a bathtub and even if we did, we have not the servants and I don't have the inclination required to heat the water and fill such a thing."

Jules, stop talking! You don't need to call attention to the disparity of your stations.

A rumble came from his chest before the sound released into the air as a chuckle. He kept his attention on the fountain. "There is nothing wrong with that, Julianna. In fact, I think bathing in nature is possibly one of the most freeing acts a person can indulge in. As for not having a secret life." He shrugged, and it was such an elegant affair she wanted to sigh again. "I wouldn't worry too much about that either. Sooner or later, we find what is meant for all of us."

She nodded, silent, for not a blessed intelligent word came into her mind. What was he insinuating if anything? Not knowing, she stood beside him and watched the water trickle from the statue's urn. Every once in a while, a sparrow would alight, tap a sip, and then flitter away. People bustled through the village, intent on their daily tasks. If a few of them cast curious glances at Arthur, he didn't seem to mind, but she wondered if they knew who he was.

After a few moments, he turned to her once more. "How does your father fare today?"

"I assume he is well. He was quiet when I left, but the house-keeper is there, and she'll keep him company while I'm out."

"Oh?" One of his blond eyebrows rose. "Your afternoon is uncommitted?"

"Yes. I'd hoped to find the clue within the statue. However, I now think it was naught but a lark, an excuse to have me here for whatever reason." She peered up at him, for he was a good five inches or so taller than her. The silver at his temples fascinated her and that dratted jaw crooned, called out to dance her fingertips along it. "Were you able to discover anything out of place on the statue?"

What was wrong with her? She'd spent an hour with this man last night on the hill, and not once during that time did she have such scandalous thoughts.

"I have not. Perhaps there is nothing abnormal about the fountain and that note was merely a ruse to put us both in the same place at the same time."

"Like the note from yesterday." But who had sent them and why? Perhaps years ago, her father might have played at such deviltry, but not now.

"Indeed. I'm rather annoyed at the prankster who thinks to dictate our lives." He cast a glance about the village square. "This is a quaint area, regardless. I haven't visited as much as I perhaps should. After all, shouldn't the Earl of Ettesmere keep a finger on the pulse of the areas his tenants utilize?"

"He should, and if you'd like, I can give you a quick tour. I'm familiar with the shops as well as the shopkeepers."

His grin had returned. "That would be lovely. Thank you, for I rather doubt we'll find a clue in this fountain."

"Agreed." At least in this way it would keep him in her company for a while longer. And she could pretend as they strolled side by side that she was a grand lady of the *ton* worthy of his attention and regard. There would be time enough to coddle her disappointment when reality crashed into her later.

The next hour passed in a blur as Julianna introduced the earl to various shopkeepers. She had to make a conscious effort to refer to him as the Earl of Ettesmere instead of his Christian name. When they weren't doing the pretty, she pointed out items in window displays that had caught her eye. He shared a pint at the local tavern as she waited outside, and when he returned, they talked briefly with the butcher as well as the owner of a pastry shop. Everyone was pleasant toward him, though they sent surprised and curious glances her way, no doubt in the attempt to puzzle out why she accompanied him. Some even mentioned that she was the odd one of Wokingham with her penchant for stargazing, but Arthur quickly and gently told them it took many people to make up a village. Everyone had a place.

He was the epitome of a polite and gracious gentleman. As they'd gone on, he'd asked intelligent questions and handed out praise as if it came from a bottomless bag. Many of the people they met had known his father when that man held the title, and there were plenty of stories shared between them. It gave her a greater understanding of the sort of man Arthur was, which edged her respect for him higher.

Eventually, they returned to the fountain at the village square. "Well, thank you for that little diversion." She offered him a smile. "I hope you've gained a better insight into village life, and I also hope you won't be a stranger to these people. They work hard; it's good that you acknowledged them and their efforts."

"I've been remiss in my duties of late. At times, grief steals large portions of my life and I've discovered I have used that as an excuse all too much." Tiny golden flecks floated within his irises in the sunlight. "It is something I need to make an effort to curb."

"I suppose we all do." Surprise gripped her chest. "Have a lovely evening, Arthur." When she turned to leave in the opposite direction of where he would head, the fleeting touch of his hand on her arm stayed her course. She glanced at him in confusion. "Did you have need of me for something else?"

At the last second, she realized her inquiry sounded all too open ended, perhaps like an invitation. *Oh, dear.*

A slow grin curved those sensual lips. "I do, actually."

Heat jumped into her cheeks while silly little flutters went through her lower belly. "Oh?"

"There's a quaint tea café on that corner." He gestured with his chin. "Would you do me the honor of taking tea with me? I'm rather not inclined to return home just yet."

"I would enjoy that very much." As if to put credence to

those words, her stomach growled. When he snickered, she couldn't help but smile. "I *did* forget to have breakfast today."

That's what I get for mooning about this man and a kiss that was no doubt an accident.

"Then we shall rectify your hunger immediately." He stepped aside so she could proceed him toward the tea café. "A repast with such wonderful company sounds like just the thing for this summer afternoon."

"Such gammon, my lord. I can assure you I'm nothing special." Though she smiled as she led the way across the square. For the moment, having an earl wish to take tea with her was a thrill of a lifetime. She'd worry about his intentions later.

CHAPTER SEVEN

N O SOONER HAD the first cup of tea been poured out than Arthur was temporarily distracted by the play of sunlight over Julianna's face and how it brought that sprinkling of freckles to the forefront. As such, his fingers went lax, which in turn spilled the hot beverage down the front of himself and into his lap.

"Hell's bells." He quickly returned his cup to its saucer then took up his napkin and dabbed at the worst of the mess. Heat flooded his neck and cheeks as he was forced to attend to his lap while Julianna looked on. Did she think him a nodcock, an imbecile, because he couldn't apparently hold a teacup?

"Are you quite all right, Lord Ettesmere?" Her low-pitched inquiry held concern, but damn if that tone didn't send a thrill of *something* down his spine.

That depended on the context. "Yes, I believe so." He did his level best to clean the spill, but the damage had been done. The satin of his waistcoat was stained, to say nothing of his breeches.

Or his ability to appear sophisticated in her presence.

It had been easy to converse with Ellen. So what had brought on the fumble-fingers? Why was it different now? He surreptitiously peered at her while tending to the mess.

Because Julianna was different. Arthur scrubbed at his breeches as surreptitiously as he could.

Where Ellen had been blonde and perfect, the daughter of an earl, Miss Quill was dark-haired, a commoner, and everything *ton* women were not. She went about the countryside alone at night, had vast knowledge about astronomy, which of course set her apart from every other woman, and she had a penchant for plain-speaking he found quite refreshing. And when he'd courted Ellen, it was with the caveat that she would be his countess, bear his children, become his helpmeet with everything the title would entail once it passed to him. Both of their lives had led to making an advantageous match, to strengthen position in society. While Julianna had never known any of that. He didn't know how to square with the problem, but then, as he completed dabbing at the liquid on his clothes, he supposed it didn't matter because he wasn't of a mind to court her.

Was he?

When he once more glanced up, she regarded him over the rim of her teacup. Her slim fingers curled elegantly around the delicate porcelain. What would it feel like if she were to dance those digits over his naked chest?

Good God, man, get hold of yourself. You're no longer a randy youth.

"Should we leave do you think?" When her lips curved into a soft smile, he simply sat there and stared like he had not a brain in his head.

"Uh..." He peered about the interior of the tiny café. All six of the intimate round tables were filled. Other people lingered about the entrance, clearly waiting their turn. "During the height of the crowds so everyone will see my wet breeches and think the worst of me?" Arthur snorted at the picture he made and shook his head. "No, thank you." With the decision having been made, he dropped his damp and stained linen napkin into his lap.

"Very well." Julianna put her cup into its saucer with nary a clink. Then she poured out a second cup for him. "Do you take cream or sugar?"

"Cream, please. Just a dash." When she did so and slid the cup his way, he sighed. "Thank you."

Now don't act like the school dunce, Ettesmere.

She selected a tiny jam tart from the tray. "Do you believe whoever wrote those notes wishes to make jest of us?"

"It's entirely possible, and since they didn't start until I arrived in Berkshire, there must be someone in the village or the surroundings who wants to watch me behave as if I'm a marionette puppet." He narrowed his eyes as he sipped his tea. "I don't appreciate it." Even if it had put him into her company twice now.

"Don't be so harsh." When she delicately licked at a bit of jam that clung to the corner of her mouth, Arthur stared. Never in his life had he been as jealous of a condiment than he was in that moment. "It's all terribly amusing."

"For you, possibly." He hurriedly took another sip of tea to banish the sudden graveling of his voice due to nothing except stark desire. What the devil was wrong with him? Yes, it had been at least five years since he'd had anything to do with a woman, yet here he was fairly marinating in sudden lust. It wasn't well done. "For me, I don't like being manipulated."

Julianna rolled her eyes briefly heavenward. "Then don't think of it that way. Instead, concentrate on the adventure. Obviously, someone has too much time on their hands and for whatever reason they've chosen us as their targets of the day. However, we had a nice evening of stargazing out of it last night, and now we're having tea after you made a few connections. That's nothing to sneeze at."

"Perhaps." Arthur conceded the point to her. "However, I don't appreciate being thrust into the unknown." That was perhaps the crux of the problem. With Ellen, he'd known exactly what to expect, for they had been both reared to attain a good match and start a nursery. But now? He gazed at Julianna, swept his attention over the planes of her face, wished to count those freckles—and to discover if she had them on any other places—and was obliged to stifle a sigh. Now, he felt a bit at sixes and sevens. What should he expect?

For that matter, what *did* he want at this point in his life?

"Everything is unknown until we become acquainted with it."

"True." When he reached for a honey seed cake, she apparently had the same idea. Their fingers met over the tray and warmth shot up his arm to his elbow. "Please, you go ahead." He eased back, glad the pleasure in her expression had come from something he'd done.

"Thank you. These are a favorite of mine."

They were his as well, so at least they had that in common. Then, because he was still incredibly curious, he centered his line of inquiry on one subject. "How did you become interested in astronomy? It's rather an obscure course of study for a woman."

Her snort of derision made him grin. "Isn't anything learned from a book instead of in a drawing room an obscure course of study for a woman?" The light of determination gleamed in her sapphire eyes. She tapped a fingernail against the side of her teacup. "None of it would have been possible without my brother Ned. Edwin, really, but everyone called him Ned."

"Oh? Does he live around here?" Since she hadn't spoken of him before, he wasn't sure.

"No." To his mystification, tears sprang to her eyes. "I lost him six years ago. At first, we thought he'd caught a head cold, but then it settled into his lungs. He had trouble breathing, was so weak for so long." She shook her head. "I can still hear his horrid, wet coughing at night. By the time the doctor was called for—at great expense—it was too late. Ned had contracted pneumonia, and in the end, he just wasn't strong enough to fight it off."

"You have my condolences." It was never easy to lose a loved one.

"Thank you." After rooting around in her reticule, she pulled forth a brass pocket watch. As it dangled from its partially tarnished chain, he caught glimpses of etchings on the front that depicted a crescent moon as well as a constellation. "This was his.

My father gave it to me following Ned's death. It's a constant reminder that I have much work to do in his name." A tear slipped down her cheek. She dashed it away. "Forgive me," she said in a tortured whisper. "Though it's been many years, it sometimes takes me by surprise, for I always forget he won't be coming 'round the corner to speak with me, and I'll never again see his goofy grin when he'd discovered something amazing."

Her grief bumped against his own and his chest tightened. "I understand all too well." As much as he wished to touch her hand that rested on the tabletop, he resisted. The café was full of people and prying eyes. It wouldn't do to land in the gossip mill for more than he was already doing by being here with her. "It's especially hard when you turn to tell them a particular tidbit you know they would like... but they were never there to begin with."

"Yes. The pain just means we loved fiercely." Julianna dabbed at her eyes with her napkin. For a moment she kept her focus on her plate. Then, with a sigh, she once more met his gaze. "Ever since Ned came back from university, he had an interest in the stars. Perhaps before even that. Oh, he was so excited about the possibilities." Though her chin trembled, she went on. "Since I had nothing pressing on my schedule," she uttered a self-depreciating laugh, "I never do, you see, I tagged along with him on his nightly visits throughout the countryside where he first charted the stars. Immediately, I fell in love with the heavens."

"I don't doubt that." How she talked about the stars was unique and full of wonder. It was contagious, made him want to learn everything as well. "You seem to enjoy the science."

"Oh, I do! I'm so... alive whenever I see something new. It's quite the thrill. Once I became proficient in using the telescope and identifying stars and their patterns, that's when Ned told me about seeing a comet." She tucked the pocket watch back into her reticule.

"A comet." It wasn't a question, and the awe infused into those two words was genuine. "How fascinating."

"I think so." She frowned into the contents of her cup. "I've seen it every day this week, which is the same month that Ned saw the comet six years ago before he got sick."

"How can you know it's the same one?" Did celestial bodies have personalities?

"There is a certain way the main part of it wobbles, as well as telltale signs in the tail." She chuckled and raised her gaze to his. Excitement warred with grief in those cool pools. "It's not a tail in the usual sense, more like a field of small pieces of debris that trail after the comet due to its gravitational pull."

"You can see that through your telescope?" As she spoke, he surreptitiously roved his gaze over her person. Though he'd seen her in that dress before, the striking color was quite pleasing, and he couldn't keep his regard from her décolletage. What would that soft skin feel like on his tongue?

You're bordering on a letch, Ettesmere. Stop it.

"Yes. It was Ned's, but I appropriated it once he passed." She drew abstract patterns on the tablecloth with a forefinger. The subject matter properly redirected his attention from cataloging her charms. "When you look at the comet through the lens, it's glorious. Shimmering. Silvery. Ethereal in some respects. It's quite peaceful, and I wonder, when I look at it, if it has a sound as it makes its way through the heavens."

"I'd like to discover that answer too." Her face was so animated as she spoke about the stars that it transformed her into quite the beauty. Was she aware of that?

"You may come with me the next time I go out. In fact, come meet me on Otis Hill tonight. I'll give you my telescope and you can see the comet for yourself."

Perhaps I can steal a second kiss and give her a better showing than before. Yet, he was loathe to commit, for Ellen's memory was at the back of his mind. "I will surely consider that."

"It's my wish to save up enough coin to purchase a more powerful instrument, but until that day comes, I'll make do with Ned's." A dreamy smile took possession of her mouth, and he couldn't stop staring. "According to the arrogant arses of the Astronomical Society of London, no one has seen a comet during this time of the year before, so I intend to chart the whole of its flight while it's visible, present my findings to those men, and once I have undeniable proof of the discovery, name it after my brother. To honor him."

God, she was incredible. He had no doubt she would accomplish that goal. "That's very noble of you." His heart ached at her fervor. Perhaps he should have done more to keep his wife in remembrance.

Julianna nodded. She wiped at another tear. "I think he would have liked that."

"And I suspect he would have been proud of what you've made yourself into." Arthur drained his teacup of its contents. "As would your mother."

"Well, there you'd be wrong." When she giggled, his lower jaw dropped as he rested his cup in its saucer. What a marvelous sound! It was pure joy. It was like sunshine, and all he wanted to do was bask in it. "My mother was second cousin to a doddering, childless viscount, and as such was loosely connected to the *ton*."

"Oh? What was the viscount's name?"

An expression of concentration crossed her face. "Uh… Lord Addington? Asherman? Atherton? It escapes me at the moment, but I can ask my father. I'm afraid I don't follow the aristocracy; they've never seemed that important to me." Then she gasped. "I beg your pardon. I didn't mean to offend."

"There is nothing to apologize for. Honesty is appreciated." And she was certainly that. "Lord Atherton sounds vaguely familiar. I didn't know him personally before he died, but I remember my father speaking of him from sessions in the House of Lords." The revelation of her connection—however slim—to the *ton* was startling and gave him a modicum of relief. Not that bloodlines mattered, he was quick to remind himself. *She is a delightful friend, nothing more.*

And then that damned imp of his conscience laughed at him

as if he were the greatest nodcock to ever walk the earth.

Julianna smiled. "How interesting. My mother was every bit a lady. She taught me everything a genteel woman of distinction should know."

He couldn't help but laugh. "Then she would have disapproved of you running after your brother at all hours of the night to study the skies instead of the latest rage in embroidery or dancing?"

"Indeed. Her fondest wish was for me to marry someone out of the village."

"Did she not like Wokingham?"

"Obviously, she did, for she met my father on the grounds while in Berkshire at a house party. They were married shortly afterward, but I suspect she wanted a better life for me." She shrugged. "I hadn't the heart to tell her that no man—local or otherwise—had ever shown an interest in me."

His chest tugged from the confusion and defeat that flitted through her expression. "That doesn't mean you have failed in your life. Why, I rather believe what you've accomplished is staggering and amazing." When hope sprang into her eyes, that invisible pull between them tightened. "You have been quite distinctive already, I'll wager."

A blush stained her cheeks. "Your kindness is quite lovely."

He didn't want lovely or appreciation or respect for his title; he wanted... what? Damn it, he wanted her to like him for himself. Panic climbed his throat, for they couldn't linger much longer in the café. "Julianna?"

"Yes?" She drained her teacup and once more looked at him with those remarkable blue eyes, stunning in the afternoon sunlight.

"My mother is throwing a rout tomorrow evening. She said some gammon about being an appetizer of sorts ahead of her midsummer masquerade." Arthur cleared his throat, for this was the height of awkward. "I... ah..." He heaved out a frustrated breath. "Would you like to attend? It would be a good evening for you, to see the world your mother was connected to." Good lord, had he even thought of the implications of extending such an invitation? He ignored the warning bells ringing in his mind. "Additionally, you could meet my sister as well as say hello to Emily." Wouldn't Sophia have a merry time in teasing him about that? To say nothing of his mother, but he would weather that storm with aplomb. Julianna was an acquaintance who deserved to dip a toe into the world her mother came from.

Her lower jaw dropped as she replaced the cup into its saucer. "You have a sister?"

"Yes, and a brother who isn't in residence at the moment." He shrugged. "My mother wanted the family around her at this time, for she and my father married during the midsummer. She's feeling lonely, I think, as well as suffering ennui."

"Understandable." A frown curved those kissable lips downward. "I only possess one gown suitable for such an event. Even then, I sewed it myself and it's probably not fancy enough for—"

He stopped her words with a fleeting touch to her hand before withdrawing his. "It will be wonderful." With a nod, he held her gaze. "You've not worn it yet."

"No. I meant to save it…" Her words trailed off in confusion.

"Don't. Life itself is a special occasion, and if I've learned anything over the course of the last several years it's to seize the day when I can." His conscience laughed again. Perhaps he should take his own damned advice. "This rout won't be nearly as bright if you don't come."

Truly, Ettesmere, have you forgotten how to talk like a charming gentleman?

"Do hush, Ettesmere." Her cheeks blazed with a renewed blush.

Instead of making a witty rejoinder, he froze, for Ellen used to say those exact words to him when he was about to make a cake of himself. Immediately, a swath of hot guilt cut through his chest. *What the devil am I doing? This is no way to honor my wife.*

Julianna cocked her head slightly to one side. "Have I said

something untoward? You've gone white as if you've seen a ghost."

"I'm fine." All the gaiety seeped from the afternoon. Was he betraying his wife by courting—not courting—desiring—surely appreciating was the more correct word?—the woman before him? He couldn't look her in the eye, so he turned his attention to the nearby window. That damned fountain stood in the middle of the square, appearing the height of innocence, yet it had been that sculpture that had thrown him into Julianna's company once again.

Only to land him in this maudlin coil.

"I rather think you aren't." The nearly whispered words skittered down his spine and put him in mind of dark, shadowy places where kisses might accompany that same tone. "Am I the first woman you've befriended or even talked at length to since your wife passed?"

Was it that obvious, then? "Yes." He swallowed around a wad of unexpressed emotion in his throat. Finally, he dragged his gaze back to hers, reeled at the compassion found in those blue depths. "It feels much like a betrayal to my wife."

This time, it was Julianna who stroked her fingertips over the top of his hand, and that fleeting touch sent tiny fires into his blood which worked to further confuse him. "She has been gone for a while now. Anyone can see how enamored of her you were, but I rather doubt she'd want you to spend the remainder of your life racked with grief and shut away from things that might bring you an ounce of enjoyment."

"My mind knows this, but my heart is resistant." The effort of speaking felt enormous, but somehow, he sensed she would understand. "Ellen thoroughly adored everything about life. She often spoke about mine if she were to pass on first."

"And?"

"She urged me to move forward, find happiness, marry a second time if I wished."

"Then perhaps you should honor her memory by putting one

foot in front of the other and taking it slow." Again, her fingers glanced over his hand before she pulled away. "Dance at your mother's rout; I'm certain your family is concerned about you. Laugh at the antics of your daughter. Let some of the light back into your soul. Then you can go from there."

For long moments, he regarded her. How was she so wise when she'd experienced nothing in life that could compare to his loss? And she'd spoken nothing about courtship or romance, only about other aspects. If he concentrated on those things, perhaps his mind would be clearer to think about how her presence into his life would affect the future.

One step at a time.

Yes, that seemed manageable.

Finally, he nodded. "I shall attempt to seek out the light. It has indeed been missing for some time, and..."

"Yes?"

"I've rather missed it," he finished in a choked voice. To his mortification, moisture welled in his eyes. "Thank you for opening the door and letting it come back in."

When she smiled, his chest tightened. "It was my pleasure, and something I needed myself after my brother died. Perhaps you can do that for someone else in the future."

This afternoon wasn't anything he'd expected, but it had been proved a catharsis of sorts. There would be plenty of time to marvel over that fact later.

Until then, what the devil should he do about Julianna now that he was obliged to introduce her to his family tomorrow night?

CHAPTER EIGHT

June 15, 1819

J ULIANNA'S NERVES BESET her so much that she feared she would cast up her accounts all over the sofa she sat on in the parlor she'd been shown into.

There had been no fear when she'd walked over to Ettesmere Park, for the twilight shadows had been interesting, as was watching the various stars pop in the sky. However, once ushered into the large manor house, doubts and insecurities raised their heads and she suddenly wished she hadn't come.

In an effort to circumvent a reaction, she smoothed her hands down the front of the deep rose-colored gown she wore, but her palms were sweaty inside her kid gloves. The silver embroidery featuring whimsical scrollwork on the bodice and hem—which had taken her the whole of the wintertime months last year— didn't bring her comfort. What was taking the earl so long to come down and greet her? Now that a day had passed, did he regret offering the invitation to someone obviously not of his world? She moved to one of the windows that overlooked the circular drive at the front of the manor. Carriages arrived and guests spilled out. Even in the fading light, their fine clothing and aristocratic bearing was unmistakable.

I cannot do this. She frowned at her reflection. Though her housekeeper had assisted in piling her hair atop her head and securing it with pins as well as a double Roman-style silver band, she still appeared like a country bumpkin playing at being a lady. It mattered not that her mother had instilled manners and proper etiquette and deportment into her from a young age. The *ton* wasn't the place for her. *At seven and thirty, I'm naught but a coward.*

Just as she'd turned about to flee, the earl appeared in the doorway, trailing his daughter and a young man in his wake. There was no escape now. She had no choice but to paste on what she hoped was a bright smile and come forward.

"Miss Quill!" The young girl shot across the room to take Julianna's hands in hers. Her white satin skirts rasped with every step. "How wonderful to see you again." Her eyes twinkled with excitement; a mother of pearl broach gleamed from a pink velvet ribbon at her throat. "Papa told John and me that he'd invited a few people. I'd hoped one of them was you."

"Hullo, Lady Emily. How have you been?" Some of the elation over the evening deflated. So, she wasn't a special addition to the night if he'd invited others. How silly of her to think otherwise.

"Wonderful, thank you."

"I'm glad to hear that." As best she could, Julianna masked her disappointment. "Yes. I'd unexpectedly come upon your father in the village yesterday. We took tea together and he mentioned that I might enjoy coming tonight."

"Well, you are marvelous in that gown. That color suits you." Then she stepped aside and gestured with a hand. "This is my brother John... er, rather, Lord Eglinton." The young man, probably not more than five and twenty and no doubt bearing one of his father's courtesy titles, executed a half-bow from the waist.

"It's a pleasure to make your acquaintance, Miss Quill." He had his father's features but there was a mischievous air about him that gave her pause.

Never in her life had she seen more blonde-haired people in one room. Truly, Arthur had gorgeous children. "Good evening, Lord Eglinton. Your father has been remiss in telling me about you."

Emily giggled as Arthur sputtered. "And of course, you already know Papa." She bounced her gaze between them. "Everyone is gathering in the drawing room. That's where Grandmama is presently. Shall I show you the way?"

"That won't be necessary," Arthur interrupted as he came forward. "I'll take her there, but I'd hoped to give her a quick tour beforehand. Unless one of you wishes to do that?"

"That sounds rather dull, Papa." The young lordling shook his head. "I'd rather have a round at the card tables before they're crowded."

"And I promised Grandmama I would see how many of the guests wished to dance. It will make a difference in when the rugs are rolled back, you know." The girl winked at her father. "You owe me a country reel, Papa." Then she gave Julianna a cheery wave. "We'll talk later, Miss Quill."

As suddenly as they'd come, the two departed, leaving her alone with the earl. Julianna peered at him, but somehow, he wasn't the same man she'd come to know the last few times they'd met. Instead of his English gentleman about the country outfit, he now wore black trousers with a black jacket that had tails. The fine lawn shirt was offset by a silver satin waistcoat embroidered with dark blue birds, while an emerald stickpin provided a pop of color and interest within the snowy folds of his intricately tied cravat.

"Hullo, Arthur. Or should I refer to you as Ettesmere for the remainder of the evening?" In his natural habitat as it were, he was vastly unapproachable, and she mourned the loss of the easy camaraderie that had been between them.

The rumble of his laughter sent skitters of awareness over her skin. "That is entirely at your discretion. However, it would cast a more proper light if we remained formal at the moment." He raked his gaze over her person. "Emily was correct. That gown is more than flattering on you. In fact, you shine in that color."

"It is a favorite of mine." Heat slapped at her cheeks. Did his notice and compliment mean anything more than an acquaintance acknowledging a pretty frock?

"You should wear that hue more often." Admiration reflected in his brown eyes. "I'm impressed with your needlework skills."

"At least I have that." She clasped her hands before her. Never had she felt more exposed. "I assumed I would despise it, but embroidery especially relaxes me, makes me forget my situation at times."

"Ah. That's how I feel when I tote up columns of numbers." He shifted his weight from foot to foot. Surely, he wasn't a victim of nerves too. "Well, in any event, there is a rout underway. Will you come up with me and meet some of my family members?"

Her stomach roiled. "I'm not certain I fit in here." Though she was confident of her needlework, the guests mingling throughout the house had no doubt spent more coin than she could imagine on their clothing.

"If you truly wish to leave, I will, of course, understand. However," he lowered his voice, "let me confess something to you. That night when we watched the stars and I kissed you? Well, I was terrified, just as you are now because I assumed it was something I never wished to do again."

It was the first time since it had happened that he'd spoken of it. The honesty was endearing. "Are you still afraid?"

"Every damned moment I'm in your company." When he shrugged, he flashed a wry grin. "I'm woefully out of practice in flirting and being charming."

A tiny gasp escaped her. "Then you were indeed flirting with me?"

"Apparently, I'm trying." His laughter swept away pieces of her worries. "Truth to tell, I don't know to what end, but if you don't mind, I certainly don't."

"I... I..." She blinked, shook her head. "I look forward to the challenge." Julianna pushed down the remainder of her concerns. "Though, how do you plan to introduce me?" It was much too early in the conversation to assume there was anything else between them than acquaintances.

"As a friend, perhaps. Are we not that despite my poor attempts at appearing something... else?" When she slowly nodded, he grinned. Shivery sensation drifted down her spine. Had he always been so potent? "Right, then." He offered her his arm, bent at the elbow. "Shall we?"

How bad of a faux pas was it to retch upon an earl's shoes? With a shaking hand, she laid her fingers on his sleeve. "I'll give you an admission of my own. I don't have any experience in doing the pretty, especially amidst so many people high on the instep." She cleared her throat. "However, I look forward to it."

"Ah, Miss Quill, you are not a very good liar." He chuckled again as he led her from the room. "You have a wild look about the eyes as if you wish to escape."

Heat went through her cheeks. "Perhaps I do." As he drew her up the grand staircase, and the closer they came to what she assumed was the drawing room, the din of talking and laughter grew louder. "This is not my world." How would these people, most of the *ton*, perceive her?

"Yet it is in a way." He patted her hand that lay on his arm. "Aren't you curious?"

"A bit." That couldn't be denied. "Mama always talked of the year she had a Season."

"Then consider this an abbreviated introduction to society." Arthur paused at the doorway. "If you still find you don't suit with the people here, I will immediately take you home. However, I think your mother would have been proud of you."

Her eyebrows rose in surprise. "I... Thank you." She glanced into the room filled with a crush of people and then back to his face. There was nothing except interest and perhaps indulgence in his expression. "Without you, I never would have had this opportunity."

"Then come inside and enjoy yourself. Have a glass of champagne, perhaps share a dance, if not with me then with the man of your choosing." With a mysterious grin, he proceeded her into the room while she followed in his wake.

Julianna's hands shook so badly that she attempted to hide them in the folds of her skirts. She held back as he forged through the crowd. Every once in a while, he would pause and speak to a few people before he continued. Only when he reached two blonde-haired ladies did he stop and buss their cheeks, respectively. When he half-turned and didn't immediately see her, he frowned. With a sigh of resignation, she came toward him. His eyes lit with relief.

"Mother, Sophia, this is Miss Quill." He stood slightly aside so she could draw abreast of him. "I met her in the village yesterday and before that when her dog ran away. Miss Quill, may I present the Dowager Countess of Ettesmere and my sister, Lady Sophia."

To say nothing of the evening they'd spent on the hill watching stars when he stole a barely-there kiss.

"Ah, the interesting stargazer our Emily met a handful of days ago." The older woman flicked her gaze up and down Julianna's person. "Apparently, you made quite the impression upon her." She glanced to the side where the young girl stood. When Julianna peeked that way, Lady Emily shrugged but grinned. "You must have been why my son came home looking like a dog's breakfast yesterday afternoon."

Another round of heat fired in her cheeks. "Uh, I did nothing other than take tea with His Lordship. It wasn't my fault he forgot how to hold a cup and subsequently spilled all over himself." At least it was the truth, but if her penchant for speaking her mind wasn't accepted by these ladies, she'd surely be asked to leave.

Remarkably, Arthur's sister chuckled. "How lovely to know there are still people in this world who have no time for dissembling or talking in riddles." She gently shoved her brother aside and then took possession of Julianna's hand. "It's nice to meet you, Miss Quill. Perhaps you and I should go for a glass of punch. We can have a good gab about Arthur."

"I don't believe that's necessary," he was quick to insert. "I didn't invite her here to spend time in gossip."

"Oh, ho! Never say you're finally showing interest in a woman." Lady Sophia winked at Julianna. "Perhaps it's you I need to drag to the refreshments table." She latched onto Arthur's arm. When he threw her a panicked look, Julianna giggled. The sibling interaction fascinated her; she missed that since Ned had passed. "Come, brother. Let Mama have a chat with the little gazelle you've brought into the lion's den while we have a cozy talk."

"But I wanted to—"

The lady tsked her tongue. "You knew what would happen when we reached this point." She tugged him away, and Julianna's stomach roiled with greater insistence.

"Don't fret, so, dear." The dowager linked her arm with Julianna's and led her toward one side of the room. "Your surname sounds familiar."

"My father was a bricklayer in his prime. He once worked on a few outbuildings on this property." The pedigree wasn't much, but she was proud of her history. If the dowager countess couldn't accept that, then this wasn't the place for her.

"Ah, that's right. I remember my husband was so thrilled with how professional those buildings were once they'd been completed." A ghost of a smile curved her lips. "In those days, he was anxious to make a good impression on the tenants as well as the villagers."

Julianna nodded. "My father still lives in the same cottage he built for my mother when they married."

"It sounds as if they had a wonderful union." A faraway look came over her face. "That's how it was with Ettesmere. He was so gallant and charming, but only after he decided he could be even in the face of tradition."

How interesting. "Your son seems to have done splendidly with the title." She glanced at the crush of people in the drawing room then caught her breath when her gaze alighted on Arthur. He'd either eluded his sister or had returned immediately after securing a drink. But now he stood talking to a woman near his age and who was ravishing in red. Gray strands glimmered in her brown hair as did jewel-encrusted combs.

"He struggles with it, the same as every man in his position, but now his children are grown and he conducts his duties by rote, his time is much more his own. I hope he'll puzzle out how to enjoy himself again." The dowager followed her line of sight. "That's Lady Drummond. She's a recent widow, and from the gossip I've gleaned, she's on the hunt for husband number three."

"Is she a good match for the earl?" She didn't like the stab of what felt all too much like jealousy that went through her chest. Who was she to have such a reaction? What Arthur did with his time and life was none of her concern. Yet, flirting wasn't courtship and neither had it been a declaration. Indeed, they were friends alone.

"Oh, I'm sure she is for someone. *I* don't particularly care for her." The dowager snorted. "Too overblown and bold for my tastes. Quite selfish, really. She wouldn't fit into the family, I think." Before Julianna could comment, the older lady continued. "It seems you're spending time with Arthur. I'm glad for that."

"Oh?" That was surprising. "How so?"

"Ever since his wife died, he's kept himself aloof from practically everyone—even the family. Rarely does he come to Berkshire. I nearly had to beg him to do so for the summer." She flashed another faint smile. "However, it's refreshing to see he's got a bit of a kick to his step these days."

"Perhaps he's entertaining the widow. She is of his same class." And Julianna despised the woman for that.

"My dear Miss Quill, class is much more than one's ranking in society. It's how one thinks and acts. It's what one puts out into the world, and how one thinks about others." She held Julianna's gaze. "One can hold a lofty position but have an ugly heart, so when I think he looks forward to his outings with you, I mean it.

Don't doubt your influence."

"I see." Yet she somehow didn't. What influence could she possibly hold over an earl? Heat smacked her cheeks once more. "Our meetings have been purely accidental." She refrained from mentioning the notes. Or the kiss. That was her memory alone. "However, he's pleasant company and quite intelligent."

"But lonely, wouldn't you say?" The dowager's gaze was intent upon her.

"Possibly. Grief has certainly touched us all." When he laughed at something the widow said, she frowned. "Sooner or later, he'll tire of the plain, uneventful life I lead, tire of the stars or the stories I tell about them. He'll be back underfoot until he finds a proper companion."

Not for worlds would she ask what the dowager thought of him spending time with her. Nor would she try to puzzle out the whys behind him seeking her out. Perhaps it didn't matter. She would enjoy his company for as long as she could. It certainly had provided a splash of color into her life.

"Time will tell." The dowager chuckled. "Arthur is quite willful, as are all of my children. He's slow to make decisions, but once he does, he doesn't waver."

Julianna frowned. "Then he spends much time thinking before acting?"

"Oh, indeed. In fact, it took him over a year to propose to his wife when we all knew they were right as rain for each other from the first."

That didn't make sense, for as long as Julianna had known him, he appeared to make decisions on the spur of the moment. One good example of that was the invitation he'd offered her to attend this evening's entertainments. Was it possible men could change after so many years in one pattern? If so, that was encouraging.

"Don't fret so, my dear. Life isn't supposed to be figured out in one go." The dowager nudged her arm. "Arthur is coming this way and it seems dancing will start soon." She patted Julianna's arm. "Have a gay time tonight. We shall talk later."

But why? After this evening, there would be no need for her to ever seek the dowager out. Yet she nodded politely while the older woman sailed off to talk to a cluster of friends.

"How was your conversation with my mother?" Lines of worry framed his eyes and mouth as he came close to her position.

"She is a wonderful woman and devoted to her family." She scooted to the wall as some of the younger men in the room began the task of shuttling the furniture to the sides in anticipation of rolling back the carpets. "I had the feeling she is a woman of many secrets."

He snorted. "Perhaps. Did you like her?"

Julianna shrugged. "I suppose, but I don't know her all that well."

"She's a real brick."

That remained to be seen. After all, why wouldn't the dowager have been polite to her—a guest? "How did you escape your sister? She seemed incredibly determined."

When he laughed, it resonated in her chest and left delicious tingles behind. "Vexed I wouldn't tell her intimate details of my life."

Relief twisted down Julianna's spine. She cast a glance at the young men who rolled back the carpets with more haste than finesse. "What will happen after the dancing?"

"Who can say? Mother doesn't often tell me her schedule for these events. There have been times when she's gotten up play-acting or games." His eyes twinkled. "Does it matter?"

"No, I don't suppose it does." Across the room, someone had thrown open both sets of double doors that led to a shadowy terrace. The addition of the summer breeze was quite welcome. "Will you dance with that, uh, widow I saw you speaking with earlier?"

"Her?" Arthur shook his head. "I should think not. Lady Drummond is a social climber, and since her last husband was a viscount, she's looking to reach the next rung. I will not be a steppingstone."

That mollified her slightly. "Surely, you'll dance with your family." It would be thrilling indeed to observe him in this setting.

"Of course." He winked. "As I will with you if you're agreeable."

The worry came rushing back to smack into her chest. "It's been an age since I indulged. I'm not sure I can remember the steps." Long ago her mother had taught both her and Ned how to dance. Many evenings she would demonstrate with their father while Julianna had to partner her brother. Those times produced copious amounts of laughter. "There's not much call for astronomers to grace ballrooms."

And if she wasn't thrust onto the floor, no one would see her flounder when she missed steps or fell into mistakes.

"Then we shall have to change that." His grin sent flutters scudding through her lower belly. "Remember, Miss Quill, no one makes glorious history by standing on the sidelines."

The smile she gave him felt a trifle forced. "Perhaps you should remember the same, Lord Ettesmere."

For the space of a few heartbeats, he regarded her before nodding. "Touché."

Then the dowager called for his attention as musicians came into the room, and once more she was left alone, even more confused than when she'd arrived.

CHAPTER NINE

ARTHUR DID HIS duty as the earl by dancing with his mother and sister as well as Emily. All the while, he remained distracted by Julianna. She kept to the outskirts of the room, watching the entertainment with wide eyes and a faint smile on her lips. The silver bands in her black hair winked in the low light.

Damnation, but she was ravishing.

His daughter chuckled. "It would seem I'm not enough to hold your attention tonight, Papa. I wonder why that is."

He gazed down into her face as heat crept up the back of his neck. "I suppose there is rather much to take in at present since I haven't been out in society for an age."

"That is your own fault." His daughter searched his eyes for something but didn't comment on it. "Have you danced with Miss Quill yet?"

"I have not. If you haven't noticed, there are entirely too many women in my family I had a duty toward first."

She rolled her gaze heavenward. "You'd best do so soon. It looks as if she's quite popular among the bachelors."

"The devil you say," he muttered, but wasn't in a position to see her.

Emily laughed outright at that. "Yet you're not all interested in her, and she is but a country friend and acquaintance, correct?"

The heat on his neck intensified, for that was the story he'd invented two mornings ago at breakfast when they kept nagging him about it. "Don't you have young pups to beguile and hearts to break?"

"Of course I do." She drifted elegantly to a halt when the dance ended. "I wish you luck tonight. Perhaps you'll discover something else you like about a certain lady astronomer that will vault your relationship over the friendship line."

"That comment does not deserve a rebuttal." But he grinned as he waved her off.

Finally, he was free.

By the time he made his way over to her location, a young pup had claimed her attention. A low growl escaped him. He didn't much care for men lining up to talk to her. Hadn't he found her first? And from the looks of it, she was overwhelmed by the attention. "I say, Miss Quill, didn't you promise this next set to me?" Let the younger men cast annoyed glances his way; what cared he? He was an earl, damn it, and he would have his way.

Get hold of yourself, Ettesmere. Throwing your privilege around merely because you're jealous. This isn't who you are.

When she glanced at him, relief reflected in her eyes. "I believe that I did, Your Lordship."

"Yes, I quite thought so." He moved a couple of the more ardent would-be suitors from his path and then took possession of her hand. "It's a country reel, so the steps shouldn't be difficult to ascertain." As he plucked her from the knot of admirers, a smug grin flirted with his lips. "You seemed to need rescuing," he whispered while leading her to an open spot on the temporary dance floor.

"I did, rather." With her flushed cheeks and sparkling eyes bringing out a wholesome sort of beauty, he had difficulty keeping his gaze off her. "It's a puzzlement to be sure, for I did nothing to encourage those men. But they kept coming and asking the most asinine questions. Not at all like the genuine talks that you and I have shared."

That penchant for plain speaking without guile or manipula-
tion left him at sixes and sevens. She didn't play the usual games
so common with women of the *ton*. It was but one facet that
drew him to her like a moth to a flame. "I am glad to know I'm
not lumped in with the riff-raff then."

Julianna's giggle went straight to his stones. Oh, what he
wouldn't give to have a few moments alone with her! "Even if
you weren't an earl, you wouldn't be that." When the opening
strains of the reel rent the air, she touched her hands to his in the
proper form. "Regardless, thank you for the rescue. I find the act
of conversing on the weather or the guests tedious at best."

"And you would no doubt wish to be free to contemplate
your stars," he added with a grin before the steps of the dance
took him away from her.

The grin she bestowed upon him once he returned to partner
her again could rival the candlelight. "Of course, but then I'm
happiest when I'm among the stars."

Feeling all too daring, he said, "Ah, you wound me, Miss
Quill. I thought being in my company might have put that smile
upon your lips and the color in your cheeks."

"Lord Ettesmere!" Then the steps tore her away from him,
but he didn't mind.

Teasing her was all too easy. In such a high-flying mood, he
even managed to bedevil his next two partners before being put
back into Julianna's presence.

"Of course I enjoy being in your company," she finally said,
and when she ducked beneath his arm as part of the dance, he
was afforded a healthy peek at her cleavage. "However, I'm more
comfortable with you when the stars are visible."

Arthur frowned. "Do I make you nervous?"

"A bit. Since meeting you, my life has been a series of helter-
skelter happenings, and each one confuses me more." Honesty
shone from her eyes. "As I've said before, I welcome the
challenge, for how else can I expand my horizons? And…"

"And?" But the steps took him away from her once more

while he died a thousand deaths wondering about what she would say.

When she took up his hand once more, he nearly shuddered with relief. "And the particular kind of nervousness and excitement you bring makes me wish to explore it further," she finally finished in a hushed voice as a blush blazed on her cheeks. "After all, what sort of scientist would I be if I didn't?"

"Indeed." As much as he wished to remain suave and sophisticated, he couldn't help a grin or feel as if he'd passed an invisible hurdle. All too soon, the country reel ended. After polite applause broke out in the room, he put a hand to the small of her back and led her off to the side. "Would you care for a glass of punch?"

"That sounds lovely, but only if I accompany you. It's quite presumptuous of me to assume an earl would fetch punch for a mere villager." She briefly tightened her fingers on his sleeve before dropping her hand. "Also, I don't want to be left to the mercy of all those prowling men."

"Put your fears to rest, Miss Quill. I won't leave you alone." Arthur escorted her from the mad crush filling the drawing room and once at the refreshment table some ways down one of the corridors, he drew her to a halt. "Most women would consider a bevy of admirers a wild success."

"Success means different things to different people, Your Lordship. And in the event you hadn't noticed, I am not most women."

"Oh, I've noticed," he added in a barely audible voice.

She looked at him as if he were the world's biggest nodcock. "Men are fickle. They'll buzz about the first pretty face they see, but their attention wavers if someone more beautiful walks by." With a nod of thanks, Julianna accepted the glass of punch he pressed into her hand. "I may not have experience in all of this," she let her free hand flutter about to presumably encompass the whole of the rout, "but I'd rather have one faithful man who adores me for everything I am—flaws and all—than dozens of adoring fair-weather suitors who don't wish to know me deeper than the surface or go running once they discover my pedigree."

Arthur gaped at her. At least she hadn't let the trappings of the *ton* turn her head. On the other hand, what if those very things proved a stumbling block? Slowly, he sipped his own punch. This woman who had her head in the stars fascinated him in ways different than when he'd courted Ellen.

How was that possible, especially when he assumed it would never happen again?

"Very astute musings, Miss Quill." The fact she was still her practical, down-to-earth self both amused him and made him proud. "After this, I'd be happy to give you a tour of the manor or perhaps show you the gardens. My mother raises prize-winning roses each summer—"

"Damnation, Ettesmere, you are a difficult man to track." The arrival of an aged peer interrupted the overture he was about to make.

"I beg your pardon, Lord Dentterton," he said, and with regret, slid his gaze from Julianna to the newcomer. "How may I help you?"

"Here." The elderly man thrust a crushed ivory envelope into his hand. "Someone in the drawing room told me to give this to you, as if I'm part of the post instead of a well-respected member of parliament."

"Oh?" Arthur's pulse increased. He shot a glance to Julianna, who shrugged. "What was the name of the person who gave it to you?"

"How should I know?" The peer shook his head. The thin strands of white that covered his balding pate were about to give up the good fight. "A servant? One of those young pups?" He blew out a breath. "I didn't pay attention. None of them are worthy of my time. Now if you don't mind, I'm going home. One of my mares is ready to foal. Those bloodlines alone will bring a fortune."

"Thank you for coming." After downing the remainder of his punch, Arthur rested his empty glass on the table. Meeting

Julianna's eyes, he gestured further along the corridor with his chin. As he moved away from the milling guests seeking out punch and a few of the sweets, he cracked the seal on the envelope and drew out a familiar scrap of paper. By the time he'd read through it a couple of times, she'd joined him.

"Is it from the same sender?" The hushed whisper sounded overly loud in the isolated section of hallway as she peeked around his arm.

"I'm not certain. The handwriting is slightly different." He held the scrap of paper out so she could see, but he rather enjoyed having Julianna so near.

Beyond the stable house near Glass Pond is a wildflower meadow. Though the New Moon will shed no light, there are still wonderful things found in the dark.

"Glass Pond? No one except my family knows about the names we gave to the ponds on the property." Did that mean the author of the notes was someone he knew or was related to? To what purpose, if so?

Julianna took the note from his hand. She held her bottom lip slightly between her teeth as she read, and it was the most sensual thing he'd ever witnessed. "A jaunt out to a meadow sounds like a rather involved endeavor at present."

"True." Relief mixed with disappointment down his spine. Having this woman to himself out in the dark could have ushered in all sorts of wicked things. He took the note back and then tucked it and the envelope into an interior pocket of his jacket.

But I'll attempt to take her out there another time.

She finished her punch and rested her empty cup next to his. "Should we return to the drawing room?"

A frown pulled the corner of her lips downward. "Only if you scowl at any of the would-be suitors who come near." When he glanced sharply at her, she giggled. "It's also the same look you give your daughter whenever she talks to a young man."

Well, buggar. "Is it that obvious?"

"Only to someone watching out for it." Amusement danced in her eyes.

Selfishly, he didn't want to share her attention. "I could, perhaps, give you a tour of the gardens. My mother enjoys puttering in the flower beds both there and in the hedge maze. As does my sister, but for different reasons. In any event, it should be a spot cooler there."

One of her eyebrows rose. "How exciting! And it's a clear night. I could show you a few constellations if you'd like."

"I cannot think of anything I'd like better in this moment." What the devil was wrong with him? Wasn't friendship the only thing he wanted from her? Yet that brief kiss they'd shared already floated through his mind like soap bubbles and wouldn't leave him alone. "However, there's no need to access the gardens by way of the terrace. We can do so from the library." Daring much, he grabbed one of her hands and tugged her along the corridor. Once in the darkened library, he ushered her across the floor, dodging groupings of furniture along the way.

"I would love to peruse your books later if we have the time."

In his mind's eye, he saw her with her nose buried in a book while he sat behind the desk there. It was truly a domestic scene he desperately wished to have come to pass, and was another stark reminder that Julianna was the direct opposite of what Ellen was. His wife seldom came into the library when they were in the country; she used to say it was a man's domain and the morning room was where she felt most comfortable.

"You are more than welcome to come by whenever you'd like." Then they were in the gardens, which stretched from the rear of the house and over the lawn for ten or fifteen yards in three directions. It was his mother's pride and joy; she often went there for hours, no doubt to be alone with her own grief and memories.

She snorted. "You might regret extending that invitation."

"I rather doubt that." Each time he was in her company was like having the sun break through rain clouds. He gestured with a hand. "I'm not certain the roses have bloomed yet, but it's nearly time. There are all sorts of interesting plants here as well."

Julianna released his hand in order to explore the vegetation on either side of the first gravel and ground shell path she came to. At the first piece of marble statuary—a sculpture of one of the Muses—she sighed. "This is all so lovely. A true haven."

"Mother will be pleased you think so." He clasped his hands behind his back, watching with a slight grin as she peered at the statue. "My father indulged my mother in all things, so when she indicated that she wished to fashion a garden in which she could escape, he wasted no time in fashioning one. He even encouraged her to order the statuary."

"Your father sounds like a generous, loving man."

"He was at that. In many ways, I modeled my life after his, with a few changes though." When she moved deeper into the garden, he followed. "That is exactly what I hope to pass down to my son. I want him to see me and think I'm a decent role model."

"Of course he will. How can he not?" At a spot where the trees formed a natural break, she tipped her head to gaze into the sky. "It's so peaceful here."

"It is." What a boon to find no one else strolling the gardens. Perhaps the terrace held more interest. "Will you tell me that story now?" How sad was it that he wished to hear the sound of her voice?

"Of course!" When she focused on him and grinned, tiny fires lit through his blood. "There are many, many stories about the constellations, but tonight I'm in the mood for a romantic tale." She paced along the path, like a goddess come to earth. "It's a myth from the Far East regarding Vega and Altair. Or more aptly put, two star-crossed lovers."

Though he was aware of the story, he hung on her every word.

"The Star of Vega is relatively close to us, at only twenty-five light years and subsequently it is the fifth brightest star visible to us."

"Brighter than the North Star." It wasn't a question since she'd already confirmed that upon their first meeting.

"Oh, yes." She happily nodded. "Vega lies within the constellation of Lyra which is said to be the harp played by the legendary Greek musician Orpheus. Altair is also another close neighbor, even closer than Vega, and is associated with the eagle constellation Aquila."

"Your knowledge staggers me." Unable to help himself, Arthur drifted closer to her.

"Do hush. Anyone can learn this." But she smiled and he basked in the pleasure of that expression. "Vega is called Tanabata and Altair is Kengyu in the Japanese version of this story. However, for ease of speaking, I'll use the western names of Altair and Vega."

"Understandable." He was close enough that each time she passed while she paced, her arm brushed his sleeve... and it was the most exquisite form of torture.

Julianna glanced at him in such a way that awareness shivered down his spine. "Vega was a celestial princess, a goddess of the sky. Immortal, surely, but she was weary because she would live in eternity alone." As she warmed to the tale, tiny inflections in her voice made him think that he was there, up in the stars with them. "One day Altair—who was a lowly mortal—caught the eye of Vega. She descended from the heavens to greet him, and as they talked, she fell deeply in love."

"And that's when the trouble started."

"Don't be a cynic." She contemplated the sky once more while he feasted his gaze on the creamy perfection that was her slender, elegant neck. "Vega promised Altair they would find a way to be together in the heavens, but when Vega's father discovered the relationship, he was full of rage. His daughter would *not* fall in love with a mortal!" She paused, whether for dramatic effect or another reason, he couldn't say, but he was enthralled. "His fury grew when Vega continued to repeat the promise to take Altair to the heavens."

"Let me guess. The father causes problems for the lovers." He couldn't resist needling her.

"Of course. Quite cruelly, Vega's father made the vow come true. The two lovers were placed in the sky as stars. I don't know how—perhaps he had magical powers—but while they were both in the heavens, they were not together. The great Celestial River, which is commonly known as the Milky Way galaxy, separated them."

"I'm shocked that a parent of a goddess would protest." He drifted close enough to stand behind her. "Though perhaps I side too much with the father for wanting to protect his daughter."

She snickered. "Because the story needs a somewhat happy ending—though no one knows quite how this event came about—"

"—fairy stories are extremely lax with details," he interrupted and made certain his lips brushed the side of her neck. When she shivered, he grinned.

"—each year, on the seventh night of the seventh moon, a bridge of magpies forms across the Celestial River. On that night each year, the two lovers are reunited when Altair dares to travel to his beloved."

"I'm certain that's not the end." Arthur slipped his arms about her waist and held her close to his body.

A tiny sigh escaped her. "Sometimes Altair's annual trip across the Celestial River is too dangerous so he doesn't come. In those dark years, Vega's tears form raindrops that fall over Japan. This has apparently sparked the Star Festival in that country in July, and if it rains, the raindrops are thought to be Vega's tears because Altair could not meet her – so like her, the Japanese mourn for the failed journey."

"It's a romantic, though melancholy, tale to be sure." Slowly, he turned her in his arms until she faced him. "I must say, I rather prefer happy endings."

"Which is surprising, coming from you and your adherence to the past." She gasped and looked up into his face. "I beg your pardon. I didn't mean to say that aloud."

"No offense was taken. Please don't change your personality." He cupped her cheek while wishing fervently he wasn't wearing a glove so he could feel her skin. "What you said is true. It's a downfall of mine, and rapidly becoming a hinderance."

"Don't let it be." Her breath warmed his chin. "Think of grief not as a prison, but as a pathway toward the next place in life you need to be."

"I like that." Because he couldn't help it, Arthur dipped his head and kissed one corner of her mouth. When she murmured a sound of acceptance, he did the same to the other corner.

For long moments, Julianna rested her hands on his chest. She held his gaze, searching for God only knew what, then she lifted up on her toes and pressed her mouth to his.

It was the sweetest form of permission he'd ever been given. With a growl, he bundled her more firmly into his embrace and set out to discover every secret of her lips. Over and over, he drank from her, taught her the basics of how to kiss—her inexperience was all too heady—and then one of her hands was curled about his nape while her other arm lay looped about his shoulders, her breasts crushed into his chest.

It had been quite some time since he'd let passion carry him away, but he welcomed the heat and the need he found with Julianna. The last six months of his marriage he hadn't lain with his wife due to her illness, and he wasn't one of those men who took a mistress. Perhaps he'd taken himself in hand while in the bath a time or two, but kissing this woman, tangling his tongue with hers with nothing but raw heat and passion behind it, was incredible, amazing—both familiar and new.

And he couldn't have enough of her.

When he pulled slightly away, she offered up a protest, but he merely pulled her deeper into the garden until he found one of the stone benches his mother had placed throughout the area. "We are merely relocating." The whisper blended in with the nocturnal sounds of the night.

"Why?" She grazed her teeth beneath his jaw, and those tentative explorations had heat pouring over him.

"So we can do this." Quickly, he dropped onto the bench, and even more swiftly, he brought her into his lap so that she straddled him. "Mind your knees and gown."

"This is odd." She clutched his shoulders in an effort to keep her balance. "Why can you not continue to kiss me?"

The inquiry, coupled with a slight pout of her kiss-swollen lips, drove him closer to the reckless edge he raced toward. "Pardon my oversight." He claimed her lips, gained deep, drugging access to her mouth, and while he explored, he cupped her breast. The thin taffeta of her gown was a mere wisp of a barrier, and all too soon, her nipples hardened when he brushed the pads of his thumbs over them.

She broke the kiss with a moan of both surprise and pleasure. "What are you..." Those words trailed off as he tugged down the plain bodice and freed her breasts.

"They're perfect." He took them in his hands. The fleshy mounds filled his palms without spilling over. "So perfect." And much different than Ellen's. She'd been on the small side, but these... "Gorgeous." Needing to taste them, he lowered his head and took one of those pebbled tips into his mouth.

"Arthur!" She hissed in a breath, but when he manipulated that bud with his tongue and lips, another moan escaped her throat.

As her fingers dug into his shoulders, he moved his attentions to her other breast. When that elicited the same response, he grinned against her skin and started the cycle all over again while his length hardened and pulsed with anticipation.

Dear God, I need so much more.

While he caressed one of her breasts, he kissed her and let the other hand wander between them. Digging through layers of fabric, he finally found her inner thigh. As soon as he touched her, glided his fingers along that soft, heated skin, she squeaked, and her body stiffened.

"Shh. I won't hurt you," he whispered against the crook of her shoulder. Again, he caressed her thigh, dared to move upward to stroke those digits along her already slick folds.

"Merciful heavens." Awe wove through her voice. Her body quivered against his. "Though I knew the finer points of this, the real-life application is quite breathtaking."

Her utterance yanked him out of the passion-fogged haze he'd tumbled into. Ellen never talked during intercourse. She merely let him do the needful, and it had been a pleasant intimacy over their twenty years together. Yet Julianna was altogether different; she looked at relations much differently. It captivated but terrified him.

What the hell am I doing?

If he didn't stop, he'd take this woman right here in his mother's garden. She deserved much more than a frantic tupping, especially since she was yet an innocent. Hot guilt and shame slammed down his spine. Not to mention this was an insult to his wife's memory. He'd promised her when she lay dying, he would never kiss another woman, to say nothing to touch one as intimately as he did Julianna.

Oh, God.

The ardor in which he'd begun the evening fled. In its wake was chilling self-recrimination and even more guilt. Even as desire still lurked on the fringes, the other emotions were too strong. All he could see in his mind's eye was his wife lying in their bed, naked and waiting for him to join her.

"I cannot do this." Without ceremony, he gripped Julianna's hips and more or less evicted her from his lap. She'd barely gained her footing when he shot to his feet with one hand to his chest. "I'm sorry." Then he proved he was naught but a coward and a cad by darting down the garden path, leaving her disheveled and no doubt confused.

And alone with scandal on her doorstep if anyone saw her.

CHAPTER TEN

June 16, 1819

IT HAD BEEN six days since she'd met Arthur, six days since everything she'd ever known had changed. Six days since he'd first kissed her, and her world went sideways.

How was any of it possible?

If he had kept his pursuit to mere kisses perhaps she might have retained part of her sanity, but after what happened the night before at his mother's rout, she was out to sea on a tide of foreign sensations and emotions she'd never experienced before. Never had she been introduced to the raw passion he'd exhibited nor had any man wanted her as much as Arthur did that night in the gardens.

The remembrance of his hands, his mouth, his fingers on her body, the caresses that awakened a primal hunger deep inside sent heat skittering through every nerve ending and need throbbing between her thighs. So much so that she squirmed on the battered quilt she'd spread over the ground on Otis Hill. A tiny moan escaped her throat before she could recall it, but then those amazing feelings dimmed because he'd abruptly cut off that intimacy. The man had turned tail and run from her as if she'd suddenly grown two heads and a huge wart on the end of her nose.

But why? What was he so afraid of?

Not knowing, she trained her telescope on the night skies. After visiting all her favorite stars and constellations, she searched for the comet. Ah, there it was, farther than it had been before, which meant it was on the last arc and would probably not be visible to her past tomorrow night.

Once she'd dropped the telescope into her lap, Julianna quickly took up a mariner's sextant she'd bought second hand at a shop years ago. Tarnished and stiff in places, it still worked. She held it up to the sky and then jotted down the coordinates of the comet's last position with a few notations of which constellations it had cleared and what it was nearest to. Over the course of her note taking, the comet's path had been meticulously plotted, and she couldn't wait to take her findings to London to challenge the pompous male astronomers.

Now that she'd done her due diligence with the comet, she allowed her mind to wander back to the problem of Arthur and his odd behavior. If he hadn't essentially dumped her off his lap last night, would she have let him take further liberties? Would that passionate embrace have ended with a rushed coupling? Heat stung her cheeks. It was impossible to say, and continually thinking about it would drive her mad.

One thing was all too certain. Such kisses and caresses couldn't happen again. It didn't matter if he'd set her aflame and had opened doors to new worlds. She was a self-taught astronomer of no consequence, and he was an earl, a lofty personage in the beau monde, and she certainly wouldn't fill a void for him if he only wished for somewhere to plant his prick.

The thought made her chuckle. Julianna lifted her gaze to the star-strewn night, and she sighed. Though she would have been quite interested to see what that portion of his anatomy looked like, perhaps his defection had been the best course of action. It would have been all too dangerous—as well as scandalous—to encourage such wicked behavior. So, she would remain a virgin for the rest of her days. That was her lot, and she'd had many years to square with that.

But it didn't make that acute longing, the restless hunger deep inside her, fade. He'd ignited those feelings in her, yet she couldn't allow him to fulfil them. It would provide her nothing but heartache and regret.

I have too many other goals I wish to achieve, and I won't allow a guilt-ridden widower with unclear intent to take them away from me.

For a long time, she communed with the heavens before a rustling from the shrubbery alerted her to the presence of another living thing.

"Miss Quill? Are you up here?"

She smiled at the sound of the familiar voice. "Lady Emily!" The young girl materialized out of the shadows. Her dress, no doubt of ivory muslin, made her appear as if she were a ghost in the dim illumination. "How lovely to see you again."

Without ceremony or hesitation, the girl came over to the quilt and plopped down, apparently as at ease as if she were in a drawing room. "Where is Regent tonight?"

"When I left, he was asleep next to my father in their favorite chair." Julianna chuckled. "I didn't have the heart to wake either of them."

"That's just as well. That dog is a menace and he no doubt terrorizes the countryside." She flashed a smile. "But he's endearing, and I'm trying to think up ways to lure him up to the manor so that I might play with him."

"Oh, you won't need to lure him. Just show him the property once. Then he'll think it's part of his territory. Before you know it, he'll be quite the nuisance, showing up at the kitchen door and begging." She shared a laugh with Emily. "You are more than welcome to come to the cottage anytime if you'd like to take him out."

"Oh, thank you, Miss Quill." Genuine delight wove through the girl's voice. She drew her knees up to her chin and wrapped her arms around her legs. "Do you mind if we talk intimately?"

Julianna's eyebrows rose in surprise. "Of course not. Are you in trouble?"

"No, nothing of that sort." A sigh escaped the younger woman. "You see, this summer has been the first time I've been allowed to mingle with members of the opposite sex. To tell you the truth, I'm finding it both stimulating and confusing."

"How well can I understand that," she answered in a soft voice. The earl's attention had certainly knocked her off balance and set her at sixes and sevens. "Enjoy this time of stretching your wings. I wish I'd had the opportunity."

Why did I tell her that? No one needs to know how pathetic I really am.

"You would have been snapped up had you had a Come Out year, Miss Quill."

"I rather doubt that." But it was fun to think about.

Emily giggled. She flashed a grin Julianna's way. "Do stop. You were magnificent last night at the rout. That gown was quite eye-catching. I particularly adored the embroidery at the hem and bodice. Did you do that?"

"I did." She couldn't help but grin as well. "I might not have all the skills ladies do, but I actually enjoy embroidery work, and since there is nothing wrong with my eyesight, I wield a needle whenever I have the time."

"That's wonderful. I find that sort of handiwork woefully dull." Emily contemplated the sky once more. "However, I do love to paint. Portraits especially. I did one of Papa a few years ago, but he hasn't let me paint him since, but I've done portraits of Grandmama, my brother, my aunt, and my uncles many times. Some are even as good as the professional artists they hire for official paintings in the portrait gallery at the park."

"How lovely! It must be so freeing to lose yourself in painting." What a marvel. "The closest I've ever been to painting was to watch my father whitewash my chicken coup."

"Aww, you keep chickens." Excitement threaded through the response. "I adore chickens."

"It's a nice little hobby. I keep some for daily use then go on to sell the remainder to the baker in the village. That provides for a bit of pocket money to spend at my leisure." Or save up for her next trip to London.

"In many ways I envy you, Miss Quill." She rested her chin upon her knees once more.

"What?" Now that *was* a surprise. "Whyever for?"

"You have a certain amount of freedom. Papa watches me like a hawk, and when he's not on the job, it's my aunt." She blew out a breath. "They are all so concerned I'll tumble into scandal, as if I don't know how to conduct my own life."

Julianna bit the inside of her cheek to stave off a smile. She didn't want Emily to think she made jest of her. "Well, I suppose there is some truth in their vigilance. You are the daughter of an earl. You command a certain level in society. There are plenty of men who would take advantage of that."

"Perhaps." The young lady was silent for a long time. "Miss Quill, answer me this. How does a woman know she might be in love with a boy? What does love feel like?"

Oh, dear. What a sticky wicket this conversation is turning out to be.

"I'm afraid you are asking the entirely wrong woman. I've never been in love to know." Julianna shrugged. "However, I imagine it's an all-encompassing feeling where a woman would forever think about her suitor, wish to be everywhere he is, strain to hear his voice when they're in the same room."

At least she assumed.

"Yes, it does feel rather like that, doesn't it?" With a sigh, Emily flopped down on the quilt, laying on her back as she kept her gaze to the sky.

"I'm going to give you some advice that might sound too bold or harsh, especially since it comes from someone not related to you." Julianna placed her notebook, pencil, and telescope into her basket. Then she scooted closer to the girl on the quilt. "Quite frankly, you are too young to even consider thinking that you're in love with a man." For the space of a few heartbeats, she thought about what she would say next. "You have your whole life ahead, Emily. There is no rush to marry and bear children if you harbor other aspirations and goals."

"Oh, dearest Miss Quill." The younger woman laughed. "I adore your ideals and your urging to have everyone around you buck tradition and societal roles."

Julianna frowned. "I'm only looking out for you. Too often, tradition and generational expectations can become prisons if a person isn't careful."

"While that is true to an extent, isn't love the singularly most important thing someone can find? Why not begin the search for it at an early age and enjoy a lifetime of it with that same person?"

Merciful heavens. What a question.

However, now that it had been posed, she had no choice but to examine it as fully as she would any statement that ran contrary to her beliefs. Feeling comfortable in Emily's presence, she laid down beside the girl and stared at the comforting blanket of the stars. "I used to think that, especially when I was your age, and my mother was alive. She trained me up as if I would suddenly attract a man of the Quality."

Emily turned her head and met Julianna's gaze. "And then what happened?"

"When the years kept passing and there were no suitors who wished to take a chance on the daughter of a bricklayer, I found other more important things to chase. My brother had the chance at an education. Each time he was home, he'd share knowledge regarding astronomy and a bit of science with me. It was so exciting and fascinating! I wanted to learn all that I could about those subjects."

"But when your brother died, everything changed. Isn't that right?"

She didn't question how the girl knew that; perhaps Arthur had told her some of the history she'd shared with him. "Yes." The bright dot in the midnight velvet sky that was the North Star recalled her attention. With a finger she traced the outline of

Ned's pocket watch in the pocket of her dress. "Once Ned passed, I wanted to carry on and continue his legacy. He was so close to discovering something of importance and value but died before he could accomplish it. With this comet, I know it's just the thing I've waited for that will honor him as well as gain me entry into the Astronomical Society of London. It's been my life's work. If that means I've sacrificed everything else to attain it, I'm at peace with that."

Was that true, though? The more she thought about it, the more confusion danced about her brain. In the end, she felt nothing but peace. It wasn't as if there had been men who'd wished to court her over the years. So, really, nothing had changed. This was her goal, and she'd chased it with all the energy and passion she had within her.

Emily sighed. "But if you had the chance and found love now, would you still want it?"

"You have quite a knack for asking difficult questions. Perhaps you should pursue a career in journalism."

"Ha! Wouldn't Papa have an apoplexy over that?" Her tinkling laughter reminded Julianna of the stars themselves. "I'm merely trying to find my place in the world. That's all."

"I understand. We all go through periods like that, at least a few times in our lives." She remained silent for a long time. "In answer to your question, I don't know. The man would need to be extraordinary. He would have to present a compelling enough reason for me to leave everything I've ever known, and he would need to respect the fact that I won't give up the pursuit of knowledge or the stars merely for him."

As she talked, images of Arthur flitted through her mind. Heat infused her cheeks, for those kisses had been all too delicious, and those intimate touches had made her wish for so much more even if it would have led her directly into scandal. Of course, all of what happened in the garden had been an aberration. It was merely a product of high emotion and mutual attraction. There was nothing compelling that bound her to

Arthur, for hadn't his flight shown that?

"You are clever to think that way, Miss Quill. It's never a good idea to give up one's identity for a man." Emily sighed as she kept her gaze on the stars. "They can be nodcocks at any given time and don't know what they have even if everyone around them can see it."

Julianna frowned. What did that mean? "Perhaps, and even the best of men is still a man when the day is done. Unfortunately, our world is dictated by them, and women are thought of as little more than property, when they're thought of at all."

"I wonder if that will ever change," the girl said in a dreamy sort of tone. "Imagine seeing such upheaval and a turn of the tide in my lifetime. It boggles the mind."

"One never knows what the future holds." As Julianna watched, a shooting star streaked across the sky. "How lucky to see one of those."

"It's truly wonderous."

It was rather pleasant to spend this precious time with the impressionable girl. "I suppose the best advice I can give you is by all means follow where your heart leads. However, make certain you invite your brain along for the journey. Make intelligent choices. Don't put yourself into a situation where your integrity is in danger. If a man is doing that, he isn't the noble sort and will never have your best interests at heart."

"I hadn't thought about it in that way before."

"I hope you will after tonight." Julianna offered a smile when Emily turned her head and met her gaze. "A woman—perhaps even a man—needs more than love to sustain them throughout a lifetime. Don't discount the yearning for companionship, understanding, humor, the ability to compromise, support in less-than-ideal situations. That is only a few. Assure yourself that it's quite fine if love *never* comes. You will come out just as amazing." She wasn't used to giving advice, but she hoped the young lady would pull out those words and think upon them in the coming years.

Emily pushed herself into a sitting position. "But Miss Quill, what of desire and passion and the carnal pleasures I've heard some of my friends whisper about? Shouldn't a woman investigate those with the man of her choice?"

Oh, dear. Julianna had no choice but to laugh. She struggled upward and then crossed her legs in a Western style. "My girl, a woman won't die if she's not bedded." Should she reveal this next bit? *Please God, keep Arthur from discovering what I'm about to say next.* Yet, when she was a handful of years older than Emily was now, she'd wished someone had told her this advice. It wasn't until much later that she'd come upon it herself. "If it's the physical release you want, that is easily enough found with your own fingers if you put in the time to study your body."

"Surely that's too shocking! I'd be embarrassed to even try, Miss Quill."

"Again, that is your prerogative." Julianna held up a hand when the girl would have protested. "Life is long, so a woman needs to do what she must. However, there is much to be said for kisses from a man and feeling his caress, but don't make that your guiding light."

The young lady's face scrunched up with a frown. "What do you mean?"

"Everyone is unique in this world; don't tamp your light to let a man's shine brighter or to chase him if he's not certain of his own intentions." Perhaps she should take her own advice. If Arthur couldn't decide if he could kiss a woman who wasn't his wife without being beset with guilt, then she shouldn't make herself so easily available. When the twinkling North Star caught her attention, she pointed it out to Emily. "See that bright star just there? That's the North Star. People cast wishes upon it."

"Do you?"

"Yes, almost every night. You should try it." Wishes gave hope, and everyone needed that in their lives.

"Very well." She closed her eyes for a few seconds, and when she popped them back open, she grinned. "I sent up a wish."

"Good. Perhaps it will come true."

"Thank you, Miss Quill." Emily grabbed one of Julianna's hands and squeezed. "I'm so glad I can come to you with these questions that I dare not ask my aunt or grandmother."

"You're welcome to seek me out anytime you wish to talk." No doubt the girl missed her mother, for these were the types of confidences a young lady might exchange with her. "And don't forget about your promise to play with Regent. No doubt he'll wear you out long before he tires."

"I won't." Emily gained her feet then helped Julianna to hers. "By the by, did you enjoy the rout last night? I absolutely adore dancing."

"I rather did. Most of the evening was quite nice. Only a bit of it was baffling, but that's easily forgotten." If that were so, then why did her traitorous body still tingle every time she thought of Arthur's amorous attentions?

"That's wonderful. Perhaps I'll see you again in a societal setting soon."

Julianna frowned. Whyever would that happen? "Do you want me to walk you home?"

"There is no need; I know the way quite well. And rest assured, I don't have an assignation in mind. Your advice has given me much to think about." With a wave, the girl set off and was soon swallowed by the shadows of the night.

With a sigh, Julianna gathered the remainder of her items. Then she straightened and took the basket in hand. At least there was one good thing about counseling a young lady: it gave her clarity of mind as well.

Stars came first. The earl would need to prove his interest before she'd allow anything else to occur between them.

CHAPTER ELEVEN

June 18, 1819

J ULIANNA HADN'T SEEN or heard from Arthur in two days, which was odd in and of itself. Neither had the anonymous writer of those notes sent another. Could be that the earl had written those notes, and when matters between them had become too much for him to bear, he'd ceased with the pranks?

There were no immediate answers, and though disappointment had stabbed through her chest, she'd shoved it away. Truly, there had been no harm nor foul because nothing had been promised between them. He had been a temporary diversion, had expanded her horizons a tiny bit more, and she would take that knowledge and hoard it to herself like a dragon with treasures.

It was certainly more than she'd had before.

Yet a restlessness had stolen over her since the night of the rout. Something that she couldn't quite put a name on buzzed through her veins. It had only been enhanced by the rains that had plagued the area for the past two days, and now, finally, the weather had cleared. Desperate to do something that didn't require being trapped inside the house with her father who hadn't remembered who she was for the same number of days, Julianna told the housekeeper she intended to take a walk and perhaps visit the village to clear her head.

Mrs. Draysley clucked and waved her off. "Go. I don't blame you for wanting some peace. Your father will be just fine until you return."

She nodded and gathered her basket full of supplies. What she really wanted was a nice, soothing dip into the stream, where she could wash her hair and not have to think about life or its confusing aggravations. "I might not return until well past sunset."

"You and those stars." The housekeeper shook her head. "Not a day goes by that you don't look at them." She grinned. "Go. Go. There will be time enough for everything else."

By the time she'd run her errands and made it to the stream, the western skies were ushering in a spectacular sunset full of vivid colors that rivaled a painter's pallet. "You never fail to disappoint," she whispered to the panorama in front of her. With a smile, she made her way past the bend where the stream disappeared into the trees. Bushes and shrubberies shielded one side while the trees kept the place hidden on the other side. Only about a mile and a half from her cottage, the area was a true gem.

As the shadows of twilight descended, Julianna had undressed down to her shift. She padded over the cool, springy mossy ground, and with a comb, a bar of fine-milled French soap, and a dried sponge sent from Brighton, she waded into her favorite place in the stream. The relatively cold water came up to just below her knee. For the first few minutes, she stood there and let the gentle current pass her legs and wet the hem of her shift. Then she laid her bathing accompaniments on the lichen-green bank. Here and there, a few cattails had sprung up. They were a cheerful sort of plant. When a pair of ducks paddled by with a wary eye on her, she grinned and waved.

Then, with a sigh of pure enjoyment, she lowered herself down into the water, found a relatively comfortable spot to sit, and then proceeded to take down her hair and begin the arduous task of washing it. The length reached her waist, which meant it truly was a chore to wash, rinse, comb, and then let it dry before she could put it back up, but Julianna didn't mind. It was a soothing task and let her enjoy the world of nature around her.

"Good God, Julianna, you're magnificent."

She gasped at the sound of *his* voice, and then she froze with the sponge in her hand. Darting her gaze about as he materialized out of the shadows, she covered herself the best she could, for the shift was completely soaked and rendered sheer. Heat slapped her cheeks the longer he stared, but she couldn't reach her clothing without coming fully out of the stream, and the water wasn't deep enough to hide her figure besides.

"For all that's holy, Arthur, please either go away or turn your back. This is hardly decent." Her hand shook. Thank the heavens she'd completed bathing, for it would have been all too embarrassing to know he'd probably watched. Except... how long had he been there? Her cheeks blazed all the more.

"That would mean a surcease of looking at a veritable goddess." Reverent awe threaded through his voice.

Though logic told her she should remain angry with him, she couldn't quite hold onto that emotion. Not in the face of his charm and obvious appreciation. That was something she'd never experienced from a man, and despite the ridiculous situation, she wished to revel in it. "People have to bathe, Your Lordship. It's not unique to me."

"This is true, but you *are* exquisitely unique." He raked his gaze over her form, and as he came closer, there was no denying the light of need in his dark eyes. "Would that I were a sculptor or a painter, for I would surely immortalize you just as you appear tonight."

It was exceedingly awkward to sit on her knees in the gently moving stream while trying to shield her private parts from him as her thin shift clung to her body. "Do stop, Ettesmere. The overt flattery is not needed." But it was rather nice, and it warmed her quite deliciously.

"Your hair is like a curtain of midnight, as if you came from the stars themselves.

She pointed her gaze to the heavens. "Now that is much too grandiose." What ailed the man? Two days ago, when he'd put her in a scandalous position, he'd quickly dumped her from his lap as if she had vipers for hair. He'd run away in apparent fear. Now, here he was, fairly gawking at her and paying her lavish compliments. Yes, he'd opened new paths to her, and she couldn't fault him for battling with his own fears, but this was outside of enough.

"Uh, how have you kept yourself since I last saw you?" He came closer still, pausing on the bank when the toes of his boots hit the edge.

"You wish to conduct tedious conversation while I'm basically sitting here nude in front of you?" Had the man taken leave of his senses? Could he not see she was embarrassed and two seconds away from becoming the talk of the village?

"I…"

She blew out a frustrated breath. The man either needed to come to the point or leave her in peace. "What do you want, Your Lordship? I think it's past time for the truth."

"You are quite correct." For long moments he stared at her as his mouth worked but no sound emerged. Then, he'd apparently come to a decision, for he nodded. "You, Julianna. Right now, in this moment, I want *you*."

Gooseflesh raced over her skin. "I beg your pardon?" Her heart beat out a rapid tattoo while she struggled to puzzle out this change.

"It means nothing for the future—I think—and I can't attach promises to this desire I have, but I want you."

This was perhaps the most honest he'd been with her. Raw emotions left his voice graveled, and in her surprise, she dropped the sponge. "Well, then." Scrambling to catch it before the current took it away, she probably gave him quite the show. Thank goodness for the rapidly gathering cloak of darkness. "The words would cause any woman's heart to skip a beat, but after that night in the garden, you ran away… I'm afraid that's rather a mixed message."

"I quite agree, and I apologize for that." A muscle in his cheek ticked. Did he still have reservations? "It's been difficult for me to acclimate to the changes my life has seen since I've met you, difficult to try to fit both halves of my life together."

She quirked an eyebrow. "Your society self and the one who wants a romance?" There needed to be clarity for her to make a decision.

"Yes, of course." He rubbed a hand along his jaw that was shadowed with light stubble. "Surely, you've felt the attraction, the desire, between us?"

"I have." She might be advanced in age, but there were proprieties, after all. "This is highly scandalous." To say nothing of embarrassing. And sitting there in a wet garment was ushering in a chill even though the night was warm. "You have much more to lose than I."

The earl scoffed and waved a hand. "I care not for that." When he cast a glance about and then returned his gaze to her, a gleam had entered his eyes. "There is no one around and the night has already descended." He grinned and her heart fluttered. "Afterward, we could star gaze...."

"But I... But how do I know you won't turn tail and run just when things grow interesting?" It wasn't an acquiescence, not yet.

"I promise I won't show myself for a coward a second time. It is my fondest hope that I've gotten myself sorted. Though I will admit to being as flummoxed as I was prior to courting my wife. Yet, this is... different." Arthur moved away, went into her hidden nest. He took the tattered quilt from her basket only to spread it on the ground within the shelter of the trees and shrubberies. When he returned to the stream bank, he looked so much like a hopeful young man that the rest of her resistance crumbled. "Will you let me share the greatest intimacy with you?"

Oh, merciful heavens! If she agreed, she would finally know the joy of being desired carnally by a man and wouldn't go to her grave an innocent. And she did adore learning above all things. "I wonder what it says about me that I'm going to agree to this preposterous scheme."

His grin was this side of wicked as he waded into the stream regardless of his recently shined boots. "That you have fine taste?" Before she could offer up a protest, he scooped her up into his arms. "I have long wished to explore every inch of your body."

"Such gammon." She snorted in derision, but at the same time, there *was* something romantic about being in a man's hold as he carried her to bed... er a pallet in the woods, rather. "Our association hasn't been long at all." A handful of days, really. Perhaps around ten if she had to hazard a guess.

"That doesn't matter, not when there is an invisible connection between us that has bedeviled me from the first." He had barely released her, let her feet find purchase on the quilt when he dropped to his knees and tugged her down with him. "You're certain? The consequences...."

"Hush, Arthur." Julianna smiled. She dropped the sponge in favor of tugging at his cravat. It was an adventure she'd only dreamed about until this point. "I'm of enough advanced years to know my own mind, and frankly, after observing the world around me, I rather doubt pregnancy is that large a threat to a woman my age."

At least she hoped that assumption was true, but her studies rarely led her astray.

"Good." He held her head between his large hands, stared into her eyes and searched for heaven only knew what, and then he claimed her lips in a gentle kiss that managed to both steal her breath and ignite tiny fires in her blood.

Almost immediately, Julianna was lost to the tide of sensations he invoked within her. She looped her arms about his shoulders—oh, they were so broad!—and sought to kiss him back. One only improved one's skills with practice, right? But then that wasn't enough. Selfish or not, she needed more of him.

"Touch me, Ettesmere. Show me in no uncertain terms how much you want me."

He made a sound of soft satisfaction in his throat. "I adore how forthright you are in every endeavor." Without further comment, he dragged his lips down the side of her throat. When he reached the crook of her shoulder, he spent time nibbling and licking her skin while tangling one hand into the damp mess of her hair.

Down, down, down he went, nipping and kissing and teasing. With a few yanks and tugs, he had the wet shift up and off her body, then there was truly nowhere she could hide from his intense regard. And still he caressed and touched until her bones held the strength of cooked porridge and she toppled backward onto the quilt. Quickly, he followed. Breasts, nipples, ribcage, naval, nothing escaped his attention.

When she thought he'd leave off to undress, he didn't. Instead, he slid down her body, exploring with hands and lips as he went. Arthur encouraged her to bend one leg at the knee merely so he could press feather weighted kisses to the inside of her trembling thigh. The slight scrape of his stubble created another layer of delight, and she quite lost the ability to breathe normally the longer he teased. When he moved on to her other thigh, Julianna shook from anticipation and raw need. Every time she reached for him, he batted her hands away.

"This is your first time; I want you to enjoy it without the distraction of worrying over my pleasure." And he was once again over her, his fully clothed body layered to hers. The drag of the fabric over her sensitive nipples made her catch her breath; the cold press of the buttons on his jacket to her belly elicited a sigh of pure appreciation.

"But I'd like to—"

"All in good time." He claimed her mouth with such drugging kisses that her mind spun and then promptly vanished beneath a haze of passion. Over and over, he drank from her, and when he probed the seam of her lips with the tip of his tongue, she gladly opened, invited him in.

Dueling with his tongue was rapidly becoming one of her favorite things. There was simply nothing quite like the slide of silk against satin, and with each pass, heat seeped into her veins to form a molten river of need. Every time he thrust and chased her tongue, she could only imagine him thrusting into her with a very different part of himself.

Was there a limit to how long one could be kissed? Julianna didn't know, but she gave as good as she got, let him teach her the finer points so she could mimic what he did. All the while, she plucked at the buttons of his jacket, removed each one from its holes.

"If you'll just let me—"

"Not yet." He encouraged her arms over her head, and with his lips against the underside of her jaw, said, "There's something else I want to initiate you in before I undress."

She hadn't a clue as to what that could possibly be. Hadn't he already explored her body sufficiently? But when he put a hand between her thighs as he had the night of the rout, her legs shook. Still bent at the knees, they provided a cradle for him to rest, and as he stroked his fingers along her folds from top to bottom, an involuntary sigh of pleasure escaped her.

"I suppose I haven't forgotten how to do this," he whispered into her ear while he continued fondling her. Every time he slipped those talented fingers downward, he dipped one of them into her passage. "That is a marvel unto itself."

Did he truly wish for her to invent a response while he did such wonderful things to her? At the moment, all she could do was attempt to regulate her erratic breathing and keep her eyes open, but whenever one of those digits invaded her channel, she sucked in a surprised breath. Again and again, he stretched her, mimicked what he would eventually do to her once his length had been employed.

And the anticipation of that worked to drive her mad.

But the earl wasn't done in his conquest or lecture. Not at all.

The sneaky man parted her flesh and encouraged her swollen nubbin out of hiding. She gasped. Surely, he wouldn't... "Dear heavens!" He *did* and with gusto. The touch of his fingers and the application of various degrees of friction quickly sent her hurtling toward the glimmering edge. "Arthur, I... I..." What the devil was she trying to say?

The words fell right out of her desire-soaked brain, for with every pass and circulation to that tiny bundle of nerves, she felt as if she'd jolt right out of her skin. It was one thing to pleasure oneself in the privacy of one's bedroom, but quite another when a man did so, and right here in the open where anyone could see if they were out for a nighttime stroll.

Perhaps that gave this illicit meeting more of an edge, of danger; she didn't know. Her whole world became the heated kisses he continued to give her and the insistent strum of his fingers on that little button at her center. Bands of pressure built and stacked low within her belly. Though Julianna writhed beneath him, he didn't leave off with his torture.

"It's quite all right if you fly, Miss Quill. That is the point, after all."

His breath steamed the shell of her ear, the weight of him pressed her into the soft quilt-covered grass. She grasped the blanket in her fists as the sweet torture went on, and then, quite suddenly, her whole body stiffened. A wave of bliss smacked into her, and she succumbed to it. He truly did send her flying into the heavens with the stars that she admired. Shivers went through her body, tickled into her nerve endings as she shook with the releasing tension.

"That was wonderous indeed," she finally managed to gasp out when her faculties returned. Her body felt pliant and lethargic, yet a sense of restless hunger remained. Much better than what she'd found sometimes with her own fingers.

"I'm glad you're so satisfied, but don't run away just yet." Arthur eased off her, and as she watched behind slitted eyes, he divested himself of every stitch of clothing he wore.

As men's bodies went, his was magnificent. Lean and slightly muscled in all the right places, his belly was only slightly soft in accordance with his age, but he hadn't let himself devolve into a paunchy wreck like so many men did once they were past their prime. "Oh, goodness." As he came near, she stroked a hand along his flat abdomen, and when the muscles contracted beneath her fingers, her mind drifted to all the naughty places she'd like to visit with him.

On him.

"I suppose I'm not hideous," he said as he took her into his arms once more and reacquainted himself with the crook of her shoulder.

"No, no you are not." *What a fortunate woman I am this night!*

The hard, hot length of his manhood twitched insistently against her thigh. Oh, she couldn't wait to feel him moving inside her! She occupied herself by exploring his back, his shoulders, his chest. The bay rum and lime of his shaving soap clung to his skin. It was quite intoxicating. She kissed as many parts of him as she could before he once more took possession of her lips with a kiss of his own.

When she encountered a ring of seed pearls about his neck on a black chord, she paused. "What is this?" Her fingers had barely brushed it when his body went taut.

"Nothing that has bearing on this moment." Yet his voice was tight, rough with emotion.

"It must mean something to you if you wear it close." Had it once belonged to his wife?'

"I promise to tell you about it, but not tonight." He kissed her again, preventing further discourse, and as he settled himself more comfortably between her splayed thighs, the tip of his member bumped her opening. Tingles of need cascaded down her spine and tightened her nipples. Feeling oh so daring, Julianna slipped a hand between them to cup his equipage. His hiss of surprise echoed in the night, and wishing to experiment, she gave him a gentle squeeze.

"You're going to make me spend prematurely." He chuckled but removed her hand from his person. "It's been years since I've done this, and I've been primed for quite some time."

Had his relationship with her enhanced that need? There were so many questions she wanted to ask, but the primal feel of his body pressed into hers as well as the throb of need deep in her core whisked all of them right out of her mind.

"Then you shouldn't wait any longer." She wrapped her legs around his, and when she slid one of her hands down his back to squeeze a buttock, he groaned and ground his hips into hers. "Take me, Arthur. This wanting will surely cause my expiration if you dawdle."

"We wouldn't want that." Amusement warred with desire in his voice. He pushed one of her arms up above her head, put his other hand beneath her hip, and then with one powerful thrust, he penetrated her body, crashing through the slight resistance of her maidenhead as if it were naught but tissue paper. When he was fully seated, he paused and searched out her gaze with his. "I apologize for the pain."

There had been a sensation of that, of course, but it wasn't so uncomfortable that she couldn't appreciate being filled by him, stretched by him, completely claimed by this man she'd known less than a month. "It is nothing. Truly." Once she'd wriggled beneath him and into a more comfortable position, she gave him a nod. "I rather like this."

He grinned and she was out to sea again from the wickedness in that gesture. "You are such a refreshing change that you make me feel as if I'm not a relic consigned to a corner of my study just yet." Then he moved, slowly in and out of her passage, and each push and pull gave her different layers of friction and pleasure. "Lift your hips each time I stroke into you. That will help you find a rhythm faster."

As with anything in life, there was much to learn on a new subject, but this one was so interesting, she took to it rather quickly. And it was so enjoyable! How fascinating that the press and surge of two bodies coming together in the most ancient of ways provided so much pleasure. With her feet flat on the quilt, she was better able to meet his thrusts, and all too soon the crude slap of flesh against flesh echoed in the night around them, punctuated by sighs and moans.

Then the cadence changed. Arthur dug his fingers into her hip as his pistoned ever faster. "I'm not going to last," he bit off on a tense whisper.

Deeper. Harder. Shorter.

She peered into his face. Such intense concentration held his expression, and then she didn't care. Every time he speared into her, that familiar pressure mounted, bigger and bigger, until finally, she shattered again, and the surprise of that second pinwheel into bliss provoked a keening cry that she didn't bother to try and stifle.

As contractions rocked Julianna's core, the earl thrust once more. He immediately followed her into that void full of white light and then no light at all as stars twinkled through that velvety nothingness. His member pulsed and jerked. Warmth spread through her passage and drat if that wasn't the most intimate thing she'd ever experienced.

Seconds later, he collapsed on top of her, and his weight further worked to bring her closer to him. She wrapped her arms around him, holding his head to her shoulder while her heartbeat hammered, and her breath rasped.

"Without question, that was the most amazing discovery I've ever made. To know that the human body can withstand such pleasure before breaking? I'm in awe."

"You never cease to amuse me and draw my respect." He rolled onto his side, taking her with him, then he held her in his embrace while she listened to the strong, fast beat of his heart. "But you're right. That was incredible. I'm glad I could share it with you."

Though he said nothing about his feelings or the state of his heart, she didn't care. What they had right in this moment was enough. He hadn't promised the future and she hadn't demanded it. Perhaps that wasn't where their paths would lead. But for now, she basked in the glory of finally being bedded, and it had been everything she'd dreamed it would be.

A midsummer tryst. She giggled against his shoulder. Well, one only lived once. Perhaps it was best to make that time on this mortal coil memorable. There was plenty of time for regret and wishing later.

CHAPTER TWELVE

June 19, 1819

ARTHUR HAD RISEN late in the morning, which meant he'd missed breakfast entirely. That suited him just fine, for he hadn't wished to see his family. Especially since he hadn't gotten in last night after being with Julianna until well after one in the morning. He'd gone directly to his study to indulge in brandy, which was the reason he suffered a megrim now.

Where he thought that indulging in carnal pleasures would finally push her from his mind, he'd discovered the exact opposite. After intercourse, he was even more captivated with her, and he hadn't the first blessed clue what to do about that.

Oh, God.

He stumbled into his study and had just dropped into the chair behind his desk when his sister sailed into the room. "What the devil do you want?"

"And a good afternoon to you, too." She crossed the room, and once at the window, opened the drapes, unlocked the catch, and then pushed the glass panel outward. "You need fresh air. It's overcast and looks like rain, but there's a relative breeze that will do you good."

"How do you know I'm ailing?" He didn't care his tone was gruff. His sister had the tendency to meddle, and today, he hadn't the wherewithal to indulge her.

"First, you're slumped over in your chair and holding a hand to your head, which indicates you have a megrim." She turned about and ticked off the items on her fingers. "Second, because your head pains you and since there is a nearly empty bottle of brandy still sitting on your desk, I believe you came in late last night and took refuge in spirits. Thirdly, because you did that, you *must* have done something that severely preys upon your conscience. And fourth, your cravat and its intricate knot, cannot quite hide the edge of that love bite on your neck." Dear Sophia arched a blonde eyebrow. "Shall I go on or will you tell me what happened to you last night?"

"Do I have a choice?"

And when the hell had she become so accomplished at discerning little details? He put a hand to his neck. Last night, shortly before he'd left Julianna's company, she'd been rather frisky during a bout of kissing, and since he'd just shown her how to make such a mark, she wished to experiment on him. Thus, the resulting bruise. Though his head ached, he couldn't hold back a grin, for the woman was certainly a quick study. He had hoped no one in his family would prove so observant.

"You do not." Sophia flashed him a grin of victory. She approached his desk then perched on the edge of a chair that faced his desk. "Did the ingestion of too much brandy help you forget or come to terms with whatever you're grappling with?"

He heaved out a breath of frustration. "Not really."

"Then you deserve the megrim." She clasped her hands in her lap, looking for all the world like a proper *ton* lady, but there was a rebellious streak in her a mile long when she chose to unveil it.

"Thank you for your assessment." Arthur leaned back in his chair. The springs creaked, for it had been the same chair his father had used in this room. He planted his boots on the desk and crossed them at the ankle. "Do you have other questions?" The sooner he appeased his sister, the sooner he could seek out something that would ease the ache in his head.

"Of course I do." For long moments she stared at him. "Who were you with last night?"

If he didn't answer her, she would keep digging until she discovered the truth. "Julianna, er rather Miss Quill." With her, over her, inside her…

"Oh, ho!" Sophia's eyebrows soared. "How delicious." Her eyes twinkled with mirth as she regarded him. "Did you kiss her?" She looked pointedly at that spot on his neck. "You must have."

There was no way *not* to remain smug about it. "Perhaps we should go back to the night of the rout."

"Whyever for?" Her smile faded into an expression of confusion.

"Because… Because I first kissed Julianna in the gardens that night. When things grew heated, I…" Briefly, he closed his eyes. "I was hit with so much guilt and shame for doing that, for betraying Ellen's memory, that I left Miss Quill in the garden in a state of dishevelment."

"Arthur, you cad." Twin spots of color blazed in his sister's cheeks, whether in indignation for what he did or his treatment of Julianna, he couldn't say.

"Spare me the lecture." He held up a hand to ward off her chastisement. "I hated myself for what I did. So, I screwed my courage to the sticking place and sought her out last night."

"And?" Sophia leaned forward. Her eyes were round with anticipation. "Did she hate you?"

"Obviously not." He indicated the mark on his neck. "However, I did have her at a decided disadvantage."

"How so?"

The memory of coming upon Julianna while she bathed in that stream had awareness shivering over his skin. The sodden black mass of her hair had fallen over her shoulders and down her back like spilled ink. That coupled with her in the sheer, wet shift had put him in mind of a Greek goddess, straight out of mythology. Struck dumb for a few minutes, he'd spied on her, looked his fill at the various pieces of her body as she'd scrubbed.

Then, with a raging cockstand, he'd finally found the bravery he'd previously lacked and had approached.

Knowing his sister required an answer—a full confession more to the point—he sighed and winced when his head ached all the more fiercely. "She was bathing in a stream."

Sophia uttered a squeak of outrage. "Oh, Arthur, you spied on her?"

He shrugged. "It wasn't well done of me, but what was I to do?" That image of Julianna would forever be seared upon his brain. Lowering his voice, he gave her the most succinct version of the story. "Suffice it to say, after she and I talked, one thing led to another, and I bedded her." Best have the confession over and done instead of drawing it out.

"That's wonderful!" She bounced in her chair with a squeal. "You stepped out of your self-imposed exile and rejoined life in the most primal of ways."

"Please, do not make that sound again." As pain ricocheted through his brain, Arthur rubbed the skin between his eyebrows.

"How do you feel about... *that*? Does it make you want to do other things? Like court romance? Will you offer for her now?"

Bloody hell.

"I don't know, to tell you the honest truth. Marriage wasn't my goal, yet for all intents and purposes, I've ruined her." He drew a hand along his cheek as he thought over the events of the last twenty-four hours. "Like the night of the rout, I'm beset with confusion, shame at what I did, and the fact I didn't have enough control over my base urges. Julianna didn't deserve to have her first time take place outside, and not even on a real bed." When his sister snickered, he pulled a face at her like when they were children. "To say nothing of the ever-present guilt. I have betrayed Ellen's memory, and that doesn't sit well."

Would it ever? How could he move forward with his life—if he even wanted that—if he couldn't free himself from the emotional prison he'd fallen into?

For long moments, Sophia stared at him with varying degrees

of understanding and compassion. "I know exactly how you feel. That's what I struggled with after my first husband died and I faced my wedding night with my second husband."

"How did you overcome it?"

She shrugged. "For a bit, you learn to make room for all the feelings. You give yourself permission to feel everything regarding your deceased spouse." With a sigh, she looked at her hands in her lap. "Eventually, the urge for companionship and the thrill that comes along with a new romance comes bubbling to the forefront. Those other emotions fade. Of course, you don't entirely forget the people who have left, but you do embrace life again. That is as it should be."

"Perhaps. I'm still mired in the struggle."

Sophia smirked. "Did you enjoy being with Miss Quill in that way? Ooh, I wonder what she thought of it? Did she think you marvelous with manly prowess?"

"Just stop. I refuse to discuss the finer points of my conquest with you."

"Spoil sport."

"As to your first question…" If he denied that he'd enjoyed himself, his sister would see right through him. She'd always been able to do so. "Yes. I enjoyed it very much." Though, had it been merely the need for a physical release with a woman instead of by his own hand?

"Excellent. Then we're making progress." Once more she leaned forward. Excitement filled her expression. "How does Miss Quill feel about you now that you two have expressed yourselves physically? Especially since you've introduced her to the carnal world?"

Arthur frowned. "I would have no idea." They hadn't talked about the deed once it had ended. Instead, he and Julianna had remained tucked away in that hidden spot for an hour then they had dressed, and he'd been true to his word. They'd stargazed, indulged in heated kissing, before he'd escorted her home.

"No, I don't suppose you would. You're a man, after all, and it's probably escaped your notice." His sister tapped a finger to her chin. "Did she seem properly enamored of you?"

"I didn't notice." He'd been rather preoccupied at the time. When Sophia didn't immediately offer a comeback, he sighed. "What of Ellen?"

"What of her?"

"She was my wife."

"Yes, and the key word is 'was.'" She shrugged. "Whether you want to believe it or not, Ellen is gone, Arthur. She's never coming back." Empathy filled her eyes. "When she died, your union ended. Perhaps it sounds harsh, but it's the truth. You can carry her memory in your heart, you can remember what it felt like when you were with her, but you'll never have that same *exact* romance again."

"But I—"

"No." Sophia shook her head. She wagged a finger at him. "Miss Quill is a different woman entirely; it would stand to reason that *everything* with her would also be different. And that isn't a bad thing. Having a different woman in your life will make you think beyond what you already know."

What she said made sense. Of course it did, but he fought against accepting it. Why?

His sister rose from her chair, only to perch on the corner of his desk. She crossed her legs at the knee and swung her foot. "The solution to your problem is quite easy."

"How so?"

"Do you enjoy spending time with Miss Quill outside of the bedroom—or wherever the two of you choose to copulate?"

Heat crept up the back of his neck. "I do. In every aspect, she holds my attention. She's different from Ellen in every way. And I… Well, I enjoy the challenge." He shot her a wry look. "If I'm being honest, I enjoy the chase as well."

"There's something to be said for that. I do so adore it when men give chase." Sophia winked. He didn't quite trust that mischievous smile. "Does Miss Quill make you feel as if you could conquer the world if only she would look at you in a certain way again?"

Did she? The heat on the back of his neck intensified. When he was with Julianna, he didn't feel quite so alone or so gutted over the loss of his wife. He felt as if happiness was indeed possible again. "She does."

A slow smile bloomed over his sister's face. "And you find her fascinating, do you not?"

"I do. She's one of the most intelligent people I've ever met, and she has goals beyond the typical wishing to keep a house, etc... However, I'm unsure on many things. She's not truly of the *ton*. If I decide I wish to marry again, could she withstand the rigors that being a countess will bring?" He shook his head, and the damned thing ached all over again. "For that matter, would she even want to be part of this world?"

Why the devil am I even talking about this? Marriage was never the plan.

"In matters like this, there are no exceptions, Brother."

"I think it would a bit. There's the title to consider." Then a new thought occurred to him. "What of John and Emily? How would they feel if I married again?"

Sophia's laughter bounced through his brain and made his head ache. "I wouldn't worry about them. Both are nearly grown. Surely they want to see you happy." She sighed. "As I've told you before, life is short and all too precious." Shadows pooled in her eyes. "Don't waste it. If you've found something wonderful, keep it close."

Arthur huffed out a breath. "Even if it terrifies me? What if I lose Julianna too?" He met his sister's gaze and his chest tightened. "I am not strong enough to survive that again."

"I know." Sophia leaned across the desk to pat his knee. "More than anyone, I know." Her smile had faded in intensity. "But I still have advice. Pursue this woman with all you're worth and enjoy what is bound to come out of that pursuit."

"Even with the risk?" How could she say that?

His sister nodded. "Even with the risk. Is finding love a second time the worst thing that could happen?"

Was he on the path to falling for Julianna? It was difficult to say, and it was all tangled up and lost in the miasma of other emotions besetting him. "No, of course not. It's the potential losing that love I fear the most. It almost makes me not want to try again."

Never had he been as candid with anyone as he was right now.

"Yet you won't know if that's true until you try." Sophia hopped off the desk. She came around that piece of furniture and hugged him. That modicum of comfort, that human touch, made him relax bit by bit. "Even with my history I chase love because there is nothing else like it. Connecting with another person so deeply that your souls shiver together?" She sighed and her bright smile was back in place. "Oh, Arthur, it is so worth the heartache."

That remained to be seen, but if his sister was convinced after losing two husbands, then perhaps there was a grain of truth there. "Then you'll marry again?"

"When you'd asked me that before we ever came to Ettesmere Park, I had honestly not been convinced I would. But now? After watching you rediscover the wonder of an unexpected romance, after seeing those glimmers of joy in your eyes when you think I'm not looking, yes." Her own eyes twinkled. "I think I will. The trouble is finding a man suitable."

Arthur righted himself. When the ache in his head made him wince, he sighed. "It's a lovely sentiment, and you've never been as happy in life as when you're content in a marriage."

"You either. Just think about what I've said. In the end, let go of everything else you think you should be feeling and just focus on her. The answer is usually simple. Oh, and don't forget to invite Miss Quill to Mama's midsummer ball. That should prove fun." She tugged on his hand until he stood. "Come. Let's see if Cook has some special concoction that can soothe that megrim."

With a shuddering sigh, he nodded. "I never thought at this age, at this juncture in my life, that my insides would be tied in knots over a woman."

Sophia's laughter both annoyed and encouraged him. "Yet isn't it wonderful? Romance is a thrill everyone should experience at least once in their lives. Twice if one is fortunate."

"Or three times in your case?" he asked as they quit the study.

"From your lips to God's ears."

Perhaps he didn't need to have everything figured out all at once. For the time being, he would enjoy the journey and attempt to work through the things holding him back.

If he wished to move forward.

CHAPTER THIRTEEN

June 20, 1819

J ULIANNA GLANCED AT her reflection in the cracked mirror that hung over her washbasin. Color bloomed in her cheeks and her eyes had a definite sparkle to them that hadn't been present before. Perhaps that was because she was different; she certainly felt different. The logical reason was that she couldn't stop thinking about that evening two days ago when she and Arthur had come together in carnal pleasure.

It had been the single most glorious event in the whole of her life.

"Get your head out of the clouds and back to the stars, Jules. It doesn't change anything. Hasn't he stayed away for two days without a word?"

It had been remarkably silent on that front. Neither had there been any more anonymous notes. What had changed? She giggled, turned away from the mirror, and grabbed her plain bonnet from the back of the one wooden chair in the room.

Everything had changed.

In fact, she swore that she still felt the delicious tingles dancing through her body that his attentions had invoked. The heat had certainly lingered. Even her muscles retained a vague ache from having suddenly been used in ways she could never imagine.

If this is what being ruined feels like, no wonder the whole of England is scandalized whenever it happens.

Yet, why would anyone wish to deny themselves or others those brilliant feelings? There were no regrets on her part. If given the chance, she wouldn't have changed a thing. For better or for worse, she'd consented and had given the earl her innocence, such as it was at this advanced age. There had been a certain freedom in making that choice merely for her.

"Regent? Where are you, boy? We're going for a walk." The dog had gone out of his way to find trouble these last couple of days. Perhaps he missed Arthur too.

By the time she'd come down the narrow stairs and into the common room, her father had entered from the garden door to take up a spot in his favorite chair.

"Where are you going, girl?"

Julianna glanced at her father as she grabbed her trusty willow basket. "Into Wokingham. I need to post a letter, pick up two things at a shop, have a book I must return to the lending library, and Regent could do with the exercise besides. He's become something of a sloth of late."

As if on cue, the overweight beagle surged into the house by way of that same garden door. With a series of happy barks and many tail wags, he danced about her legs.

"Settle, boy. I don't need you shredding my skirts. I've precious little in the way of a wardrobe as it is." Once again, she'd chosen the dress of robin's egg blue. It was a favorite and it was the dress she felt the most beautiful in with the exception of the rose gown she'd worn to the rout.

"What are you doing wasting time writing letters for?" her father wanted to know. "Your time is better spent looking for a man to marry you."

At the last second, Julianna stopped herself from rolling her eyes. "The choices in men around Wokingham are slim, Papa. I'd rather have none at all then settle for less than I deserve."

Especially after she'd shared the greatest intimacy with Arthur... the man who'd been suspiciously silent after said life-changing event. Did that mean he didn't think it as special as she? After all, he had, of course, done that deed many times over during the course of his life.

Had he only used her to scratch an itch?

She shoved that thought away. There was time enough to think upon that.

The letter was to the Astronomical Society of London. She'd written it the night before, requesting an audience with the head of that austere organization, for she meant to lay out all the information she'd gathered about the comet, and then more or less demand those white-haired men show her the respect she deserved in the field.

Over the course of the last month, she'd taken most of the coin from selling eggs and bought herself a fine, ladies' fan of silk with a pretty picture of lords and ladies dancing upon it stamped onto the fabric. It had finally come in, for she'd ordered it from a catalogue all the way from London. Yes, it was a frivolous purchase and one in which she had no need, but it would make her feel as if she belonged to the world of the *beau monde*. And June was proving to be a hot month indeed. If she didn't pamper herself, who would?

Of course, that meant she'd dipped deep into her savings meant for a London trip, but she would find a way to go there regardless.

"Why are you not happy with staying here in the cottage with me?" It was a rare day when her father groused, and the fact that he was hinted at his worry.

"I have much to do just now. The comet discovery is nearly over, and with that knowledge I intend to challenge those arses at the Astronomical Society of London. Their assumptions that only men can make interesting discoveries is pure gammon. I will prove them wrong."

"Your spirt reminds me of your mother." He thumped a

gnarled hand on the arm of his chair. "Never lose that, Julianna. It'll see you far."

"One would like to hope, Papa." She frowned. "You seem distracted. Is something amiss?" What must it be like to live with a mind that constantly flashed between the present and the past? To never know which timeline one lived in?

"The earl's son has knocked about my brain of late."

Julianna frowned. "When did you meet Lord Ettesmere's son?" She'd only met Lord Eglinton once that night at the rout. He'd been eager to make her acquaintance and he was an accomplished dancer. Like his sister, she'd given him snippets of advice when asked. Hopefully, he would take the words to heart and choose not to follow the path of a rake.

"I already told you. He spent part of the summer with me and my mates when we built some of the outbuildings at Ettesmere Park." His voice rose with his agitation. He thumped a fist on the armrest. "That fool boy came around searching for the missing signet ring a couple of times. Says his father gave him a beating he wouldn't soon forget."

Once more, her father had slipped into the past. "But none of that concerns you. If Arthur's carelessness caused him to lose the bauble, it's lost to the ages." That was years ago, and it was highly unlikely such a thing would ever be unearthed now.

"What ages? He lost it last week, girl. Don't you listen?" Her father's eyes flashed blue fire. "I need to go out there and search. It's the least I can do for the lad. He didn't set out to act irresponsibly."

Oh, dear.

She glanced at one of the windows. The day was overcast with dark gray clouds looming on the horizon. "It will undoubtedly rain in a few hours. If I promise to pay the park a visit and poke around while I'm out, will you promise to stay here?" The housekeeper wasn't due to pop over today, which meant the whole of the responsibility for his care fell to Julianna.

"You don't know where to look." So, he would be recalcitrant to the end.

Tact and patience were required, but she was growing increasingly tired. What would happen when his mind went entirely? "This is so, but I would if you'll tell me which building you were working on when the signet ring was lost."

"I don't remember that!" He shook his head so violently that the thin wisps of gray hair fluttered about his head. "The one going up right now. You can't miss it."

Julianna blew out a breath. She gripped the handle of her basket all the tighter. "Calm yourself, Papa. I'll visit all three buildings and see if anything comes of a visual inspection." She didn't know why he was suddenly so fixated upon that moment in the past and Arthur as a young man. It made no sense, especially when he'd not met Arthur in his capacity as the earl. To that end, she'd not talked about him either.

"I guess that'll have to do." With a sound of frustration, he took up the book he'd been reading all week. Was he even able to comprehend the words, or was he going over the same few pages each day? "Don't dawdle. It looks like rain."

"Yes, I suppose it does." Tears welled in her eyes, but she quickly blinked them away. He was growing steadily worse. How long would it be before he no longer remembered who she was? "Well, then, I'm off. I shouldn't be away long." She whistled for the beagle. "Come, Regent. We're going for a walk."

As soon as she'd closed the door behind her, Julianna leaned her back against it and closed her eyes. She pressed the heel of her free hand against her mouth and bit down to keep from screaming out her frustration and sorrow. Would that life were different, but it wasn't, and nothing would be gained by lamenting about it.

Drawing in a deep breath and letting it ease out, she dashed away the remaining tears, pushed off the door, and with the dog frolicking about her, she set off down the lane.

AN HOUR LATER saw her on Ettesmere property. It was a ridiculous quest, of course, but at least she could return home and tell her father the truth: that she'd looked around the outbuildings. The third one proved an icehouse. Currently, the door was securely locked but the coolness of the interior was evident when she rested a hand against it.

"Julianna? What the devil are you doing here?"

She turned about at the sound of surprise in Arthur's voice. How to explain her trespass without appearing like a resident of Bedlam? "I am... well, I promised my father I'd poke about a bit."

"Whyever for?" The earl frowned. He glanced about the area. Happy barking from Regent drifted to her ears, for he'd decided to run with gladness over the countryside. No doubt he'd bedevil a few sheep on this jaunt.

For long moments, instead of answering, Julianna studied him. No doubt fresh from walking the acreage, his boots were a trifle scuffed and there was a tiny stain on one knee of the buff-colored breeches that hugged his legs a bit too well. The sleeves of his ivory lawn shirt were rolled to the elbow, and that sight of his strong forearms put a hitch in her breathing. A few streaks of dirt that marred that once pristine garment, but his waistcoat of blue tweed provided a welcome pop of color in the otherwise gloomy day.

Good heavens. Did he always appear so delicious, or was he mere enhanced to her since that wonderful day at the stream?

Finally, she forced moisture into her dry throat and met his questioning gaze. "You must understand. My father's mind isn't what it used to be. Today, he is firmly in the past, thinks he's still the man who laid bricks to build these outbuildings. To him, none of these buildings are finished." After gesturing with her free hand to include the general area, she shrugged and was suddenly at sixes and sevens regarding the situation. "He was concerned there was something lost over the course of the bricklaying."

"I'm sorry to hear that." Compassion lined his face. "Even if there was something left behind, that was decades ago. It's highly unlikely anyone could find it now."

"Oh, I'm quite aware of the futility, Your Lordship." When her words were waspish and bitter even to her own ears, she sighed. Her shoulders sagged. "I apologize. The state of his mind has declined in recent weeks. I'm so afraid that soon he'll not remember who I am. And then what shall I do?" On the verge of tears, Julianna looked away to hide that emotion.

"You have my full sympathies." One moment he stood a few feet from her, and the next, she was bundled into his arms for no other reason than support. When she attempted to push out, he tightened his hold. The basket fell to her feet, forgotten for the moment. "Just let me hold you for a few minutes. Lean on my strength. It's quite all right to admit you cannot do this on your own."

"Oh, Arthur." Knowing he understood broke the barrier that acted as a dam for her tears. She relaxed into his embrace, her fingers curling into the thin fabric of his shirt, and when he stroked a hand down her back, she let her reaction flow. Tears wet her cheeks. In some embarrassment, she buried her face into his chest, his cravat, and he simply held her, slightly rocking her in silence while she cried out her frustration and fear. "In some ways, it would have been kinder if my father died instead of being made to suffer a stolen mind and memory."

"I know it's difficult."

That was an understatement. "When Papa is lost to the past, his whole demeanor changes and he's gruff, angry, at times belligerent." She didn't mean to wipe her streaming eyes on his cravat, but she did it anyway. Seconds later, he pressed a crisp linen handkerchief into her hand. "If he becomes violent as well, I won't be able to care for him any longer."

What would happen to him then she couldn't say.

"Shh." The rhythmic stroke of his hand on her back lulled her into a cloud of security. For the first time in her life, she realized how much she'd missed in not having someone around she could lean on or talk to about such things. "Please know that I am here if you should have need of me." The soothing rumble of his voice in her ear provided another layer of strength she so desperately needed.

If she wasn't careful, she would grow all too used to being held by him.

"Except once the summer is over, you'll return to London." The reality of that sank into her head, and the tears fell a bit harder. She hadn't meant to think that far in the future, but there it was anyway, and as much as she kept telling herself it didn't concern her, the bald truth was, it did. She and Arthur shared a bond, a connection. Would he leave it to a brief summer romance and then forget all about her?

"Let's not visit trouble before it arrives." He pulled slightly away to cup her cheek. With the pad of his gloved thumb, he brushed at the lingering moisture on her skin. "You will come through this valley."

Did he refer to her father's illness or the state of loneliness that would descend once he departed Berkshire?

"Undoubtedly, I will, but just now, I'm taking comfort in the tears. They're cathartic in a way." When he tilted her head up until their gazes connected, she sighed. "What are you doing out here. You've got dirt on various places of your person."

He chuckled. "I thought to try my hand at putting two ponies out on the loop since one of the stable lads has a summer cold. One was docile enough, but the other?" The earl shook his head. "Well, he's stubborn and absolutely refused. To which he broke away from me, dancing always out of reach in the stable yard. It took two grooms as well as me to bring him back and have him hooked to the loop."

"After a few tumbles to you, I would imagine." The scene in her mind was so vivid and funny that she couldn't help but see it as it might have unfolded. Him running about, tripping over tufts of grass or rocks on the unfamiliar yard, the pony snickering as it watched the antics of the humans.

"Nothing escapes your notice."

She offered him a smile. "Why were you even out here assisting the stable hands to begin with? Surely there are other things that would hold your attention."

"I have much on my mind and needed a distraction." Would he admit to thinking about her, about that night at the stream? When he said nothing of the sort, she stifled a sigh. Arthur put a hand to the small of her back and propelled her around to the other side of the icehouse. "Come and sit with me for a while."

"Where?" Hurriedly, she scooped up her dropped basket. Thankfully, the contents hadn't fallen out.

"Here." He dropped to the ground and leaned his back against the brick wall. Then he patted the grass next to him. "We aren't immediately seen in the event some of the staff are wandering about the property."

"Ah." Not ready to return to the cottage, Julianna gratefully sank to the ground beside him. He wrapped an arm about her shoulders and pulled her close to his side. The scent of bay rum and lime teased her nose, and another sigh escaped. "Thank you."

"For what?"

"Being here for me. I hadn't realized I needed the support until it was offered." After setting her basket at her side, Julianna turned into him and laid a hand on his middle. Muscles clenched beneath her touch. Did he remember how it had felt when she'd briefly explored his body that night? "It seems an insurmountable challenge at present."

"Everything does until we square with it or make a plan to rout it."

"True." She rested her head on his shoulder. "I've written to the Astronomical Society of London demanding an audience and a review of my discovery and charting of the comet."

"I wish you good fortune in gaining it, but you'll be granted that meeting by sheer tenacity above everything else." When he chuckled, the sound reverberated in her chest and provoked delicious tingles down her spine.

"Perhaps."

For long moments, they sat together without speaking as the dark gray clouds rolled closer and a slight breeze kicked up. The companionable spirit soothed her troubled soul and she rather thought it might be nice to indulge in such things for the rest of her life…

Eventually, Arthur stirred. "By the by, my mother is throwing a midsummer masquerade ball in three days. Do you have an interest in attending?"

Julianna gasped. A masquerade! She'd always wanted to go to something like that, but then reality once more tempered her excitement. "I'm afraid I couldn't."

"Why?" He turned his head and met her gaze.

"For the simple fact that I have nothing to wear." She snorted. "You've seen practically the entirety of my wardrobe. I'm not one of those ladies who have more dresses than sense."

His sensual lips curved into a grin that lit tiny fires in her blood. "Is that your only excuse?"

"I suppose. Other than the fact another society event is daunting."

"I'm sure something will come to light. I'll speak with my sister. She'll know how to solve the problem." He brushed his knuckles along the side of her cheek. "In all honesty, I would really like you there. To be a part of my mother's special day… at my side."

So much meaning hung on those last three words that she could scarcely breathe. What did that mean? Did he want her for more than a summer tryst after all? "Then, I should be delighted to come, *if* I have an appropriate costume."

It would be a small miracle in and of itself should that come to pass.

"I look forward to it." He leaned close and when she assumed he'd kiss her, he instead pressed his lips to her forehead. It was such a tender gesture that tears sprang to her eyes for a completely different reason. "When you are near, some of my own insecurities quiet. Thank you for that."

"Truly, it's been a pleasure." When he didn't appear to want to move, neither did she. As she snuggled back against his side, she smiled.

Perhaps the key to puzzling out a relationship was to invest in patience.

CHAPTER FOURTEEN

June 21, 1819

ARTHUR CHUCKLED AS Regent's leather lead tangle about his ankles for what seemed like the twelfth time that afternoon. He'd met Julianna at the village's midsummer festival by accident, and since his children had abandoned him for their own pursuits, and her father had claimed exhaustion and had gone home, he'd asked her to accompany him around to the booths.

Now, after a few hours, it was nearing time for tea. The sun in a cloudless sky had made his throat quite parched. For the twelfth time he untangled the lead from his ankle and guided the dog to trot along beside him.

"Your beagle doesn't really care for the lead. I believe he makes walking with it so difficult and obnoxious that the people he's with will grow frustrated enough to remove it."

Her laughter wrapped around him and the invisible connection between them strengthened. "That's the best explanation for his horrid behavior I've heard." She swung her familiar willow basket from one hand while her other rested lightly on his sleeve. The longer they'd tarried at the festival, the more goods she'd acquired. Roasts and sugared nuts. A small tin of biscuits. A rag doll he'd won from a game of strength which she'd probably give to her dog as an incentive to obey. To say nothing of a new handkerchief, a beaded bracelet he'd bought for her when she'd shown an admiration, and a red ribbon he hoped she would wear in her hair soon.

What the woman needed was a decent reticule, a bag she could carry with her for everyday occasions. Perhaps he'd go 'round to the shops next and see if he could acquire one. Leave it on her doorstep with an unsigned note so she'd be more willing to accept the gift.

"It would certainly explain his apparent hatred for someone else being in control." Again, Arthur tugged on the lead in an effort to curb the dog's willingness to thrust himself into every bush, dart beneath every table, chase each rabbit or rodent he came across.

"I'm afraid Regent is a free spirit." She squeezed her fingers on his sleeve as they approached a handcart whose vendor sold lemonade. "Perhaps a pause to alleviate thirst is in order."

"Indeed." It was all too easy to let himself think being with her was an ordinary part of his life, but if he thought too hard about what was happening, the twin bastards of guilt and panic reared their heads, prompting him to put distance between them. "Let me fetch a glass for you."

"You're too kind, Ettesmere." Arthur couldn't decide if he enjoyed hearing her use his title or his Christian name more. When it came down to brass tacks, he didn't care as long as she consented to remain in his company.

She took the lead from him and stood beneath an oak tree in the shade while he asked the hand cart owner for two glasses.

After he'd dropped the requisite coins into the man's hand, he took the glasses. "Thank you."

The man nodded and then narrowed his eyes. He pulled a familiar ivory envelope from a pocket of his homespun shirt. "I was told to give this to you, Lord Ettesmere."

Arthur frowned. "Upon whose authority?"

"Don't know. As soon as I got here this morning, a man came over, gave me a guinea to hand this to you if you patronized my cart." He shrugged. "I don't question the travelers. They keep to their own code."

"A traveler gave this to you?"

The man shrugged. "Who can say?"

Well, that told him absolutely nothing. "Thank you again." He tucked the envelope into an inside of pocket of his jacket, picked up the glasses, and then joined Julianna beneath the tree. "You'll never guess what I was just given," he said as he handed one of the glasses to her.

Regent kept up a string of barking as he ran about her, winding the lead around her legs as if she were a Maypole.

"A note?" Her eyes rounded with surprise and anticipation. "Truly?"

The sentiment was infectious, for it had been days since he'd last received one of the anonymous missives. "Yes." He took a large gulp of his lemonade. As the sweet, tart, and slightly watered-down taste of the beverage hit his palate, Arthur took the envelope from his jacket. "Can we dare to assume where we'll be 'led' next?"

"I couldn't begin to guess." She watched intently while he broke the seal and pulled the scrap of paper from the envelope. When she licked her bottom lip to catch an escaped drop of lemonade, Arthur stifled a groan.

Dear God. No, he hadn't gotten her out of his system at all. If anything, the need—the hunger—for her had increased. "'On the grounds of Ettesmere Park, there is a seldom-used maze. It's said there is something of great value waiting at the heart. Do you dare to find it?'" He laughed and shoved the budding impure thoughts away. "That's the clue, but whoever wrote this is wrong. I know that maze like the back of my hand. There's nothing in the heart except for more of my mother's rose bushes."

"Perhaps the writer of the note considers them valuable." Julianna took another sip of her beverage. "From all the work your mother apparently put into them—"

"—they *are* award-winning roses—"

"—then why shouldn't he or she wish to show them off?" she continued as if he hadn't interrupted her. She flashed a smile. "The question is, why does the person who penned the note want you to go there if you're already familiar with the maze?"

"Who can say?" He shrugged. "When once I thought this clandestine business over, now it's suddenly resurrected itself." As he stuffed the note and envelope back into his jacket pocket, he frowned. "But to what end?"

Julianna wrapped a length of the leather lead about her hand in the attempt to curb Regent's penchant for running around her. "The note is hardly threatening, so it's not an enemy who is dictating to you. Perhaps someone you know is having a good laugh in watching you dance about like a puppet?"

"For what purpose, though?"

"I would have no idea." She took another sip of the lemonade and then handed the glass to him. "Regardless, are you curious enough to investigate? Perhaps there is another clue in the heart of that maze."

That was something he hadn't considered. Arthur's pulse kicked up a notch at the impending adventure. Truth be known, it was fun following the notes, even if he found himself distracted most of the time. "There might be." He swallowed the remaining contents of his glass in one gulp and wished it was something stronger. "Do you care to accompany me? I understand, however, if you want to return home to your father." After what she revealed yesterday and how disheartened she'd been about it, he rather suspected she needed a break.

For a brief moment, sadness gathered in her eyes but cleared at her next blink. "That sounds like a delightful excursion."

"Capital. I'll just return these, and we'll be on our way." In any event, it meant she'd remain in his company for a little longer.

By the time the three miles from Wokingham to Ettesmere Park had been accomplished, Arthur could honestly say that walking with the highly exuberant, rotund dog had been quite the chore. Several times the dog had darted into his path and tripped him. It had caused him to flail about like a nodcock to prevent himself from falling. Julianna must have found the antics amusing, for her laughter continued to ring in his ears long after the journey had been accomplished. They'd taken turns in handling the lead, for Regent was a handful. And he was rather strong when he strained against the hold.

As soon as they entered the hedge maze, Julianna spoke. "Did your father have this designed?"

"He did. Early on during his reign of the title. He and my mother had been married for a few years." Arthur grinned, for his family history was a happy one. "She wanted something to occupy her time when they were in residence at Ettesmere Park, so she took to growing roses. Over the years, her skill has only improved, and now she and her hand-picked gardeners often win awards throughout the county."

"What a lovely hobby. I commend your mother on her dedication." Warmth echoed in Julianna's voice. When Regent tried to dart ahead, her arm jerked, and she stumbled a few steps to catch up with his pace. "I'll have to remember to praise her creations at the ball once I have a look at the roses."

"Mother would adore that." His respect and affection for Julianna grew; she was always so considerate even with everything she personally battled with. "She dotes on those roses. Now Sophia tends them as well."

"I can understand that. Perhaps she puts her time into those where she can't any longer with your father." Somberness reflected in her tones. "It's a nice memorial, for his memory will continue to bloom for her."

"True. I've never thought of it that way." But it made sense. She wished to spend her time in the country as opposed to in London. This was where she felt most comfortable and no doubt closest to his father.

Ah, Mother, you should have told me you still mourned. I would have understood.

Yet, she hadn't let that grief affect the other portions of her life, for she entertained and socialized. She didn't shut herself away like he had. Why didn't he ask her for help and guidance?

There were no easy answers, so he remained silent as he navigated through the maze. The familiar scents of evergreens and growing things tickled his nose. Gravel and finely ground shells crunched beneath the soles of his boots. As they made turn after turn, Regent became a tad more subdued. Perhaps he didn't know what to think about this strange new please he'd never visited, but Julianna delighted in the genius his father had when the maze had been laid out.

"One could find themselves lost here quite easily."

"Oh, yes." Arthur grinned. "When we were children, it was a badge of honor to conquer the maze by ourselves that first time. For me, it took three attempts while poor Sophia never managed it until she was nearly a girl of twelve. Gilbert cheated and plowed his way through the hedges to reach the heart."

"I like it in here. It's like the opening to a fairy land far removed from daily life." She looked about her with rounded eyes. "An escape."

"Perhaps." That was something else that had never occurred to him. Shock slammed into his chest at the realization that everyone fought some sort of battle within themselves they seldom talked about.

We all are searching for an escape...

Just like each time he'd ever visited the maze, it opened abruptly into the heart. Soft, springy grass cushioned his steps, for here the sunshine was limited to the few hours surrounding noon when the sun was high enough to filter through the hedges. Since it was nearing teatime, shade blanketed the circular area, but that was all to the good, for the temperatures were pleasant and cool here. Directly in the middle of the grassy circle, a cluster of rose bushes waited. They hadn't yet bloomed, for it was still slightly too early for that, but they'd budded. Already, hints of color peeked through: yellow, pinks in all shades, and deep, blood red. There were a couple who hosted white buds, and one of peach, all in sharp contest to the dark green leaves.

It would be a breathtaking display this year.

"What a dear little area!" When Julianna went to advance toward the bushes to join Arthur, Regent sprang into animation. He gave a few happy little barks and raced around and around them. The leather lead wrapped about their legs, but the dog didn't stop until it had pulled tight enough to crash them together. The dog only halted because the length of the lead had disappeared.

With a whine, he pawed at Julianna's legs, but the damage had been done. The hopeless tangle of the lead made standing unstable. "Well, damn," Arthur uttered seconds before he and she tumbled to the soft grass and cool moss. He cushioned her landing as best he could, shielding her body with his so that he took the brunt of the fall. Even still, she came to a rest on her back with him haphazardly over her. As she gave a breathless laugh, he shook his head. "Something must be done about that dog."

"I think he's too far gone." When the dog crept over and licked her face, she giggled. "You have displeased the earl, Regent." Julianna fumbled with the knot, and finally unraveling it, she freed the canine's collar. "Go home to Papa."

Apparently, the dog didn't need further encouragement. With a happy yelp, he bounded away, crashing through the hedges, and kept going until his barking grew ever softer.

"He'll eventually find his way to the cottage," she said as she met Arthur's gaze once more. "The sad fact is Regent adores the outdoors so much that the days are much too short for his adventuring even if he is a fat little problem."

"There is one boon to his destruction." In such proximity, how could he not take advantage? He lowered his head and claimed her lips in a kiss designed to tantalize. When she cupped his cheek and kissed him back, he was very nearly lost.

When the embrace broke, Julianna rested her head on the grass. Some of the midnight tresses had come loose from their pins leaving the hair in a spilled mess. "Perhaps I won't scold Regent when I reach the cottage."

"No. I don't suppose you should," he responded in a quiet voice. Arthur stared down at her as if finally seeing her for the first time. Laughing, sapphire eyes aglow and shadowed with the same desire coursing through his veins, lines of amusement framing her eyes, hair tumbling down. She was easily the most gorgeous woman he'd ever set eyes on.

The sensation of falling assailed him. Everything about his non-traditional not-quite-a-courtship had been the opposite of what he'd had with Ellen that he couldn't quite come to grips with it. Hell, he hadn't even bedded his wife until after they'd married, but now? A grin spread over his face, and when she gave him one in answer, awareness prickled throughout his body. Now, he wanted Julianna more desperately than he had the last time near the spring. Yet, this hunger, this need was much more than merely satisfying a physical urge. He wanted her in every way that a man could.

When the devil had that thought come about?

Julianna trailed a fingertip along the side of his face, and damn if he didn't want to remove those gloves posthaste. "You have the look of a man who has reached a surprising decision. Do you care to share?" Her words held a slightly breathless edge.

"Not now, and definitely not until I can make sense of things in my mind." But he rested his weight on his forearms and elbows, framing her face with his gloved hands, and then he once more took possession of her lips.

With a tiny sigh, Julianna surrendered to his embrace. One of her hands rested near his cravat while the other curled about his nape; her fingers furrowed through the hair there and every touch ignited his blood.

It took next to no time to convince her lips to part, and when he found her tongue with his, she was waiting. An ancient duel unfolded. She'd taken to kissing in the French style quickly enough, and soon it was him who was breathless.

And he wanted so much more, to claim her in so many other ways.

Wildly. With abandon.

But he couldn't do that while they were tangled together with the dog's lead. Uttering a sound of regret as she offered a protest of her own, Arthur broke the kiss. "There are some things a man wishes to unfetter himself with, and right now that includes this lead, these gloves," he wrenched the kid accessories from his hands and tossed them to the side, "as well as any other fabric that's proving a barrier from me and what I want most."

"I've never seen you in such a forceful mood." There was a tinge of awe in her tone as well as appreciation. "Where has that man been hiding?" Julianna removed her gloves. They landed on the grass like dropped dollops of cream.

"Perhaps he's been there all this time but has only now been unleashed." And it had everything to do with the advent of Julianna into his life. She made him feel reckless and daring, as if there wasn't anything he wouldn't do to win a smile or acknowledgement from her.

In short order he'd unwound the leather from their legs then he pounced, pinning her to the soft, cool grass, putting every ounce of feeling he had for her into that one meeting of their mouths. He pillaged her lips as if he were a Viking of old, deepening the kiss, molding his mouth to hers in an effort to memorize every one of those secrets.

When that intimacy didn't prove nearly enough contact, he nuzzled her neck, kissed and licked a path to the swell of her breasts above the bodice of her muslin dress. The veriest pressure on the back of his neck by her hand guided him closer, and when he closed his lips over a taut nipple through the fabric, she moaned and arched her back. He fell down that slope as passion clouded his brain. Never had he been so consumed so quickly with a woman as he was with Julianna. He worried that tight little bud with his teeth before moving to the other one and starting the sensual torture all over again.

His astronomer wasn't content to apparently remain docile. She kissed him with a hunger and desire that matched his own, and all the while she tugged on his cravat until the knot unraveled. Her fingers plucked at the buttons on his jacket, and when she'd finished with that, she moved on to the ones at his frontfalls.

"Now, now. There is no need to rush," he whispered against her lips. Wanting to distract her before the session was over too soon, Arthur tugged the bodice of her dress down. Once her perfect breasts were freed, he set out to pleasure her again and quite thoroughly.

Would there ever come a time when he wasn't fascinated by those two pale globes or their bright pink tips? He licked, suckled, and lightly bit those nipples, brought Julianna to the apparent brink of breaking before giving her a reprieve.

"I adore how responsive you are." And he followed the comment with rolling those pebbled buds merely to watch the emotions play about her face.

With a cry, she shoved at his chest until he levered off her. "There is such a thing as turnabout, you know." Again, her fingers wandered to his frontfalls.

"You think you can best me when it comes to giving pleasure? Where had this sudden cockiness come from? Surely this wasn't the man he'd always been.

Her laughter shivered over him as she undid each button one by one. "We shall see that evidence together, won't we?" Gently but with enough authority that he obeyed, Julianna pushed at his chest until he rolled onto his back. When his engorged length sprang free from his breeches, she gasped. "I never had the chance to see you the last time, but Arthur, you're quite magnificent." Apparently knowing what she wanted, she curled the fingers of one hand about his member.

Sensation exploded through his body to concentrate on the

flesh she held as well as tingle through his stones. "Careful." The fact that she wished to take command of this coupling gobsmacked him. Ellen had never done that. She always waited for him to initiate intercourse, and never would she voluntarily touch his manhood without invitation, had said it was a nasty business she'd rather ignore. He'd respected her preferences, for some women didn't enjoy the other more scandalous aspects of sex.

Julianna's willingness to explore and take him in hand was gloriously different, and if he didn't concentrate, he'd spend prematurely.

"It's a wonder how this appendage grows with just a touch and yet provides so much pleasure when applied to a woman's core." She glanced at him. The heat in her gaze nearly broke him as her tentative strokes up and down his shaft. "This is one mystery I can't wait to solve, even if it takes more than a few opportunities to do so."

Bloody hell. Did that mean she wanted to see more of him in this capacity or was she angling for a declaration?

Did it matter?

Not right now, not in this one moment of time when her ministrations were rapidly sending him to the point of no return. Then the amazing lady astronomer fondled his stones, cupped them, fit them into her palm as if she were weighing him, assessing him. Each pass, every squeeze had him shuddering with heightened need, but when she kneeled between his splayed legs and applied her tongue to the tip of his member, he was utterly and completely lost—at her mercy in more ways than physical pleasure.

"Dear God, Julianna, what are you doing to me?" Perhaps he needed to know the answer to that question as it applied to more than this moment.

"Conducting scientific research on how best to bring you to the edge of sanity the quickest." A wicked light appeared in her eyes that he didn't quite trust. "There is plenty of time to study how to do it the slowest way later."

Then she dipped her head and slowly, oh so gently, took his straining length into the warm cavern of her mouth.

"Julianna!" The shout wrenched from his throat before he could recall it. Such exquisite pleasure it was to feel himself slide in and out. First there was heat when she took him inside then when she came off, the moisture she'd left behind cooled the oncoming surge. Over and over, she treated him to more of the same, and he tightened, muscles clenching with both the need to spend down her throat and to hold it back. It was torture of the most erotic sort, and surely, he wouldn't survive it. To distract himself, he asked in a choked voice, "Where did you learn that?" She'd been an innocent when he'd first coupled with her at the stream. How was any of this possible?

Her chuckle reverberated around his shaft causing his stones to tingle and tighten in anticipation. Finally, after one last, lingering lick to the underside of his cock, she lifted her head and grinned. "I read, Ettesmere, and I'm often overlooked in the background at gatherings. I hear gossip and talk." When she shrugged, her breasts jiggled. "I have a curious mind. It leads me many places, and now I'm here."

"I see."

"Shall I continue? I'd like to know how quickly I can have you hit release."

Oh, dear God! Had he caught a tigress by the tail instead of an on-the-shelf woman with stars in her eyes?

"Some other time." Arthur barely got those words out past a tight throat. Already, his body was taut and shaking, to say nothing of the urgent pulsing of his prick. "There are other things we can do together." Desperate and falling, he tugged her up and over his body until she straddled his waist. His hardened length rubbed against her backside, the fabric of her skirting sliding over him, and those varying degrees of friction nearly did him in. "Ride me, Julianna. Take what you need from me."

"Oh, how interesting." She rose onto her knees and at the same time moved her skirting out of the way. Then she once more took him in hand, and he groaned. Sweat plastered his shirt to his back. With a grin that bore trouble for him, she fit his tip to her wet opening. "Forgive me if I'm adrift in the proper way to do this. Application is much different than theory."

Could he adore her any more than he did in that moment?

"I'll guide you, but for the love of Jove, take me inside you!" This was what he'd been reduced to, begging a woman for a coupling.

There were worse things.

With another laugh that was genuine and without guile, Julianna lowered herself onto his length. She didn't stop until he fully impaled her. Damn, but she was tight. That snugness added another layer to his need. A shiver passed through her body, and for a few seconds she paused as she no doubt acclimated to this new position. "Good heavens. This is quite... something."

"Yes." Arthur gripped her hips. "Come down when I thrust upward. Once you've sorted that, then you can move on me as you wish."

"That sounds reasonable." Determination lined her face as she did as instructed.

He assisted as much as he could, but she felt too good as he slid in and out of her honeyed heat; his mind was nearly gone. Soon enough, they found a rhythm, and though her movements were slightly awkward, watching her as she figured out what she liked and didn't was the most erotic sight he'd ever seen.

And still she moved, slowly at first with her hands pressed to his chest. When she gained more confidence, she straightened as she moved on him. The initial gentle, long strokes rapidly grew frantic and deeper, shorter, sharper. Her breasts bounced. He took them in his hands and teased the nipples into hardened tips once more.

Julianna whimpered with need. She arched her back, which put those charms more firmly into his care, and as she rested her hands behind her on his legs, she gyrated her hips in a rhythm all her own. With each thrust and push, her gasps and moans filled his ears. Her eyes shuttered closed. A pink stain of a blush encompassed her cheeks and upper chest. When her breathing became erratic and the first flutters of contractions gripped his length, Arthur clenched his teeth.

He'd be damned if he spent before she finished, but when she faltered, no doubt lost on a sea of pleasure, he tugged her down over his body and kissed her. Seconds later, he'd flipped them both over and speared into her so deeply they both groaned. "Julianna, look at me." Emotion and desire graveled the request.

"Why?" She looped her arms about his shoulders, frowned when he temporarily stopped his movements.

"I want to see you, *all* of you as we finish." Arthur encouraged her to pull her legs up to her chest, and when she did, he went deeper still and fell into the blue pools of her eyes. His strokes grew frantic and shorter, but as he worked her over, he kept eye contact, and in that one twinkling moment of perfection, something was exchanged between them. A few pieces of his soul were given into her care while he received the same from her. "How have I managed to exist with you so close by and I never knew it?"

She didn't answer with words. Instead, Julianna tugged him closer. A light nip to his earlobe had his stones tightening. Then she canted her hips in a way that made her cry out with pleasure as he continued to thrust, and he was done for. A rush of need roared through his length, and though he couldn't hold back the inevitable tide, he didn't need to, for on his next stroke, the woman in his arms broke.

In fact, she shattered in spectacular fashion, and that pulled him into his own release. Julianna threw back her head. Her fingers dug into his shoulders while a keening cry of surprise and bliss left her throat. In the distance, the baying of a beagle answered, and as Arthur chuckled, he pumped into her again until those contractions pulled him under.

"Bloody hell, Julianna!" Never had he spent so hard before. He collapsed over her with his lips pressed to the side of her neck.

By the time his breathing had returned to normal, exhaustion weighted his limbs and she'd gone completely pliant beneath him. "Are you well?" He moved off her enough to roll onto his side.

"There is no answer for that just yet." She looked at him with the soft, secret grin of a highly satisfied woman. Pride tightened his chest. "That was, by far, the closest I've come to soaring with the stars." A chuckle escaped her throat. "Don't ask me to move, Ettesmere, for I cannot."

"Then I suppose I've done the job correctly." And somehow, she'd managed to steal a few pieces of his heart in the bargain. "At the moment, we're well-hidden. There is no need to do anything immediately." Which was a good thing, for his mind was steeped in post-coital haze and tinged with confusion and guilt.

"Mmm." She snuggled closer to him, and he wrapped his arms around her. One of her hands drifted to his chest. As she burrowed them beneath his cravat and found the opening of his shirt placket, he gasped when her fingers encountered the chord about his neck that led to the ring. "Ah. The mysterious trinket. I'd almost forgotten about it."

Would that she had, for remembering it stole some of the joy from this coupling. "It belonged to my wife." He laid a hand over Julianna's to prevent her from exploring further.

"Why do you wear it?"

"So I will forever hold her against my heart." Was it important any longer? Hadn't he already tried to make peace with his past? "It was the ring I gave her the day we became engaged. I wasn't the earl yet and had only started to make a name for myself outside of who my father was. There was very little coin to toss on a bauble, so I found this one in a pawn shop."

"It's a dear ring. I hope it made your wife happy."

"She was thrilled with it; her father not so much. He felt it was an insult to his daughter and well beneath her station." Arthur chuckled, even if talking about Ellen made his heart ache. "She didn't care, and she wore it with enthusiasm."

"But you replaced it as soon as you were able."

"I did." He tried to move Julianna's hand away from the ring, but she refused.

Again, she fingered the circle of pearls. "It's a lovely memento, of course, but if you don't have this around your neck, you'll still remember your wife. The human heart has great capacity for love—both through memories and in real life."

"It... wearing this makes me feel as if Ellen is still with me."

"Is that what you want, Arthur? To bring her back, to keep everyone else at arm's length so those memories won't fade, so you won't be tempted to move forward?"

Damn. It was uncanny how well Julianna could peer into his soul and read him. "I don't know." It was partially true. Additionally, every moment with her confused him even more.

"Well, only you can work out what you eventually want." She slipped her hand behind his neck and drew him closer. "I hope for your sake you figure it out soon. You're a good man who still has much to give the world."

Arthur couldn't help himself. He dipped his head and kissed her as if she'd suddenly vanish from the maze and he'd never see her again. Over and over, he drank from her, put every ounce of feeling that raged through his veins into that one meeting of mouths. He hoped to God she would understand, would stick with him as he tried to pull away from that which he'd hidden behind for far too many years.

Once the kiss ended, her grin was bemused and her eyes dreamy as she rested her head on his arm. "Too much more of this and I'll be branded a fallen woman."

"Nonsense. I won't allow it." How, then, did he think he could if he wasn't willing to go the next step and offer for her? Arthur shoved those thoughts away to become lost in the haze of his mind. Slumber could have at him, for in that state he wouldn't have doubts and worries to beset him and falling asleep with this woman in his arms sounded quite perfect indeed.

Julianna snorted. "Sooner or later, you'll have to make a definitive decision. I am not a woman who will stand idly by while you play with my emotions." She sighed. "I've given you latitude, for I've enjoyed myself heartily and I wanted the couplings too."

"I know." She deserved at least that and was more than a convenient trysting partner. "Allow me until the masquerade. I promise to have sorted myself by then."

He hoped. Fear clenched icy fingers around his heart. If he couldn't pull himself from the past, he would certainly forfeit his future.

Dear God, what am I going to do?

CHAPTER FIFTEEN

June 22, 1819

JULIANNA'S HEART FLUTTERED as she gazed up at the stars on Otis Hill. Why did every constellation she peered at resemble Arthur in some way? His eyes, his grin, his form... Possibly because, like a ninny, she'd fallen in love with the earl.

She petted Regent's sleek head making sure she scratched behind his ears. "It's quite the most terrible and wonderful thing I've tumbled into," she told the dog.

He, of course, merely whined in response. If the conversation wasn't about rabbits, food, or walks, truly, the canine wasn't interested.

When such a miracle had happened, she couldn't say. Neither could she utter why. Perhaps it was a mix of things, for she admired him, and he made her laugh. To say nothing of his vulnerability, his caring, and his devotion to his family. Every facet of the man appealed to her, and if she'd been perhaps ten or fifteen years younger, she would have jumped at the chance to flirt with him, try to move him in the direction of making a declaration, but now?

I'm much too old. If he wants to marry again, to have more children, he needs to look further than me.

Even if that was the logical assumption, her heart wasn't in league with her brain. Why would he continue to seek her out for conversation, take her to a country festival, and share the greatest of intimacies if he was merely marking time? Of course, men high on the instep like the earl did that sort of thing all the time. Wasn't Town full of stories centering around titled men and their mistresses? He'd return to London and leave her behind, forgotten. Yet a man with his sensibilities and adherence to the past? No, he wouldn't do something so crass or careless.

Yet, here she was, waiting as if suspended in this sliver of life not knowing what the end result would be. *Oh, it is impossible!* The thoughts circled around her head in a never-ending loop. So, she kept her eyes on the dark, star-strewn skies and concentrated very carefully on nothing.

Eventually, the excited barking from Regent alerted her to the imminent arrival of someone else on the hill. He sprang up onto all fours, planted his front feet on her chest, and bayed as loud as he could while wagging his tail.

"Who is it, boy?" Her heartbeat accelerated as she sat up. Perhaps it was the earl coming to seek her out. It wouldn't be outside the realm of possibility, for he knew she was always on this hill in the evenings.

"Miss Quill? Are you up here?"

She frowned. No, the visitor wasn't Arthur. "Lady Sophia?" Why in the world was his sister seeking her out?

"Ah. There you are." When the lady reached the top of the hill, she waved. "I was hoping I could find you tonight."

"Whyever for?" That was strange in and of itself, but before she could say more, Lady Sophia reached the quilt and then dropped onto it, folding her legs beneath her, and covering them with the skirts of what appeared to be a gown of navy satin. "You're dressed for a society event instead of being out here."

Her trill of laughter reminded Julianna of the stars. "I do so adore your penchant for plain speaking. You never try to couch your words behind useless banter." For long moments, she looked into the sky and then finally sighed. "I'll admit, I couldn't take one more moment in that drawing room, indulging in things and conversations that don't matter. Especially when time is very precious and somewhat limited."

What did that mean? Julianna glanced at her companion, but there was nothing except sadness reflected on her face, and even then, it was difficult to read those emotions in the dim illumination. "Are you quite well, my lady?"

"Please, there is no need to remain formal between us." She reached over and patted Julianna's hand. "I'm merely Sophia." Another sigh escaped her. "And no, I'm not all that well, but I don't like to think about it, let alone talk about my lot. I'm living in the moment."

Fair enough, though Julianna wondered what it was that ailed the woman. "If you don't mind me coming straight to the point, why are you here?"

"Arthur had once mentioned you are an astronomer and liked to come out to Otis Hill for stargazing. I wanted to see for myself what wonders are contained in the heavens." Sophia once again tipped her head up to contemplate the stars. "He also told me you'd discovered a comet."

"I did." Julianna nodded. With a grin, she dug into her willow basket and withdrew her telescope. "However, it has now completed the leg of its trek that took it across our skies. It dropped from view last night, but there are plenty of other marvels to see if you'd like." She held out the telescope to the other woman. It was unnerving to sit there with this woman and not know exactly why she was there.

"Oh, I believe you." Sophia declined the instrument. "It's interesting, is it not?"

"What is?"

"Knowing there is a whole other part of the world contained in the sky, but we rarely think about it because it happens in the dark above our heads." Sophia frowned. "We as a people are often self-absorbed and oblivious to things around us. It's one of the reasons that being part of the *beau monde* has lost its charm for me."

"I'm sorry to hear that, and of your troubles." Though she had no idea what the other woman struggled with, her heart went out to her all the same. They were of an age, or a few years apart, and in a different life, perhaps they could have been the best of friends. "We don't need to speak at all if you'd rather. Sometimes, sitting in the silence is just what a person needs."

"Oh, I don't know if I want to court quiet just yet. It will come soon enough." When she uttered a wry laugh, Regent went over to her and climbed into her lap.

"I beg your pardon." Julianna tried to coax the canine back. "He'll ruin your gown."

"Please, leave him." Sophia wrapped her arms around the beagle, who snuggled up to her as if he hadn't had human contact for years. "A warm body is always welcome; I just didn't think it would be of the canine variety."

"Indeed." Julianna snorted with laughter. She racked her brain for something intelligent to say. "Are you looking forward to your mother's masquerade?" Even mentioning that event put knots of worry into her belly.

"Yes and no. There is much potential there, of course, but there is no depth to it." She cast a glance at Julianna. "Are you? Arthur told me he invited you."

How much, exactly, had the earl told his sister about her? "I am… nervous." At least that was the truth. "And it makes me feel silly to be in that state, for one would think at my advanced age, all of that would have gone away."

"If only that were true." Again, Sophia laughed. Regent wagged his tail so vigorously, it thumped against the lady's leg. "Why are you nervous?"

"Oh, pick a reason." She sighed and peered at the heavens. The stars never worried; they merely kept on shining because that was their purpose. "Perhaps the biggest worry is the fact I have nothing to wear. The ball is tomorrow. I've searched the shops, but Wokingham doesn't exactly have anything as fine as what I'll need."

Another bout of tinkling laughter came from the lady. "Perhaps you can go as Lady Godiva, then. You know, naked and on a horse. What a grand entrance that would be."

Julianna rolled her eyes even as a grin curved her lips. Her companion had a sense of humor she admired. "I rather think that's the height of scandalous, and I don't need any more of that in my life." She tamped on the urge to gasp, for that slip had nearly revealed too much.

Sophia snickered. "Then fear not. You can borrow one of my gowns. I have an armoire full of them."

"Oh, I couldn't do that. It's not right."

"Pish-posh, Miss Quill. I won't hear any protests, for the gowns are doing no good merely hanging there." She shrugged. "Come to Ettesmere Park with me tonight. I'll gather a few of the maids that do fine handiwork. We'll fit you into one of the gowns. I'll help with the alterations." Excitement wove through her voice. "In fact, it's really the only way."

Unfortunately, that was true. If she didn't accept the assistance, she couldn't attend the masquerade. Slowly, Julianna nodded. "Why would you do this for me?"

"Honestly?"

"Of course."

"You make Arthur happy." For long moments, the other woman remained silent as if pondering her next words. "I want you to feel the same, but I suspect you have reservations and fears. Not just of the ball, but of my brother." She continued to cradle the beagle in her lap. Regent, to his credit, had drifted off into doggie slumber. "Somehow, you assume you're not good enough for us, or for him because he's an earl. Yes?"

"How do you know?" Julianna gawked at the other woman. "Is it that obvious?" *Obviously, I need to do better in hiding my emotions.* Never before had she had reason to do so.

Sophia grinned. "Not to many, but I know my brother, and I've followed your relationship with interest."

What did *that* mean? She sighed when the lady wasn't forth-coming with more information. "Regardless of the relationship, yes, his position in society makes me uneasy. As does the fact that I've long passed the first and second blooms of youth." Julianna bit her bottom lip. "However, commonsense tells me I shouldn't worry, for your brother doesn't have marriage on his mind. Even if I aspired to such with him," she was quick to add lest Sophia think she'd risen above her station. "It's merely an observation." *Well, drat. I hadn't meant to admit that.* But it *was* uppermost on her mind.

"Oh, Miss Quill, you are so delightfully genuine! It's what we all aspire to be." Sophia squeezed her hand. "Suffice it to say, men are frustrating at times. Especially widowers."

"Perhaps." Julianna drew her knees to her chest in a fair imi-tation of how Emily sat the last time she'd visited the hill to talk. "If you want to know what I think, he's still in love with his wife." That much was readily obvious in his struggles.

"Possibly. The man was smitten with her indeed." Sophia sought her gaze in the darkness. "However, he's more afraid of possibly having to mourn again should he lose another wife. Trust me, no one should have to go through that more than once in a lifetime."

"Of course that's understandable. Watching my father de-cline, I have no choice but to know he won't be with me as long as I'd like." A swath of sadness slammed into her and tightened her chest. "It's a horrible proposition. I'll be alone once that occurs."

"Unless Arthur will come up to scratch, hmm?" A knowing twinkle flashed in her eyes. Sophia nudged Julianna's arm. "Do you enjoy being with him?"

"In what capacity?" The question sneaked out before she could recall it.

The other chuckled with apparent glee that woke Regent, who uttered a canine snort. "Any." She hummed with approval. "Or specifically, has he offered any romantic overtures for you yet?"

Merciful heavens. The heat of embarrassment slapped at Julianna's cheeks. "He has." Perhaps she should leave it at that.

"Lovely!" Sophia leaned a bit closer and lowered her voice, even though they were the only ones in the area. "Have you and he engaged in physical... exertions?"

"Lady Sophia!" The affront and embarrassment weren't contrived. This line of questioning was extremely personal and quite uncomfortable. "Such should never be the topic of discussion."

"Ah, then that means yes." She chuckled as if that were the best thing she'd ever heard. "I'd hoped Arthur would meet a woman with whom he felt that wonderful carnal spark. You didn't think him inept? Please tell me he didn't make a poor showing of it."

"Please, Sophia, enough." If her cheeks heated any further, she would surely dissolve into a puddle. When the lady stared at her in clear expectation, Julianna sighed. "He was everything a man should be in such an arena."

"I'm so happy to hear that!" She clasped Julianna's hand and squeezed. "And you enjoyed yourself? You and he are quite compatible?"

Obviously, the woman would continue digging regardless of if the subject should be private. "I did." She couldn't help a grin. "I think he's rather wonderful even beyond that side of our relationship."

"Then there's no time like the present to make certain you've caught Arthur's eye." Sophia bounced with happiness. Regent, apparently catching the excitement, gave a few happy yaps as if he, too, urged her to do just that.

She snorted. "For that, he will actually have to see me clearly instead of through the haze of his wife's ghost." Then her spirits sank. "He hasn't discussed the future or what will happen between us past the ball tomorrow night." Julianna shrugged. "Yesterday, Arthur asked that I give him until at least then to get himself sorted."

"I see." The earlier levity in Sophia's voice faded.

"And as much as I'm coming to care for him, I…" Her voice broke. "I cannot, in good conscience, become a summertime plaything for him, abandoned once he returns to London to take up the reins of his life. That would hurt too much indeed."

"Of course he doesn't think of you that way." The tone of her voice suggested she was scandalized at the prospect. "It has taken Arthur a long time to even reach this pass. The fact that he has and has opened up to you means you're something special to him."

"Though actions are welcome, in this case, I would prefer words spoken in honesty from him. Otherwise, it's too difficult to ascertain his intent." And she was much too advanced in age for games.

"You're very insightful, Miss Quill. I like that about you." She lapsed into silence again for several minutes. "Never doubt you've managed to sneak beneath that wall my brother has erected around his heart for protection. If he can't realize he's halfway in love with you, then he's a bacon-brained idiot and you don't need him."

"That is easier said than done, I'm thinking." How could she not need him? He was everything wonderful that she would have searched for in a man had she turned her attention to courtship instead of astronomy.

"Perhaps, but you didn't say impossible, so that means there is hope." Sophia's enthusiasm was infectious. "And where there is hope, there's life. You and Arthur will have a marvelous time of it once he figures out the risk is worth the reward."

"Oh, please stop, Sophia. That's rather putting the cart before the horse." Julianna was nothing if not practical. She gripped her telescope in her hand so tightly the dials and knobs bit into her palm. "I am not of your world."

"Oh, la!" The lady waved a hand in dismissal. "Love doesn't care about class, Miss Quill. It just is."

Perhaps that was the most profound statement Julianna had

heard from any of his family. It gave her a modicum of reassurance, but only just. "Be that as it may, I wouldn't know the first thing of what a countess does, even if Arthur were to ask me."

Which he hadn't even hinted at.

"Mother and I will educate you in that, so put those fears from your mind." She put on a bright smile that flashed white teeth. "You are so easy to talk with that the evening has slipped away." Leaning down, she placed a kiss upon Regent's forehead. "Your dog is wonderful, and having him nearby makes me feel as if everything will come out right in the end. For all of us."

"Regent does have that effect on people. No wonder he's such a fat and happy dog."

"Emily was right. Being in your company is soothing and lovely."

The fact the Winterbourne family had talked about her was somewhat disturbing, but she shoved those thoughts from her mind. "I do what I can. Everyone deserves to have their fears and misgivings brought into the light, to be heard."

"Indeed." Gently, Sophia urged Regent from her lap. "Will you come with me to the manor now? I have a few gowns in mind that will fit you. And we can talk about whether you wish to portray a character or merely wear a mask. I believe there might be some of those in the attics. Perhaps Emily or John will fetch them for us."

Was there any point in offering a protest? The bald fact was she *did* need a gown or a costume, and she hadn't any other recourse. Julianna nodded as she put the telescope into her basket. "This is quite an undertaking for all of you. Too much fuss for me."

"Nonsense." Sophia stood the same time that Julianna did. She helped fold the quilt. "I want to see my brother find love again, wish for everyone around me to have that happy ending that I had twice in my life, even if I might not have that again."

"Then you see yourself as a matchmaker?" Julianna wouldn't pry into the other woman's life, but she was curious. Was it possible she had written those notes?

"Only in this. And I had nothing to do with it. Arthur found you all on his own." Her trill of laughter echoed in the night. "Oh, tomorrow night should be such fun!"

That remained to be seen, but at least she'd see the earl again. It was up to him how the remainder of their association would go.

CHAPTER SIXTEEN

June 23, 1819

I T WAS THE night of his mother's midsummer masquerade ball. There was no doubt in his mind that she lived for this time every year, for she and his father had enjoyed a love that was from the ages. However, while she might have reached a pinnacle of triumph, Arthur had knots in his belly and sweat trickling down his back.

There was much to think upon on this night.

But none of it meant that he couldn't manipulate his own cravat. "Bah!" Once again, he'd botched the intricate knot he wanted, and since his valet had gone home to attend to an emergency with his own mother, Arthur was on his own. "What is wrong with this bloody neckwear?"

John grinned from his perch on the arm of a low sofa in Arthur's dressing room. He hadn't put effort into donning a costume. The only concession tonight was a black opera cape and a domino mask. "Nothing, Papa. You're merely frustrated."

Not that he'd been willing to pull together a new persona for the evening either. Out of respect for his mother, he would wear a mask, but the black breeches and loose-fitting lawn shirt would play the part of a highwayman if anyone were to inquire. And the mask was much more intricate than John's. "With a cravat?"

"I'll wager not only with a cravat."

"What the devil does that mean?" He couldn't concentrate on two different subjects at the same time. As the earl, should he have created a costume? But why? He didn't wish to be there in the first place, and the only reason he'd attend was for his mother... and the chance to dance with Julianna instead of meeting her in clandestine places.

"Just that there is something different about you tonight."

"Different how?"

His son left his perch and lifted an eyebrow as he approached. "Something that has changed from the inside out, as if you've suddenly found yourself happy."

"Such gammon." Yet it hit all too close to the truth.

"And now you don't know what to do about it. Perhaps you're even battling against yourself." He batted Arthur's hands away. "Let me assist."

"Fine." He lifted his chin as his son easily manipulated the length of cloth. "It's been an age since we last talked alone like this."

"Don't change the subject." There was deviltry in John's eyes that Arthur didn't quite understand. "What has you at such sixes and sevens? If you were a contemporary, I'd wager it had to do with a woman."

"Nothing I'm willing to mention at the moment." What he had with Julianna was special and he wanted to hoard it all to his heart.

"Coward," his son joked.

"Oh, indeed," he agreed, but that levity didn't alleviate the knots of worry in his gut. When he'd become what his son accused him of, he couldn't say, but where Julianna was concerned, his courage had surely deserted him.

"Ah ha! It *is* a woman, then." John manipulated the neckcloth with expert precision and soon stood back to admire his handiwork. "You'll pass inspection by Grandmama, though she will scold about the lack of a costume. She is going as the Greek goddess Hera."

"What lack? I'm going as a highwayman."

"Pshaw. Just barely." He met Arthur's gaze. "Now, tell me why you're nearly in a brown study."

Emily sailed into the dressing room at that precise time. "Oh, I can tell you that."

"Can you?" Arthur's stomach muscles clenched. What if they hit upon the truth?

"I can." She smiled at them both and then twirled. The skirts of her pink and moss green gown flared. Her golden hair had been strategically pulled back at the sides, left long in the back, and somehow, she'd managed to fashion fleshy points on the tops of her ears. "Have I managed to pull off a garden fairy well enough? After all, it *is* midsummer."

"No one would ever doubt you weren't that to begin with." To his embarrassment, tears misted Arthur's eyes. "You look so much like your mother right now."

"That is a lovely compliment." She slipped her arms around him and gave him a hug. When she pulled away, she looked John up and down. "I'm sad but not surprised you couldn't manage to put in the effort."

He stuck out his tongue like he used to do when they were little children. "Just be happy I'm attending at all. I could have gone to the festival with some of the fellows from the village."

Emily shook her head. "This is Grandmama's big night. We should all give her our respect and love. However, she has hinted that she might throw yet another masquerade soon for the joy of it all over again." Then she glanced at Arthur. "You're different."

"That's what I said, but he's denying it." John stared at him as well. "Out with it, old man. What's that secret you're keeping from us?"

Oh, dear God. Could the evening grow any worse?

"There is no secret. I merely have much on my mind."

Emily blew out a breath that ruffled a few curls on her forehead. "Papa might be in love. Can't you see it?"

John's eyebrows went up. "Right! Now that you mention it, the signs *are* there."

This was outside of enough. "Stop, children. I am not in love."

Perhaps.

Though, the signs were indeed there…

"Now who is dissembling?" John asked with a grin.

Arthur shook his head. "No lies. I'm thinking over my options." And that was where the guilt and confusion stemmed from. He glanced between his children. "You have both become admirable adults. Wasn't it just yesterday I bounced you two on my knee and reenacted some of Wellington's battles with tin soldiers and stuffed toys in the drawing room?" For his daughter refused to be left out of that merely because she was a girl.

"Don't act more ancient and decrepit than you can help." Emily shook her head. "It is the way of things, Papa. Soon John and I will leave the nest and you'll be quite alone."

"Yes, which is why it's essential you move on to the remainder of your life while you still can."

"Ah, because I eerily resemble a pile of mummy bones due to my age?" Arthur couldn't resist teasing them.

"No, because everyone deserves a second chance at love." Emily sobered. She ran a critical gaze along his person. "It's good you haven't donned a costume. You are manly and virile in your evening clothes. No doubt you'll catch a lady's eye tonight for certain."

Heat went up the back of Arthur's neck. "I don't know about that…"

John snorted. "Or perhaps you'll lead Miss Quill out. You seem to favor her company, and it certainly has given you a new outlook." He winked at Emily. "Perhaps she's why your mind is in such a tizzy."

The heat on his neck intensified even as worry built in his stomach. "Perhaps she is, but you should stay out of it."

His daughter shook her head. "Of course we won't stay out

of it, Papa. Miss Quill is a wonderful woman. She is quite perfect for you."

"And," his son was quick to add, "She's not a starry-eyed chit making her Come Out. It would be the height of awkward should you take an interest in a woman younger than me or of an age with Emily." He nodded as if that settled the matter. "Miss Quill is the best candidate we've seen in years for you."

They'd find no arguments from him. Did he have enough courage to take that chance?

Before he could reply, a knock sounded on the door. When John answered it, the butler stood in the frame.

"Lord Ettesmere, I have news from Lady Ettesmere," the butler proclaimed in what he probably thought was a thrilling tone.

"Yes? What is it?"

"These are her words, Your Lordship, so I quote, 'If my son and children don't put their arses into this ballroom within the next ten minutes, I shall disown them all.'" The butler raised one of his salt and pepper eyebrows. "That was two minutes ago, my lord."

Arthur exchanged glances with both Emily and John. All three of them burst into laughter. Finally, he raised a hand. "Tell my mother we will shall arrive presently."

"Very good, Your Lordship." Then, the butler was off.

"Well, I suppose I should hurry and finish with my toilette. This *is* Mother's night to shine." And to remember my father. She certainly had done better with grief than he had.

"Here." Emily handed him a black mask that featured loops and swirls in golden embroidery. It was also edged with golden paint. "Put this on. I'm especially looking forward to the dancing."

"Only with me or your brother, remember. You haven't had your Come Out." And that was certainly something he didn't wish to think upon, especially tonight.

Some twenty minutes later, he grinned with indulgence at his mother, who was in her element as she waxed eloquent in her speech.

"As we all celebrate tonight at this midsummer masquerade—and every one of you has put so much effort into your costumes—" She rested her gaze on Arthur and his children. "Most of you, that is," she amended with a smile, "my husband would have been so proud and excited to celebrate our wedding anniversary in such a way. He was the hallmark of mischievous."

A few murmurs of agreement went through the crowd, for those area members of the *ton* and gentry who had known the old earl would always remember him fondly.

"I hope we all remember this night in the spirit of Shakespeare and his famous play, and I hope there is magic and love and amusement aplenty in the air that will provide you with memories you can enjoy for years to come, just as I know my husband John surely would have."

"Oh, Grandmama, what a lovely speech," Emily said with tears in her eyes as polite applause echoed through the room. "Grandpapa would have adored it."

"Yes, dear, he would." The dowager's eyes were misty. She clasped Emily's hands and then grinned at John. "I want you two to have a wonderful time this evening. It took me six months to plan this ball."

"Is it true you're doing another in a couple of weeks?" Emily wished to know.

"I believe I will, for why not?"

Sophia made her way over to Arthur's side. "Mama shines more with every passing year." She linked her arm with Arthur's. "Look how some of the unattached men regard her. Perhaps she can find romance again too."

He frowned. "Too?"

"Yes." Sophia leaned into him and lowered her voice. "The same as you."

"Poppycock." He certainly didn't want to talk about this again.

Then Emily sucked in a breath. "Oh!"

Everyone in his party turned to follow her line of vision while the string quartet his mother had engaged played a song designed to enhance a party-like atmosphere.

"Oh, indeed." Julianna entered the ballroom, and Arthur completely forgot to breathe as he stared.

Dear Lord, she's gorgeous.

Her silver gown shimmered beneath the candles in the chandeliers; it was as if she'd fallen directly from the stars she watched. Every step, each movement of that taffeta gown caught the light and reflected it back. Delicate tulle lined the low-cut bodice and shoulders of the gown. Matching glitter and spangles had been glued to a silver mask that tied about the back of her head. He flicked his gaze to her black tresses, which had been piled high on her head, highlighting her slender neck, and secured with sparkling silver combs that flashed with what appeared to be tiny diamonds. But the stunning surprise to the gown were the sheer butterfly wings secured to her back. Indeed, she was a moth sent from wintertime fairyland.

And he couldn't have enough of her. The longer he gawked, the more his feet were frozen to the ballroom floor. Guests moved and mingled around him, yet he couldn't do more than try and memorize how she looked.

"Bloody hell," he whispered to no one in particular.

Both Emily and Sophia snickered.

"Since Papa is apparently addlepated this evening, I shall go and ask the newcomer to partner me in the first dance of the night." John shook his head and sent him a look that proclaimed him a nodcock. Did he know who it was behind the mask? It was too difficult to say.

"Oh, my." Sophia proceeded to laugh at Arthur's reaction. "How interesting. Isn't that Miss Quill? What a transformation she's made." She squeezed his arm before releasing him. "So elegant, so poised. How easily I can picture her hosting events as a countess."

Dear God. Arthur swallowed hard. "I don't know…"

"Oh, la." She swatted his arm. "Arthur, don't *think* tonight. Just enjoy the moment. Dance with her. Talk with her." Amusement filled her eyes as she looked at him. "Go where the wind takes you, but for Jove's sake, don't destroy your future because you have been unable to put the past behind you." She patted his cheek. "You won't find another woman as interesting or as practical as Miss Quill."

"I…" That was probably true. "Perhaps."

Sophia sighed. "And she makes you happy."

"She does." Why lie about that? It was probably obvious. He followed John as he escorted Julianna through the steps of the country reel. His children were all but grown, and suddenly he wanted someone in his life he could talk to, enjoy the remainder of it with, but fear kept him frozen, uncertain.

"There is something to be said for happiness, brother," Sophia said softly.

Emily nodded. She waved to someone across the ballroom. "Papa, promise me you'll follow your heart tonight."

"I'll do my level best."

She huffed. "Do more than that. You deserve the best that life can give you. Mama would have wished for you to do so." She lifted on her toes and bussed his cheek. "My friends are waiting. Don't disappoint me."

"I should hope not." Would he do just that if he didn't continue to court—or whatever the relationship with Julianna was—and have it end as they all wished?

When the current set ended, John escorted Julianna over to his position with her hand tucked within the bend of his elbow. Her cheeks were flushed, and her eyes sparkled behind the mask.

"Good evening, Lord Ettesmere."

The sound of her voice, the faint apricot and vanilla scent of her, the curve of her lips all worked at his undoing. "Good evening, Miss Quill." He even went farther in doing the pretty by executing a half-bow from the waist. "I trust you're enjoying yourself?"

"Oh, quite. Your son is a wonderful dancer." She glanced at John and offered him a smile. "Thank you, Lord Eglington."

"It was truly my pleasure."

Arthur lifted an eyebrow when John lingered over her hand after kissing the back of it. Surely his son didn't have designs on her. When Sophia snickered, he tempered his reaction, and as the musicians struck up chords, he sighed. "The next set is a waltz. I should really dance with my mother."

God, what a coward I am!

"Such gammon." John snorted. "I'll take Grandmama out. You partner Miss Quill. She's a lovely conversationalist and has given me a couple of things to think over for my future that never would have occurred to me."

"Such as?" Arthur gawked. How had she managed to charm his children and family so thoroughly as she had?

John shrugged. "How I might manage the estate when it's my turn, or investments I might turn my attention to while I wait." He nodded at her. "She's truly quite insightful on many things. I might need to talk with you more in-depth at another time."

"I look forward to it, and I'm happy to help."

"How fascinating," Arthur whispered. Was it possible that his children had needed—craved—the advice of a female not related to them all this time? That they'd missed the guidance of someone who could stand in as a mother figure in their lives?

Have I done them a great disservice?

"Ah, I can see the wheels are turning." Sophia openly laughed at him. She gave his shoulder a shove. "Go waltz with Miss Quill, brother dear, and remember to enjoy yourself. You two make an admirable couple." She winked at Julianna. "You are wonderous this evening, Miss Quill. That silver is simply breathtaking."

"Thank you, Lady Sophia. It's easily the most beautiful thing I've ever worn. Thank you for the wardrobe assistance."

"It suits you." His sister nodded. "I must say I'm jealous of how that gown sets off every aspect of your figure. It certainly seems made for you and is definitely your color. You'll make a sensation tonight if you're not careful."

"I quite agree," John was quick to add.

"Not if I have anything to say in the matter." Was that a growl in his voice? Good God, he was jealous, but he didn't care. He also ignored the looks of surprise his son and sister cast him, for he couldn't help it. The thought of Julianna with another man, tonight or anytime in any capacity, was enough to make him want to punch a hole in the wall. She belonged with him, at his side, in *his* life, yet he hadn't found the courage to voice those sentiments.

Would he lose her before he could ever have her?

"Enjoy your evening, dear," Sophia whispered to Julianna. She bussed Miss Quill's cheek. "I'll check in on you later."

"Thank you." She waved to John as he, too, departed. Then Arthur was alone with her—or as alone as he could be on the sidelines of a crowded ballroom. "The waltz will start presently, Lord Ettesmere. Should you like to join?"

"Of course. My apologies for the delay." In short order, he escorted her to an empty spot on the floor. "Sophia wasn't wrong," he said in a low voice.

"In what?" She gazed up at him, her eyes twinkling behind the glittering mask.

"You are stunning in that gown." When the opening strains of the waltz floated into the air, he set them into motion. "It's so easy to imagine you're a bit of the stars, tumbled from the heavens merely to tempt me." He was about to make a cake of himself over this woman, but for the moment, he didn't care. Pulling her a tad closer, he fit his lips to the shell of her ear. "There is nothing more I want to do right now than slowly remove that gown, kissing every inch of your skin as I go."

The shiver that went through her body transferred to him. A pink blush stained her cheeks. Her eyes darkened. "I've never heard such definitive confidence in your voice before." Her fingers tightened on his shoulder. "If that is what you want tonight, I won't tell you nay."

Dear God, she was so different from Ellen, so mysterious, so…
real. She didn't try to be the image of perfection the *ton* adhered
to. Arthur forced a swallow and incrementally brought her closer
to his body. The sensation of falling, tumbling, flying once more
swept over him the longer he held her, moved with her over the
dance floor. As best he could, he tamped down on the rising guilt,
the worry—everything.

Then, he grinned. "Let us see if we can't make that happen
sooner rather than later."

CHAPTER SEVENTEEN

JULIANNA HAD NEVER had so much fun in her life. As Arthur whisked her about the parquet floor, her feet scarcely touched the ground, or so it felt like. In his arms, she was secure and protected; there was the certainty that she could accomplish anything she set her mind to, and from the way he looked at her, there was no mistaking how much he wanted her.

It was simply wonderful, and for the moment, she let those sensations overtake her. In this one perfect moment, while she matched steps with the earl amidst the crowded ballroom, she could easily imagine being with him for the rest of her life. Oh, he was strong and powerful to be sure, but he was also funny and kind, dedicated and careful. His family was darling, and each time she was around any of them, it was as if she'd finally found her own family again.

Different but the same.

And she tumbled tip over tail deeper into love with him. No longer did she want to stop that slide, for it was simply amazing and was making her into a new person, a better person.

"Why are you looking at me in such a way?"

The sound of his voice brought her back to the present. "How am I looking at you?"

Arthur chuckled as he touched her hand above her head and moved away in the steps of the dance. Once they came back together, he replied. "As if you wished to do wicked things to me regardless of who might be watching."

"How could I not when you're dressed like that? Why, I'll wager half the women here are devouring you with their eyes."

"As are you." When she gasped and warmth infused her cheeks, he grinned. "You wear your heart and feelings on your sleeve, so to speak." When he dropped his voice, he pulled her a tad bit closer. "It's adorable, and it fires my own need."

"Oh?" Was the husky laugh that escaped her throat truly hers? Julianna smiled and vowed to remember how to do that. "Your need to do what, Lord Ettesmere?" She rather enjoyed the process of flirting, especially with him.

"Hmm." The next turn brought them close to the terrace doors that had been thrown open to encourage the nighttime breeze into the overheated room. "Take you out into the gardens and perhaps do unspeakable things to you?"

Tingles of anticipation shivered down her spine. "That is a splendid idea." Perhaps once they were alone, she could have a private and heartfelt talk with him in an effort to smooth out the confusion of her thoughts. Their relationship couldn't continue in the same vein if there was no goal in mind.

"I think so too." As the last notes of the song reverberated through the room, Arthur whisked her out one set of doors and onto the stone terrace. "My father often said he did some of his best thinking out here." He escorted her with a hand to the small of her back to the stone railing that was crumbling in a few places. "It was one of his favorite places at Ettesmere Park."

"I can see why." Perhaps three feet off the ground, it gave a quick overview to the nearest portion of the gardens, but if one looked on the other side of the terrace, the back of the property stretched on for miles in the distance. And beneath the navy blanket of the nighttime sky as stars twinkled above, it was breathtaking. "He must have felt truly proud of what he'd accomplished when he stood here."

"I know he did. However, it is not my favorite place on the

property."

"Oh?" They strolled the length of the terrace. A handful of other couples milled about the area. She recognized none of them, and even if they hadn't been wearing masks, she wouldn't have known them. It was one of the things that divided her from him, for as they walked, he nodded at a few and greeted others by name. "Where is yours?"

"Let me show you." After glancing about the terrace and then apparently thinking it safe to slip away, Arthur led her down the handful of shallow steps and into the gardens. As they followed various paths—going in the opposite direction of where he'd taken her the night of the rout—he finally stopped in an area where fruit trees grew in orderly rows and shaded the pathway. A tall, L-shaped brick structure—perhaps sculpture?—lay hidden among the shrubberies and vegetation. Moss clung to it and portions of the brick and mortar were crumbling away. If a person wasn't searching for it, they would never see it. "Here."

Julianna frowned. "What is so special about this part of the garden?"

"This is all that's left of the original portion of Ettesmere Park." Gently, he hooked his hand around the upper portion of her arm and drew her deeper into the garden. "It's the first corner of the house my great grandfather built on this property. Sadly, due to a fire, most of the house was destroyed, but this remains. It reminds me every time I come out here that you can be completely shaken to your foundations and fall, but there is still strength to rise again."

Tears prickled the backs of her eyelids. "What a wonderful story. Have you used that throughout your life to keep motivated?"

"Yes, especially when my grandparents died, when my father died and I was given the title, and again when I lost my wife." His voice caught on the last word. "At times I forget what it is to be strong, but then I come out here, and I regain that hope, that determination."

How often had he visited this very spot since he'd begun his relationship with her?

"I admire that you've always risen and haven't let circumstances defeat you." Yet wasn't he doing exactly that when the guilt came to call, and memories of his wife tore them apart?

"Ha." He shook his head. "I'm not perfect by any means." When Arthur drew her closer, he turned her about so that her back was to his front. In a soft voice, he added, "Unfortunately, I believe that I fail more times than I succeed, that I'm failing even now."

"More than you know, I understand that sentiment." That was what she tried to escape from each time her father took another turn into the past. How long would it be before he was permanently stuck there, and he remembered nothing at all?

"And look there." His whispered breath skated over her nape. Delicious tremors began in her lower belly to ebb outward on the wings of heated tendrils. "See the illuminated windows of the house?"

"Yes." She could hardly concentrate when he was so close with his hands on her shoulders and his lips so near her neck.

"This is another reason why this spot is my favorite. Behind me is the past represented in the cornerstones, but there is my present. My family is there, the responsibilities I currently hold are there, my memories and history are all there, and they bring me peace and comfort."

"But are you content, Arthur?" she couldn't help but ask as she gazed at the squares of golden light. She wouldn't ask him about his intentions with her just yet, not when the night was rife with romance and her head was still in the clouds from that waltz. "Will you find that in the future you never allow yourself to think upon? The future you are so afraid of stepping into?" She gasped when he drifted his fingers along her nape, the side of her throat, her jawline. After a hard swallow, she concluded her statement. "The past and present will never change; only the days yet to come can give you that."

"I'm beginning to suspect you are correct, yet there is still that part of me that remains terrified." His lips brushed the skin just beneath her earlobe. "How can I break free?"

"You must release yourself." Despite the subject matter, Julianna lifted a hand and curled it around his nape urging him closer. "Let go of all that is tethering you, of all that no longer serves your purposes."

"But—"

"Until you give yourself that permission, you will always remain trapped in fear, in guilt and regret." He caressed a hand down her arm and then ran it up her ribcage until it rested, splayed, over her middle, just beneath her breasts. Trembles of need ricocheted along her spine, and she whimpered, for she desperately wanted his touch. "It's all right to live again. You are not the one who died." That was a bold statement. Would he take offense?

"In some ways, I did."

Fair enough. Needing to see him, Julianna turned to face him. Immediately, he settled his arms around her. "If that is the case, then you are truly no longer the man who was married to your wife. You've grown." She dared to trace her fingertips along the side of his face. "Don't you think the man you are now deserves a life of happiness? Why should the man from your past be the only one to know that?"

It was perhaps the most profound statement she'd ever made, and she waited, holding her breath, for his response.

For long moments he peered into her eyes as if searching for his answers there. Then, with a sound that was a half-growl, half-sigh, he tugged her fully against his chest and brought his lips crashing down on hers. A frantic energy was shared between them as kisses were offered and exchanged. They weren't gentle embraces, oh no. These kisses were given from a man stuck within two worlds: the past and the future, a man torn in the middle. Their masks scratched against each other, and with a savage sort of sound, Arthur wrenched his from his face while she removed hers. Both of them fluttered to the ground at their feet once he resumed kissing her.

Madly, wonderfully, he demanded that she kiss him back, took everything from her while giving her the same. Somehow, he'd managed to free one of her breasts from the glittering silver taffeta and tulle. With a frenzied friction, he worried that sensitive tip into an aching peak that pulled a moan from her throat.

Julianna pressed herself closer to him in an effort to seek relief, and when pinched and plucked at that bud, pain-streaked pleasure coursed through her veins. Never had he been so intense, so masterful. She craved that power, that command, wanted to lean into that strength and borrow from it. "Arthur…"

He was a man too far gone, and with a groan, he turned her about and pressed her back against the crumbling bricks of that ancient corner of wall. Holding her there, he dipped his head, sucked that taut nipple into the warm cavern of his mouth, teased it with tongue and teeth until she shook from raw, blatant need. "Dear God, Julianna, I want you so much," he whispered against her skin. "Need you…"

"As I said before, I won't tell you nay." Her eyes shuddered closed as she furrowed one hand into his thick hair while she curled the other into his cravat. "I've never met a man like you. For that matter, I've never had a man desire me as you do. It's as incredible and awe-inspiring as each one of the stars."

Yet he'd still not come up to scratch. Because of that, she couldn't figure him out. One minute he ran cold, then the next hot. If he were still in love with his dead wife, there could be nothing between them. Perhaps she should tell him of those fears. Wasn't honesty valued above all else in any relationship?

Arthur straightened. The hard bulge of his manhood rested against her belly. "Let us go deeper into the gardens and—"

"No." Knowing it would no doubt put an end to the possibility of a coupling tonight, she planted a palm at his chest and held him at arm's length.

"No?" The inquiry was breathless and rife with confusion. "I assume you wanted me as much as I do you." His dark brown eyes glinted in the dim illumination from the manor's windows.

"Oh, make no mistake, I do." When it appeared he would stay, she put her clothing back to rights. "So much, but perhaps common sense is telling me that it's folly to encourage you in those endeavors."

"Why?" He frowned and reached for her.

Julianna danced away, drew him out of the vegetation and along the back toward a stone bench. "You remain mired in the past. With Ellen. Even while sharing intimacies with me."

Shadows passed over his face. "I... She is always with me."

"I know, and that is a problem." Her heart ached. Was this the end, then? With a hard swallow and a stifled half-sob, she pressed a gloved hand to her warm cheek. "What is your favorite memory of her?"

His frown deepened. Confusion filled his eyes. "Why would you wish to discuss her at this time? It's not conducive to amorous things."

"That is exactly the point, Arthur." Her heart was breaking, and it pained her dreadfully, but this needed to be said, brought into the light. "Until you can square with her loss and move past it, there truly cannot be a relationship between *us*." Tears filled her throat, prickled the backs of her eyelids. "Not with Ellen's ghost layering herself between us."

"She was a large part of my life. I can't just walk away from all of that."

"I'm not asking you to. Keep her memory in your heart, but unless you give yourself permission to embrace a future, you will remain behind, alone." How could she break through to him? Her eyes welled with tears when he remained silent. Emotions played over his face. After taking a deep breath and letting it ease out, she tried again. "I'm coming to care for you, Arthur." It wouldn't take much to complete the fall into full-blown, breath-catching, all-consuming love.

"You are?" He looked at her with wonder that was soon overtaken by guilt.

"Yes." A tear fell to her cheek, and she dashed it away. She hadn't meant to show her hand so soon, but perhaps this conversation was much needed and a tad overdue. "But I cannot compete with what you still feel for Ellen. And I refuse to fight for your attentions with a ghost."

"But I…" Anguish entered his expression, and for one horrible moment, Julianna assumed he would pelt from the gardens as he had the night of the rout. "I feel as if I'm divided," he admitted in a choked whisper. Arthur stumbled to the bench and dropped onto it as if his knees suddenly could no longer support his weight. "Ellen was the first woman I'd ever fallen in love with, the first woman I'd taken to bed, the only woman I thought would be with me forever."

"That's understandable." Julianna sank onto the bench beside him. She ignored how the heat of him, the brush of his body against hers renewed the awareness of him. Now was not the time to invite heat between them. "I always assumed that if I fell in love, it would be the forever kind and that I would cleave to that one man for the remainder of my days."

Except when it had finally happened for her, the man she'd foolishly given her heart to was chasing a ghost from the past. Her chest tightened and ached. What she wanted more than anything was to run away so that she could lick her wounds in private, but Arthur resembled a broken shell of himself right now; her heart went out to him.

"Ellen was a dainty slip of a thing. Emily resembles her so much right now." He sat hunched over, his forearms resting on his thighs with his hands dangling between his splayed knees. "I loved her for her looks, of course, but I also loved that she was exactly the sort of woman the *ton* accepted. I knew what to expect from her as well as our union."

"There was no mystery there?" Julianna frowned. That sounded rather dull.

"No, and I liked it that way." His grin was a pathetic affair. "We enjoyed the typical society marriage. She bore me my heir as well as a second child. Passion faded over the years, but I loved her as a gentleman should."

Oh, Arthur. "Surely you were intimate with her throughout the years, for I've never heard you talk of a mistress."

"I was faithful to my wife until the end." He didn't look at her. "There was never the thought of another woman, but the fire died over the course of our union. We reserved one night a week for our nuptial bed." He snorted. "I erroneously assumed she wouldn't want me once the children were born, and perhaps she thought the same. But there was more between us than merely the heat of physical affection." He took a shuddering breath. "We should have talked about it, but then she contracted the illness…"

"And you were busy with the duties of your title, besides." Julianna laid a hand on his arm. His muscles tensed beneath her fingertips. "Never doubt that the love was still there."

At least he'd had that. When comparing her life to his, hers was an empty wasteland devoid of romance, for she'd chosen the pursuit of knowledge above all things.

"Once, Ellen surprised me with a trip to Brighton for a birthday to celebrate my thirtieth. I hadn't assumed the title of earl yet, so we took the children down. Flew kites on the beach. Strolled the town." He chuckled. "One night, well after midnight, she ushered me outside clad in nothing but a robe because she wanted to swim naked in the sea."

Julianna gasped. "Did you go with her?"

"I did, even though I was highly embarrassed the whole time." Arthur snorted. "We made love on a deserted section of beach that night to the sound of the crashing waves. It was, by far, the most scandalous thing I'd ever done at that point in my life, but it made her happy." A trace of tears wet his cheeks. "If I had but known then I would only have eight more years with her…"

"No one can divine the future; you just put faith into it and hope for the best." Tears filled her eyes from the pain in his voice. When they slipped to her cheeks, she didn't bother to wipe them away. That memory he'd shared coupled with his tears endeared him to her more than anything else could.

"We entertained much over the course of our marriage, for Ellen was in her element during such things. She adored the attention and dressing in pretty gowns." The longer he talked, the more lost to memories he became.

Perhaps it was best that Julianna left him to it. When he found his way out, she hoped he would see things more clearly. "Thank you for sharing her with me, Arthur." She leaned over and kissed his cheek. Then she stood and shook out her skirts. "When you realize what it is you want for your future beyond everything else, come and find me. I'm not going anywhere."

He never looked up at her, never responded or acted as if he'd heard her, and her heart fractured a little bit more. Would she ultimately lose him? Was the power of a previous love greater than what he could have in the future?

With a stifled sob, she hurried up the path toward the terrace. *Please don't wait too long to find yourself, Arthur.*

Only time would tell.

CHAPTER EIGHTEEN

ARTHUR HAD NO idea how long he sat in the darkened gardens, but by the time he was ready to return to the house, all enjoyment from the masquerade ball had faded. Where he thought the night would have ended with Julianna in his bed—or beneath him in a shadowy corner of the gardens—instead, emotions and the past had caught him up in their vortex, one so intense that he couldn't escape.

As a matter of course, Julianna had deserted him, and he felt that loss all too keenly. Not that he could blame her. He was a mess, had been at sixes and sevens ever since he'd met her, and all of that was twisted up with memories of Ellen and his guilt therein. Since their first meeting, he had the feeling that she'd given him everything of herself while he'd only let her have a portion of him.

That wasn't fair to either of them.

Still in the grip of that ennui and confusion, he retired to his study with the intention of drinking away the remainder of the night. Perhaps in brandy he'd find the answer he sought, for one thing was certain: he couldn't go forward or do anything if he continued to fight this battle. The words Julianna had said to him when she'd broken their heated kisses remained firmly in his mind, and damn if he didn't wish to avoid disappointing her.

How can I move forward when I don't have a blessed clue?

Eventually, the heat of the summer night had gotten the better of him and he'd thrown open the windows. There was something to be said about the highwayman attire of breeches and a loose-fitting lawn shirt. It was deuced comfortable as well as cool, but he did remove the cravat that was trying to choke him.

Once he'd tossed it to the floor, he'd dropped into the chair behind his desk, and with his booted feet propped upon the desk, he took a brandy bottle in hand and proceeded to drink himself to the bottom.

When the long case clock down the hall chimed the two o'clock hour, Arthur groaned. He shook himself awake from a light doze. The soft sound of rain reached his ears, and he welcomed the lull it brought as well as the relatively cool breeze into the room. As he straightened his posture and planted his feet on the floor, he swore there was another presence in the room with him.

"Who's there?" The inquiry seemed to echo in the empty space.

"Arthur, we need to talk."

He squinted into the darkness, for he hadn't bothered to light a candle. Was it his imagination or was there a spirit with him in the study, and one who looked oddly like his wife during the year they'd gone to Brighton? "Ellen?"

"Surely you know this is not really me, but a figment of your imagination."

Perhaps that was true enough, but he felt her presence in that study so greatly it was as if she were truly there with him—as if she were human. Just how much had he drunk? He glanced at the bottle resting on his desk. The amber liquid cut off at the halfway mark. Not as much as he could have, and he certainly didn't feel the buzz of inebriation.

Yet none of that explained the presence of the ghost. "Are you truly here now?" He reached for his cravat, to tidy it up so she wouldn't think him a layabout, but belatedly, he remembered he'd tossed it away earlier.

"Only in your mind, which begs the question of why. You must be significantly troubled for me to manifest in this way."

While the commonsense part of him knew she wasn't real, knew that he had conjured her from beyond the grave, the fanciful part of his brain desperately wanted this to be true. He welcomed his wife's return, and his heart thumped to think he could always see her thusly.

"Let us say that is true." He reached beneath his shirt to clutch her wedding ring. "Why are you here?"

"You tell me." The image of Ellen drifted closer. He could see right through the silvery blue form, but she was dressed in a ballgown he'd particularly favored that year. The pale green was as ethereal now as it was then, but the mass of her blonde hair drifted free about her shoulders and back in pretty curls. Damn, but he'd adored those tresses, yet... Now he preferred Julianna's midnight waterfall that resembled spilled ink as it tumbled over the grass like the last time they'd coupled, at the heart of the maze. Confusion followed that thought.

"How can I know that?"

The ghost shrugged as she hovered in the air perhaps five feet from him. "Your mind is sufficiently troubled that the only way you can make sense of what's happening within you was to summon an image of me." She quirked a dainty eyebrow and he fisted his hand around the ring suspended about his neck. "Why?"

It wasn't as odd as it sounded. Perhaps if he talked to himself as if Ellen were indeed in the room with him, he could make sense of the mire his life had become.

"I have recently begun a relationship with a woman. At first, I thought all I wanted from it was friendship, for I've been a bit lonely of late, but it's matured into much more..."

"How lovely! What is this woman's name?"

"Julianna Quill. She's older, more mature, perhaps a handful of years my junior, and she's an astronomer." For the next several minutes, he waxed poetic about her. "Her intelligence and practicality are addictive. Where I thought I had learned everything I needed in this life, she shows me time and again that I have not."

The ghost chuckled. "The best women show you things you never thought possible."

"Perhaps."

"Do you enjoy a physical relationship with her?"

He shifted in his chair, suddenly uncomfortable even as thoughts of Julianna had his member slowly hardening. "I do. It came about by accident."

"Does it matter how it did?" Amusement wove through the tones.

"I suppose not." He rubbed a hand along the side of his face where morning stubble was just beginning to form. For the moment, he'd forgotten the ring. "There have been nights when we've met on the top of Otis Hill and merely watched the stars. In her, there is no stress of responsibility, no urge to do a duty to the title or play the consummate *ton* gentleman."

"Then all the better. At your age, all of those things have already been accomplished. This time around, you can allow yourself the fun you couldn't when married to me."

He harrumphed. "I don't know about that, but she's so much different than you, Ellen. Adventurous. Daring. Her enthusiasm for carnal things renews my own." Arthur shook his head. "How is that possible?" His heart ached. "But I miss you, miss what we had and shared."

Different but the same. Comforting but exciting. Day into night.

"That is as it should be, dearest, for I am not there any longer. I've moved on to the world beyond and will see you again there."

"I shouldn't feel like I do for another woman when I loved you to the depths of my being." At least they were arriving at the crux of the matter. He traced the outline of the ring with a fingertip. "It's selfish to perhaps want that again when every beat of my heart still calls out for you."

For long moments, the only sound in the room was the

steady drum of rain against the windows and the spatter of it against the pavement below.

"It isn't selfish to wish for another partner. Human nature is to love and be loved. You remain here on Earth, and I never wanted you to pass the remainder of your days alone. Surely you remember one of the last conversations you and I shared."

"I do."

"Yet you haven't been truly happy or content since I left."

He snorted. "Of course not. I remained loyal to you. In death as I did in life."

"Oh, Arthur." Ghost Ellen shook her head. "I always adored how noble and sacrificing you were. Yet you were set free the moment I left this mortal coil." When he made a sound of protest, she held up a hand that he could see right through. "There is no guilt in inviting love into your life again. It's perfectly natural. If you've found that—and more—with Julianna, why do you fight against it?"

"It's all so different this time that it confuses me." It was the truth and part of why he struggled. "She constantly has me at sixes and sevens."

"As a woman should."

"Perhaps."

"I didn't do that as much as I should have, for once I won you, I didn't give thought to the fact that I needed to keep your interest."

Was that true? "You should not have had to. We were in love."

"Oh, please, Arthur, marriage takes work and effort."

"This is so." He rubbed his eyes with the heels of his hands. This conversation was becoming exhausting and didn't help clear his jumbled thoughts.

"Do you love Julianna?"

"I…" Did he? He certainly wanted to be everywhere she was, strained to hear her voice, couldn't apparently keep his hands off her body. He heaved out a breath. "I don't know. If I do, it will be a disservice against you."

"How could it be when I am no longer there?" The ghost drifted closer. "I want you to know love again, dearest, want you to show our children there is no shame in marrying after loss."

"What?" He reeled backward as if he'd been struck. "Marriage? I'm not sure…"

"Oh, you poor man. Still cannot see the evidence in front of you with your own eyes when it's staring at you." Ghost Ellen laughed, and the memory of that sound both saddened and encouraged him. She always had the best tinkling, elfin sort of laugh… but it couldn't quite compare to Julianna's genuine bouts of hearty laughter that made him want to do the same. "You cannot continue to have Miss Quill the way you are now. You're better than that and would never have a woman in your company merely as a bedmate."

"I know." What he enjoyed with Julianna went beyond the physical pleasures he'd found with her. Everything she did fascinated him, compelled him to inquire more about her. She beguiled him and silently taught him, to say nothing of how she guided his children through various bumps in their paths. That alone spoke to her tender heart and giving soul. "She deserves more than what I've given her."

"Agreed." The ghost smiled, and there was a sad tinge to the gesture that plucked at his chest. "I suspect John and Emily like her."

"How can you know that?"

"It's merely intuition."

Or wishful thinking on his part since his imagination had conjured this whole scene.

She met his gaze. "When you listen to the whispers of your heart and remove me from the equation, you'll find that you know the next logical step."

A thread of panic climbed his throat. "But there's one large issue."

"Tell me."

"Julianna is not you." She never would be. Therein lay the struggle. Why would he want someone new when he had everything he'd ever wanted with the old?

"Of course she's not me. And why should she be?" Ghost Ellen chuckled. The sound echoed through his heart like the memory that it was. "You need someone different at this time in your life. Someone who will help teach and guide our children into the next stages on their paths to adulthood. Someone who will bring joy back to your existence."

She certainly did make him feel that. He suspected that if given half the chance, he would follow her about the Berkshire countryside merely to remain in her presence. "I do enjoy being in her company."

"I'm glad to hear it." The ghost nodded. "Besides, you're not the same man you were when married to me. Don't you think that man deserves a different woman to be his countess for the next phase of his life?"

"Perhaps." His thoughts still ran amok in his mind, but they weren't as tangled as they'd been before.

"You were always stubborn. Please don't be so now." The ghost grinned. "Do this for me, Ettesmere. I left the world knowing you would be well, that you would again find happiness, that you would flourish. Don't disappoint me now." She reached out a hand and caressed his cheek, but all he felt was a disturbance of air, most likely from the open windows and the rain-propelled breeze.

Briefly, Arthur closed his eyes. Never again would he enjoy the touch of his wife, but then, perhaps he didn't need to. There was a future stretching before him that he'd once never thought was possible. It was filled with glimmering moments still undefined, but within that he might find the peace that had eluded him for years, as well as comfort and security.

Did he love Julianna? She'd hinted at her growing feelings for him earlier that night in the garden, but he'd said nothing in return. Could he summon the courage to ask for her hand?

"Oh, no!" The ghost gasped. "Julianna is coming."

"What? Here?" Need slammed into him with the force of an escaped cannonball. Worry followed hard on its heels. "Whyever for?" Were his ears playing tricks or did he hear the excited yapping of a beagle drawing ever closer?

"Why? I suspect she loves you, but this is not the reason she's coming now."

Julianna loves me.

Warmth spread through his chest. His heart gave a mighty thump as if it were coming back to life after being dormant for far too long. "Oh?" He glanced at the brandy bottle on his desk. Should he go ahead and finish it off to help sustain this bizarre vision?

The ghost moved between him and the desk to partially block his view of the spirits. "Miss Quill is quite concerned about something. I can sense it." Her words grew faster, more clipped. "Go to her, Arthur. Be with her. Help her in this."

What the devil was wrong with Julianna that she would bring herself to Ettesmere Park at this hour? "And after?"

"Marry her. Live your life to the best of your ability. I give you my blessing. Search your heart and when you do, you'll find all the answers you need."

"Please don't go."

She blew him a kiss. "I'll always linger in your memories, but I no longer have your heart. It belongs to another, and you'll see that if you allow yourself to let me go." Before he could ask more questions, the ghost faded, and he suspected he would never see her again.

That both saddened him and gave him a modicum of relief. Perhaps in her way, Ellen had encouraged him, told him she bore no ill will if he wished to move forward. Still, it had been a bizarre conversation and one in which he'd need to ponder before making a decision.

The canine baying grew louder, and by the time Arthur had scrambled to his feet, the sleep-bleary butler was at the door trailing a highly agitated Julianna.

"Miss Quill is here, Your Lordship. She refused to return later in the morning and near woke the dead with her pounding on the front door." He blew out a breath and cast a sideways glance to the visitor. "In a scandalous state of dress, I might add."

Arthur bit the inside of his cheek to keep from laughing outright at that. Indeed, the dead did walk this night, but not because of that. "Go back to bed, Landers. I shall take over from here."

"Very good, Lord Ettesmere."

Once the older man had departed, Arthur drew Julianna further into the room. Regent bounded in after her, barking like a crazed beast. "What is amiss?" He snapped his fingers at the dog, who immediately calmed.

With a whine, the rotund beagle laid down at his mistress' feet.

"I woke from sleep and felt that the cottage was empty."

That part of the tale certainly must prove true, for she'd come here dressed in a thin night rail and an equally thin robe over it though she'd shoved her feet into a scuffed pair of brown leather half boots. Her mind must have truly been fraught with worry. "What happened?"

She shivered, for her clothing was nearly soaked through and plastered indecently to her body in places. Arthur tamped a groan of appreciation. The dark snake of her braid moved over her shoulder like a snake. "My father's gone missing." Tears welled in her eyes. "In the dark and rain, I'm afraid he's disoriented and won't know how to return home."

"Did you search the cottage?"

"Of course I did. I am not a nodcock." If her tone was sharp, she had every excuse. "I looked through the garden as well. My father is simply gone. I don't know when he left, either."

"Was there anything else odd that you could see?"

"There was." Her eyes were round as she looked at him. "His old work clothes are gone. The ones he used to wear when he was a bricklayer." She shook her head. "For years they hung on a peg in the kitchen, for he was so proud of what he'd done for a living. What do you think that means?"

How the deuce should I know?

"Don't fret." In this moment, she needed him, and he would rise to the challenge. "Come here, sweeting." For the first time, he didn't feel guilt in being with her or in using an endearment. Had Julianna noticed the slip? When a few tears fell to her cheeks, he easily tugged her into his arms and held her against himself in the hopes he'd bring her comfort. "We'll work it out. And we *will* find him."

CHAPTER NINETEEN

June 23, 1819

JULIANNA'S MIND RAN in several different directions at once and jumped to all sorts of conclusions. Fear danced icy fingers down her spine, but she took comfort in the strength of Arthur's arms around her. As she rested her cheek against him, the steady beat of his heart beneath her ear brought a modicum of calm. And in the secret chambers of *her* heart, that endearment he'd called her echoed with all the gladness of an angelic choir.

"I didn't know where else to go." Both her palms lay on his chest. The heat of his skin seeped through the thin lawn, and once again she was acutely conscious of his state of undress as well as hers. "And I figured since you've often been there for me to listen to my rambles, you might help me in this."

"Of course I will." Over and over again, he stroked a hand up and down her back. "I should hope I'd be the one you come to when you have a problem." He pulled away ever so slightly in order to peer into her eyes despite the lack of illumination in the room. "You know that, don't you?"

"Yes." In the event he didn't understand, she nodded. Another few tears fell to her cheeks. "I do."

"Good." Then he bundled her into his arms once more and held her close. There were no sexual connotations to the embrace, no heat or passion. It was simply a man offering comfort to a woman, and she was in sore need of that. "You have my promise, Julianna. We *will* find him."

"I believe you." Julianna breathed in his bay rum scent and allowed another few seconds to luxuriate in the glory of being held. There was no sense in denying it even to herself. She loved him. When she'd told Arthur that she was coming to care for him, that had been a lie, for she was already hopelessly and helplessly in love with him. Knew it deep down in her soul, but he was an earl, and she was no one of consequence if one went by the estimations of the *beau monde*. To say nothing of the fact that if he desired more children, she was probably well past an age to bear them.

One more worry to add to the pile.

It simply wasn't fair that she'd waited her whole life to find a man of his caliber and now she'd be wrenched from his life due to a trifling thing of status. She stifled a sob, and obviously, Arthur assumed it was due to fright about her father. He continued to stroke her back. Then he pulled slightly away and pressed a kiss to her forehead.

"He couldn't have gone far."

"I hope you're right." Never had he wandered off for this long, and never had he gone off in the middle of the night.

"In this, I am." He released her fully and ran his gaze up and down her person. Chill bumps popped on her skin; her nipples tightened as need shivered over her. "I'll need to find you some proper clothing."

"No." Julianna shook her head. "That will take too much time. This will suffice."

"But it's raining and you're already half-wet."

Apparently, Regent agreed, for he whined as he got to his feet.

"Then there's no need to ruin another set of clothes." She popped her hands on her hips. "Are there any other objections, Your Lordship?"

"No." He flashed a grin that was potent enough to turn her knees to cooked porridge. "We will cover more ground with a horse." As soon as the words left his mouth, he strode across the room to yank on the brocade bell pull.

"Or we can leave immediately instead of wasting time waiting."

"Steady, Julianna. We won't locate your father any quicker if we're sniping at each other." In a few more moments, the butler returned to the study. "Ah, Landers, please rouse some of the stable lads. I require my best riding horse saddled. There is an emergency."

The butler darted his gaze between her and the earl. Finally, he nodded. "Of course, Your Lordship."

Once he'd departed, Arthur escorted her to the door. "I'd like for you to wait here. No sense in the both of us getting wet."

Was he daft? "Absolutely not." She shook her head and the heavy braid of hair swung off her shoulder. "He's my father, and I won't have you going into danger on his account or mine."

"It's rain, not a storm. Besides, I know every inch of this property better than you. It will go faster if I'm alone."

As if she were a woman who hadn't intelligence or would faint at any sort of shock. "Be that as it may, I'm going with you, even if I have to hang onto your reins and have you drag me over the acreage." She glared at him. "Shall we continue to argue?"

"No." His lips twitched. Oh, what she wouldn't give to lose herself in his kiss right now. It would certainly quiet the fear fluttering through her belly. "You're quite stubborn, you know."

"I am aware of my shortcomings, Ettesmere, but I'm too set in my ways to change now."

"Not shortcomings, Miss Quill. Personality features." As he escorted her out of the room and through the dark, winding corridors, he lightly rested a hand at the small of her back. She rather liked that subtle sign of possession and support even if nothing could ever come from her silly love affair.

By the time they reached the door at the rear of the manor,

the butler made another appearance. "Your horse is saddled and waiting in the stable yard."

"I appreciate that, and Landers? One thing more." Arthur moved away from her. "If you could find either my greatcoat or one of Lady Sophia's redingotes, that would be a huge help. Miss Quill requires something to cover herself."

With a nod, the butler was off but not without another questioning glance at her.

Julianna released a huff of frustration. "He's judging me merely based on my appearance."

"Oh, quite. He's a butler; he can't help it." Amusement threaded through the earl's voice. "Pay him no mind."

"Easier said than done when he's no doubt thinking I'm trying to trap you by contrived circumstances." There were so many rules that members of the *ton* played by. She simply had no patience for those sorts of games and neither did she wish to abide by them.

"Whether he does or not is none of my concern. My life isn't dictated by the opinion of a butler. No matter how fond of him I might be."

Nothing else was said until Landers returned bearing a gray greatcoat.

"Thank you." Despite the butler's gaze on them, Arthur bundled the coat around her and made certain she'd put her arms through the sleeves. "I don't know how long I'll be out, but heated water would be nice upon my return. I can make my own tea if you'd like to return to bed."

"I shall wait up for you, of course, Your Lordship."

"Very well." Arthur glanced at her. "Ready?"

"For this? Yes." For the inevitable break of their relationship that was sure to come? Absolutely not.

In the stable yard, the rain became an annoyance, but the greatcoat kept the worst of the precipitation from her person. Arthur swung himself up into the saddle of the midnight black stallion. Then he bent and offered an arm to her. The stable lad helped to boost her up, and there was a moment of weightlessness as the earl pulled her into the saddle before him. With her legs dangling over one side, he slipped his arms about her as he manipulated the reins and brought the horse about. The stable lad handed her a lit lantern. She wrapped her fingers around the wired handle and thanked him with a nod.

"Best of luck, Miss Quill. Landers told us why you needed the horse."

"Thank you." Though how the butler knew when neither she nor Arthur had said was beyond her.

"The sentiment is appreciated, Billy," the earl said as he set them off.

Though the object of their mission kept her taut with apprehension, being so close to Arthur, hearing the rumble of his voice so close to her ear kept her nerves steady.

In the dark, the bobbing of the lantern sent golden light skittering into the shadows. The horse shied and danced each time a larger shadow came too near. The closer they came to the area around her cottage, Julianna called out for her father.

"Papa? Where are you? Please answer me." But the rain and night threw her words back at her. Due to the cloud cover, there wasn't even the familiar comfort from the stars. "It's beyond me where he could have gotten off to."

"Calm yourself. Nothing good will come from speculation."

In the face of potential disaster, she appreciated the air of command and leadership he offered. "I am trying."

"Did your father have a special place he liked to visit? Maybe somewhere that reminds him of your mother or brother?"

Julianna shifted into a more comfortable position, glad of his wide chest that blocked some of the rain. "Not that I know of. He stays close to home most times." Then she gasped. "Recently, he's told me stories of the time he worked at Ettesmere Park when he was a bricklayer." *Why didn't I see what was happening?* "That's why he took the old clothes! When he was involved with that livelihood, he used to say it was one of the best times of his life. He enjoyed all of his mates as well as the work. He's proud that those outbuildings still stand." Then her eyes filled with tears. "All too often of late, he's been stuck in that specific time of the past."

"There is no shame in growing older, Julianna." He tightened his arms about her. "We'll find him." Then he pulled on the reins and turned the horse around. "Back to the park, Avalon," he told the horse while he dug in his heels and shot them forward in a gallop.

When they reached the collection of out buildings, Julianna slid from the saddle before Arthur had brought the horse to a full stop.

"Julianna, wait!"

"I can't!" She ran through the darkness toward the first building. The lantern swung wildly in her hand while the rain obstructed her vision. "Papa? Are you here?"

Arthur quickly caught her up. "Don't go running helter-skelter through the dark without an escort," he said as he captured her free hand in his.

The comfort of that human touch plowed into her. For far too long she'd gone through life alone, and she was blessedly tired of it, exhausted from the effort of being strong. "Then keep up with me, Ettesmere."

He snickered as he took the lantern from her. "Haven't I been attempting to do exactly that since we met?"

When a shadow came lurching out of the darkness toward her, Julianna screamed with a visceral reaction. It was so unexpected that she shook from the suddenness.

Immediately, the earl moved in front of her, shielding her from possible harm, and made sure to tuck her into safety. Her heart pounded hard, and ice went down her spine. "Who's there?" He lifted the lantern. "Show yourself."

As the shadow separated itself from the darkness, it began to take shape as that of a human. "Lord Ettesmere?" Her father came into the golden pool of light. He was drenched but his slouch-style cap kept the worst of the rain from his face. The tweed of his jacket probably repelled a good portion of it too.

"Papa!" With a cry of joy, Julianna darted from behind Arthur. She rushed over the soft ground and threw her arms around her father. "Why did you wander off? I've been worried sick."

"Enough, girl." He pushed out of her embrace and gave her a sheepish look. "I didn't know I'd wandered off." Her father shrugged. "I remembered where that boy Arthur lost his father's signet ring, so I went after it before I forgot again." He unfurled a hand. A muddy signet ring rested on his palm. It was too covered in muck to tell what it looked like.

"You should have waited until first light."

He ignored her chiding. "Must have fallen off in the mud when we thought it was lost to the mortar, but I remember that boy sitting on the ground when he wasn't laying bricks. Always took it off and fiddled with it." In some confusion, he glanced at Arthur and then back at her. "Tossed it into the air and tried to catch it on his finger like he was some kind of traveler's fair performer." With a shake of his head, he sighed. "He was a foolish lad. But I remembered. Remembered metal pinging against brick that day and a flash of sun on gold." His smile revealed his two missing teeth, but it was the dearest thing she'd ever seen while he continued to hold out his palm. "Took some digging but I found it. The boy will want it back, I'm guessing."

"It was incredibly brave of you to go out in this weather, Papa." Her relief was so great that tears coursed down her cheeks again. "I'm glad you've been found, and am grateful to Lord Ettesmere for helping with that." When she looked at Arthur, he stared at her father with amazement in his expression, brought into sharp relief from the lantern's light.

"You're right, Mr. Quill. I *did* have a habit of throwing the ring into the air and catching it on my finger. It was a particular skill I'd practiced on all summer." His chuckle was tinged with sadness. "My father was livid when I told him I'd lost it, for he'd given it to me for my twelfth birthday."

Her father snorted. "Can't be your ring. Belongs to a boy."

"Yes." Like a man in a dream, he approached her father. "Mr. Quill, I *am* that boy, er, at least I *was*. I'm Arthur, all grown and now the earl."

"Ah." Her father frowned, as if he didn't quite understand what was going on. No doubt in his mind, Arthur was still that boy, and her father still was a bricklayer. He handed over the muddy ring with fingers just as dirty. "Best not lose it again, son. I won't be around to dig it up the next time."

"I won't." So much gratitude threaded through those two words that Julianna became a watering pot once more. "You have my promise, Mr. Quill." He wiped the worst of the mud from the bauble and then slid the ring onto the pinky finger of his left hand.

"Good. Good." Her father laughed as if he'd just quit the company of his friends at the local village tavern. "While I was digging out here, I thought about my Julianna, that she should have the best of life, should marry a gentleman." He shrugged and his gaze faltered. Was his mind playing more tricks on him? "I thought she'd be a good fit for that young lad who didn't seem to have a grasp on his future…"

"I still don't, Mr. Quill," Arthur added in a barely audible whisper.

"Bah." With a shaking hand, her father edged his hat up and scratched his brow, leaving a streak of mud behind. "Too bad she's let the years pass her by. Gone off chasing stars with her brother." He shook his head. "Imagine the earl is married now. Seem to remember his little slip of a wife. Real toothsome thing, but I would have been so proud if Julianna could have been his countess. Would have led him around by the nose. She's so clever…" A frown overcame his expression as a gasp escaped Arthur. He glanced at her with sudden fear. "How'd I get out here? And in the rain?" Obviously, his mind was slipping in and out. He couldn't linger in the past nor stay in the present.

"Never you mind, Papa." Julianna tried to stifle the worst of her tears while Arthur glanced at the signet ring on his finger. "At least we found you. All is well now."

"Indeed, it is." Arthur impulsively gave her father a hug. "Thank you for this. You have no idea what it means, what your words mean." He gestured ahead of him. "Come, let me take you home."

"Bah." Her father waved him off. "I'm capable of walking home myself, Your Lordship. Got my Julianna to help me."

"But it's three miles in the rain and—"

A glare from her father quelled his words. "There's still life in me yet, boy. And look at my daughter. She's dripping wet and trailing scandal under that coat." He narrowed his eyes. "Whose coat is that? Are you dallying with someone?"

"No, Papa." Heat slapped at her cheeks. "It's nothing."

Her father sniffed. "Don't want her catching cold." He took her arm. "I'm tired," he groused. "Need tea and my bed. Standing around in the rain is a sure way to encourage sickness."

"Yes, it is." It would have been amusing if she wasn't so overwrought. Now that the immediate danger to her father had concluded, the worries regarding her relationship with the earl had come back front and center. She looked at Arthur. "Thank you for accompanying me tonight. It means so much."

"I'm glad I could be of assistance." He nodded but dejection had descended. His shoulders slumped. A frown took possession of his mouth. "I shall call on the morrow to inquire about your health and that of your father's."

She nodded. "Come for tea, then. I imagine we'll both rise late after this." Would he realize that she wasn't best suited for his life once he'd gone home and thought more about it? Surely after their conversation in the garden such things would be inevitable. Perhaps she'd tell him gently he should seek out someone else and let her fade into memory. Especially since he apparently had the capacity to only think about one woman anyway. Turning away, she guided her father over the ground toward the country lane.

"Damnation," Arthur muttered beneath his breath. "I just

cannot let this happen." With the authority of the earl in his voice, he ordered them both onto his horse. When they both protested, he physically picked each of them up and tossed them into the saddle with her mounted in front of her father. "I'll walk beside the horse and lead. I won't have you falling prey to disaster while on my property. It's the least I can do."

"Though wildly unnecessary, I thank you, for my father is tired." Her heart squeezed. He was such a wonderful man. How did she think she could live without him in her life?

Why is being in love such a terrible prospect?

CHAPTER TWENTY

June 24, 1819

ARTHUR PEERED OUT his bedchamber window as knots pulled in his belly and apprehension sizzled through his veins. Downstairs, the long case clock struck the four o'clock hour. No doubt right now, Julianna was puttering about assembling the needed items for tea.

He should be there, except he was nothing more than a coward. After everything, he couldn't find the courage needed to leave the house, couldn't find the words he would need to say once he arrived at her cottage.

So he watched out the window in a horrid attempt to see past the three miles that separated them, and he worried.

"Dear heavens, Arthur. Why are you still here?"

With a huff, he turned at the sound of his sister's voice. Of course it was her who would track him to earth. She was the only one to whom he'd told his plans. "I'm having second thoughts."

"About wishing to ask for Miss Quill's hand?"

"No, about whether she'll accept once I do." For he fully intended to declare himself once he could make his feet move.

"Why wouldn't she?" Sophia came further into the room with a frown. "The two of you are well-matched, and it's rather adorable how you feel about each other."

"She could do better."

She snorted. "Than an earl?"

"No, choose a better man than me, one who has struggled this whole time."

"Everyone has something, Arthur." When she reached his location, Sophia laid a hand on his arm. "Besides, this morning at breakfast, you seemed a man who'd recently found lucidity."

"I did." When he'd seen that muddy signet ring that he thought he'd lost in childhood, words from his past bubbled to the surface, words his father had said to him that were eerily apt today.

This is a sign of your destiny, his father had said upon giving him the signet ring. *Winterbournes don't allow themselves to stagnate. We're a willful lot. We shape the future. You will too.*

The moment he'd seen that ring again, it had brought true clarity, far more than his talk with Ellen's ghost. The moment Julianna searched through the rain, frantic to find her father, he knew he wanted to take care of her, support her, love her, for the rest of his life. He wished to see her realize her goals, wanted to laugh again, and make new memories... with her.

And no one else.

His sister nudged his shoulder. "Then why are you here and not with her?"

"I'm afraid." Everything came down to that. "Afraid she'll reject me. After all, we've only known each other for ten days." God, had it only been days? Each time he was in her company, the bond they shared felt as if it had been there for years.

"You won't know until you try, but speaking as a woman?" She smiled at him. "Miss Quill won't reject you. In fact, I'm so excited for you, and a tad bit jealous, that you'll usher in this wonderful new life with a new love. You are most certainly fortunate."

"Perhaps." Their whole courtship-that-wasn't-a-courtship had been bizarre and not in the usual style. "I did a slipshod job of romancing her though." Why should his declaration be any different?

"Does it matter? The results are the same as if you'd courted her for a year."

"No, I don't suppose it does." From the pocket of his waistcoat, he brought forth a ring. "I couldn't find exactly the right piece of jewelry in the estate collection, but I hope this will suffice." A dark sapphire in an oval shape winked in the sunlight. Surrounded by tiny diamonds and set in delicate silver filagree, he could easily imagine it on Julianna's finger. "It reminded me of the stars and the color of her eyes."

"Oh, Arthur, it's lovely." Sophia glanced at it and then him. "It was Grandmama's, wasn't it?"

"Yes. The engagement ring Grandfather gave to her all those years ago." He tucked the bauble away. "I think they both would have liked that."

"They would." She grinned. "Have you told Mama of your intentions?"

"Not yet. I thought I'd try my luck with Julianna first, and if all goes well, I'll bring her up here, perhaps for dinner, where we can make an announcement."

Sophia nodded. "And your children?"

"I couldn't locate either of them this afternoon, so everyone will hear the news together."

"It will certainly be the sensation of the summer." Though she darted her gaze to the window, a mysterious smile remained. "So, what are you lingering here for? Go." She gently shoved at his shoulder. "I wish you the best fortune."

"Right." In addition to the ring, he'd spent the bulk of the morning memorizing what he hoped was a romantic story pertaining to one of the constellations in the hopes that might help an acceptance along. "Well, I suppose there is no sense in delaying further." Yet his stomach muscles knotted with worry.

"No, there is not. Oh, Arthur, I'm so proud of you." Her smile widened. "However you managed to move past everything holding you back, I'll never know, but I'm glad you did."

"As am I." Perhaps it had been a mixture of things, but finally, his future wasn't cloudy and hidden. No longer did he have that block of guilt sitting heavily on his chest. "There is one thing more I need to do before I leave." Quickly, he pulled the old signet ring from his finger and then he removed the chord from his neck. Glancing one last time at Ellen's engagement ring, he pressed both baubles into Sophia's hands. "Put them in a safe place for me, but know this. I don't need either of them any longer."

He'd firmly closed the door on his past.

WHEN HE RAPPED upon the Quill cottage door, he blew out a breath to help calm his nerves. He was never this nervous proposing to Ellen; that match was expected, a *ton* union, like so many others. There had been no large dips or swells of excitement in the marriage. It was the calm waters of a pond in summer.

But Julianna was different. She represented the constant ebb and flow of the ocean and was just as mysterious.

When the door swung inward, he gawked with a gaping lower jaw when his son John stood there wearing a wry grin.

"Good afternoon, Papa. We hoped you would *eventually* arrive."

Like a man in a dream, Arthur entered the cottage, and when he was shown into the common room, he received the second shock of the afternoon, for Emily shared a sofa with Julianna, and they were both calmly taking tea with Mr. Quill, and of course, John.

"What the devil is going on here?" He didn't care to watch his language, so great was his shock.

"Welcome, Papa." Emily sprang from her seat. She took his arm and led him to a sofa opposite hers and gently encouraged him to sit. He glanced at Julianna. The expression of bewilderment on her face spoke to the fact that she didn't know either. "Don't be cross. John and I only arrived thirty minutes ago. We came because we owed Miss Quill an apology."

"For what?" He wasn't best pleased at having his plans interrupted or his momentum scattered. By rote he accepted a cup of tea that his daughter thrust into his hand.

John cleared his throat. "It was us."

"I beg your pardon, but what was?"

Emily sighed. The curls on her forehead ruffled. "John and I penned those mysterious notes that were sent to you and Miss Quill."

"What?" Both his exclamation and Julianna's rang through the room.

A pretty blush spread over Emily's cheeks while John had apparently found something vitally interesting on Regent's coat, for the dog lay at his son's feet. "After I met Miss Quill that first time on Otis Hill and we had that lovely talk and she escorted me home because she didn't want me out alone late at night, I knew she would be perfect for you."

"Oh, dear, you probably shouldn't have told him that," Julianna whispered with a hand on Emily's arm. "That wasn't exactly the story I told of our first meeting."

Before Arthur could respond to any of that, John rushed to fill the silence. "And once Emily told me of her findings, and I had the opportunity to meet Miss Quill for myself, I threw in my lot with hers." His grin was tinged with apprehension. "We sought to throw you two together, so you'd make a match of it."

Pregnant silence reigned through the room. Arthur stared across a low table at Julianna, while she met his gaze with shock in her eyes.

"None of this," Arthur waved his free hand to indicate himself and Julianna, "happened organically?" What the deuce was he to do now?

"John and I were only responsible for putting the two of you into locations at the same time." Emily once more shoved to her feet. She skirted around the table and stood near him with a hand on his shoulder. "But then it was such fun seeing if Papa would go through with our hints."

John nodded. "You always came home in such high spirits that it was like having our old father back." At least he had the grace to blush. "That's why we continued to do it."

"Exactly." Excitement wove through Emily's voice. "We merely gave you locations and suggestions."

While heat crept up the back of Arthur's neck, his son flashed a grin full of cheek. "Right. If you couldn't ascertain what you were supposed to do with a beautiful woman, I considered you a lost cause and a hopeless nodcock."

Hopeless nodcock. That was exactly what he felt like presently. *Like a puppet on a string, my own children orchestrated everything.*

An unexpected laugh from Mr. Quill drew all attention to him. "Looks like they've routed you lock, stock, and artillery, Your Lordship." Perhaps he enjoyed a lucid day, but there was no mistaking the gleam of interest in his faded eyes.

"So it seems," Arthur said as he rested his teacup on the table. He didn't quite know how to feel about anything that had occurred. Was the romance not of his own making? Had it been manipulated and contrived, and would he make a fool of himself?

Emily leaned down and bussed his cheek. "I knew from the first that Miss Quill would change our lives. She's easy to talk with and gives the best advice." The soulful look she gave him went straight to his soul. "Was I correct, Papa?"

Every person in that room stared at him.

Regent lifted his head and gave him an encouraging bark.

Oh, God. The moment of reckoning had come. Arthur tugged on his suddenly too-tight cravat. Thank heavens he'd dressed with more care than usual, but this wasn't how he'd envisioned the day. Yet... He frowned as he met the gazes of the people in the room. Perhaps it was as it should be with her father and his children here. "I think what we need in this moment is a story to dispel any hard feelings."

And it would give him much needed time to find the words to win her. As he peered at Julianna, his heart squeezed. By Jove, she was indeed as beautiful as John said. In the dress of robin's egg blue he'd seen a few times before, he would forever associate that color with summer and her. A blush raged on her pale cheeks, and though there was a sparkle in her sapphire eyes, they were also tinged with sadness.

But why?

Not knowing, he slowly rose into a standing position. "I'm not one for stories of romance or love, but Julianna adores everything related to the stars and the heavens, so I searched like a madman through my library this morning to find one she might like." He swallowed heavily to encourage moisture into his dry throat. "It's the maudlin and emotional saga of King Cepheus and Queen Cassiopeia and their never-ending celestial romance."

"Oh, Papa, what a lovely gesture," Emily whispered as she sank onto the sofa next to John in the space Arthur had vacated.

Yes, well, he hoped it would have the desired effect on Julianna.

He cleared his throat, clasped his hands behind his back, and then began his tale. "This story doesn't start out as a love story. According to Greek legend, Cassiopeia and her husband, King Cepheus, were the royalty that ruled ancient Ethiopia. King Cepheus enjoyed entertaining and wasn't a complicated fellow. He enjoyed fishing and hunting as well as drinking to excess." With too much pent-up energy, Arthur took to pacing. Regent found this pleasing, and thus trotted behind him. "On the other hand, Queen Cassiopeia was anything but easy going. She was self-absorbed and narcissistic, ruled her kingdom with a will of iron." He couldn't help but chuckle. "Of course, as is typical for these stories, she was also exceedingly beautiful with a high opinion of herself."

"Oh, she probably had a mirror in every room that she peered into," Emily said in some excitement. Already she'd been caught into the tale.

"It wouldn't surprise me," Arthur said with a grin. "The queen was well aware of her looks, and they were always uppermost in her mind. As such, she boasted of her beauty often, and encouraged everyone far and wide to acknowledge that fact."

"One would assume," Julianna said. "Since this is but a fiction."

"I wouldn't be so sure. Stories come from truth somewhere." Feeling more comfortable with his role as orator, Arthur winked. "In any event, Cassiopeia's ego grew until she became impossible to live with. No doubt that led to King Cepheus abandoning many of his duties at the royal court as well as spending much time with her. Despite her dreadful penchant for boasting, he loved his wife to distraction. Perhaps there is something, after all, in the old adage beauty is in the eye of the beholder."

John snickered. "You won't find me married to a woman like that."

Giggles came from both Emily and Julianna, but Arthur ignored them.

He continued to pace about the small space with the beagle on his heels. "One day, while Cassiopeia was walking along the seashore, trouble found her. Stupidly, she blurted out to Poseidon, the god of the sea, that she was more beautiful than his wife and all of his ten daughters."

Emily gasped. "Oh, no!"

"Indeed." Arthur rather enjoyed being a storyteller. His audience was enthralled. "Poseidon was a hot head and easily offended. And he was livid at such a slight. He called forth a giant sea monster from the depths of the sea and sent it to destroy Cassiopeia's kingdom."

"As well he should," John added in a horrible stage whisper to his sister.

"The queen deflected this horror by offering her daughter, Princess Andromeda, as sacrifice to the sea monster to pacify him and spare the kingdom. Because, of course, I'm convinced the gods and goddesses only had children for moments like this," Arthur couldn't help but adding. With a shrug, he continued. "But, as luck would have it the Greek hero Perseus rescued Andromeda and killed the giant sea monster, but that has no bearing on my story."

Julianna kept her gaze on his face, his lips, watched him with fascination and something else in her expression that sent heat through Arthur's person. *Dear God*, what he wouldn't give to have her alone right now!

After clearing his throat, he shoved the budding inappropriate thoughts from his mind. "Despite the bad blood she'd created between her and her daughter, Cassiopeia didn't learn her lesson. Seeking more attention, one morning, she shook her fist in the direction of Mount Olympus and screamed that she was more beautiful than Hera, Zeus' wife. Well, Hera possessed an ego that surpassed Cassiopeia's, and immediately her ire was stoked. Hera came down from Mount Olympus in a temper. She confronted Cassiopeia, quite violently I'd imagine. Hera asked Cassiopeia if she truly believed what she'd said. Of course, Cassiopeia was not intimidated, and she repeated the slight."

"This is why it's a horrible idea to have more than one beautiful woman in the same room," John interjected. "It won't end well."

Arthur snorted. "This verbal battle escalated. Hera conjured a rope and tied Cassiopeia to her throne. Then, in a fit of pique, she launched Cassiopeia, throne and all, so high into the sky that she was trapped in the stars, hanging nearly upside down. Hera wasn't done with her taunting, though. She said to Cassiopeia, 'Now you can show the world how beautiful you *think* you are for all eternity.' And she walked away, never looking back, which is why we, as mere mortals, can see Cassiopeia tied to that throne to this day."

Emily frowned. "Of course, this is a lovely story, Papa, but I don't understand why this is supposed to have romance in it."

"I'm coming to that part, poppet." He smiled at his daughter who was so much like Ellen. Yes, perhaps she *did* need Julianna's practical influence as she grew into adulthood. "King Cepheus came home after a day of chariot racing. When he arrived at the castle, his staff informed him of his wife's horrible fate. After peering into the heavens, grief took hold, and it was all he could think about. He was heartsick at the prospect of going through the rest of his life without his beloved, self-centered queen."

The irony of being frozen with guilt wasn't lost on him, which was one of the reasons Arthur had chosen this story.

"Cepheus called out to Zeus on Mount Olympus. He begged the god to send him up to the stars to be with his wife and share her celestial exile. As much as Zeus wanted to help, he was terrified of invoking Hera's wrath. Cepheus remained adamant. He wailed and cried in lament. Zeus took pity upon him. Without further comment, he flung the king to the stars, and Cepheus landed next to his wife. Despite their banishment, the love between them ignited. To this day, they cling to each other among the stars, more in love than ever."

Silence wrapped about the room at the conclusion of his tale. When he didn't gain the reaction he'd hoped for, Arthur sighed. He moved toward Julianna's position and peered down at her as she stared up at him. It was now or never. "What I'm trying, unsuccessfully, to say is that I don't want to wait until it's too late to be with the woman I love."

Gasps came from both Emily and Julianna while John gawked at the scene.

And still there were no words of love offered or a declaration from Julianna.

Wanting to put a bit of the theatric into it to match the story, Arthur kneeled on one knee. He scooped one of Julianna's hands into his. "We haven't known each other long, but that has no bearing in our romance. Sometimes two people just know they belong together." He searched her eyes for the answer he sought. "But over the course of these handful of days, everything I've come to know about you leads to more questions. I want to be everywhere you are. I need to have you by my side for the remainder of our lives. I wish to be with you when you meet every goal and plan you have, merely so that I can tell the world that you are mine and that I'm so proud of you." As her eyes welled with tears, he rushed onward. "Please, Julianna, please say you'll make me the happiest of men and marry me. Either after a long engagement or with a special license, it matters not as long as you're mine."

The silence in the cottage was deafening.

"I…" Slowly, she pulled her hand away. "The story you told was lovely, and I'm impressed you memorized it for me." Despair lined her expression. "And the speech you've given me just now was as romantic as any woman could ever hope for."

"But?" His stomach muscles clenched. Belatedly, he realized he'd never uttered a word of love to her. Already, he'd cocked this up.

She pressed her lips together. The delicate chords in her throat worked with a hard swallow. "The length of time that we've known each other is not what bothers me. I well know that love and romance can happen in the blink of an eye. And you are the best of all men, Arthur." With a shaking hand, she trailed her fingertips along the side of his face, fussed with a shock of hair that had fallen over his forehead. He trembled at the slight touch. "However, you are an earl and command a certain station in life that I cannot possibly match. Even if I were to accept your proposal and dress in fine clothes, I would still be a commoner, a country bumpkin with her head in the clouds. What do I know of your world?"

"But, I—"

"Hush, Ettesmere." Her eyes were sad even as she smiled at him. "You are also a father. I know nothing about being a mother. Along those lines, should you wish for a second family, I am too advanced in age to provide you that. And finally, by my own choice I had never given thought to marrying, for I've chased my own goals that will never align with anything the *beau monde* would consider proper." At the last second, she stifled a sob. "For those reasons, I must decline your proposal."

Both of his children gasped at the refusal. Then Emily bounded to her feet. "No! Miss Quill, you simply *must* marry Papa. I've never seen a couple more in love than the two of you."

"I've quite made up my mind, Lady Emily," Julianna said in a soft voice as she stared at the hands in her lap.

"Do something, Papa," his daughter implored with mild panic in her voice.

This cannot be happening. I'm going to lose her for this?

Well, not if he could help it. Never in his life had he come up to the mark until now. "Julianna, listen to me." Again, he took possession of her hand. "Yes, there are many things you can use as excuses that might keep us apart, but we shall face each challenge as it comes—together, because that is what a married couple does." When she didn't look at him, he put the fingers of his free hand beneath her chin and lifted her head until her watery gaze met his. "I don't give a fig what the *beau monde* will say about this match, but I *do* care about you. I had proper before. Now I want the adventure, I want to have the sheer joy that being with the woman who holds my heart brings." Acutely aware of his audience, he lowered his voice. Yes, this was very different than the last time he declared himself to a woman, but he wouldn't have it any other way. "The truth of the matter has never changed. I need you in my life because like that long ago king, I love you to distraction."

As Emily murmured a sound of possible encouragement and even Regent whined, Julianna stared at him with moisture-spiked lashes. "You do? But this whole time you've warred with yourself…"

"Yes, I know. I apologize for that; it's all behind me. I've finally made peace with my past. Last night, before we went out searching for your father, I came to terms with Ellen's death and my grief. I'll hold her memory in my heart, of course, but she was my past. *You* are my future. My North Star, guiding me when I'm lost, doing nothing except shining because that is what you've always done." Emotion thickened his voice, made his throat, his heart, ache. "Please say you'll marry me. Now that I've come back into the light, I'd like a companion with whom to find happiness again."

"Oh Arthur." Tears fell to her cheeks. For long moments, she stared at him, and then the sadness in her eyes changed to joy. In that moment, he knew he'd won, and he nearly wept from the relief of it. "How can I say no after that?" She leaned forward, held his head between her palms as she met his gaze. "I love you, Arthur. There is no great explanation of why or when it happened. It just did. And I will only be your guiding light if you'll do the same for me. No doubt I'll need that since you intend to thrust me into society."

In silence, he nodded while his pulse hammered hard through his veins.

"And you'll be there in defense if rumors fly?"

"Of course."

"Then yes, I will marry you and gladly, for I cannot contemplate a life without you in it."

"Oh, thank God." Relief poured through him, enough to make him dizzy with it. As Emily and John whooped with victory, Arthur dug the ring out of his waistcoat pocket. Without comment, he slipped the bauble onto the fourth finger of her left hand. "I cannot wait until you're my countess."

With a smile that could rival the stars, Julianna put her lips to his ear and whispered, "And I cannot wait to couple with you in a proper bed, Ettesmere. As your wife."

Bloody hell. Perhaps there was something to be said for finding love later in life. Both parties knew exactly what they wanted. He chuckled even as heat swept through his person and his member twitched to life. As his children surged forward, he groaned. "Now that this is settled, please, John, help me off the floor. My age is catching up to me and my joints don't work as they ought."

Laughter from Mr. Quill accompanied that feat. "Wait until

you're my age, Your Lordship. It doesn't get any better."

Everyone shared another chuckle. Emily gently moved Arthur out of the way so she could hug Julianna.

"I'm so delighted you'll marry Papa. We're going to have such fun together!"

Julianna grinned. "So I suspect."

Then it was John's turn to hug her. "Please don't refer to me as a matchmaker, Miss Quill. I do have a reputation around Town."

She giggled as she released him. "Your secret is safe."

John shook Arthur's hand. "Good show, old chap. I'm going to the house to share the good news. I imagine Aunt Sophia and Mama are anxiously awaiting word."

"No doubt they are." He would forgive his meddling children everything, for he'd won Julianna.

Emily bussed his cheek. "I'm going to refresh the teapot." She moved toward Mr. Quill's chair. "Come help me, Mr. Quill. I want to hear more stories about my father when he was a youth." She assisted him out of his chair and together they moved into the kitchen beyond.

Finally alone, Arthur tugged Julianna into his arms. He kissed her, treated her to gentle kisses borne from love and gratitude. When he pulled away, they were both breathless and grinning like nodcocks. "I should have known the answer to my ennui would be in the stars, especially after that first evening with you."

"Indeed," she whispered and claimed his lips in a kiss of her own. "I have always found a certain comfort in the midnight heavens, and if you contemplate them long enough, you'll find exactly what you're seeking."

"Thank God for that." Then he set out to kiss his bride-to-be senseless regardless if they'd soon be found out.

Yes, the past should remain in its place, but the key to stepping into the future was to never forget those who went before as long as one didn't let themselves be trapped in that grief. For there was much life yet to live if only one opened their eyes to all of it.

EPILOGUE

Six months later

"**I** HAVE IT!"

Arthur heard the hail from inside the coach where he waited for her to join him from the curb of the Astronomical Society of London. Julianna had practically haunted those vaulted halls every other day since she'd applied. If they didn't hurry, they'd arrive late to the Christmas Eve event. Yet, excitement buzzed at the base of his spine as he watched his wife approach. This was the news they'd been waiting on for months. The sound of her running footsteps echoed off the pavement as she came closer in a flurry of crimson silk and a black redingote.

With a grin at the carriage driver, Julianna accepted his assistance into the closed coach with a letter clutched tight in her fist. "It's here, Arthur."

"And?" They'd been married for five months, and it had been as glorious having her to wife as he'd imagined. Many changes had occurred since that summer's day when he'd finally proposed.

The driver put up the steps and then closed the door. Seconds later, the equipage rocked as he took his seat.

"They've agreed." She perched on the bench opposite Arthur's and handed him the letter. The ivory envelope sailed unheeded to the floor. "The Astronomical Society of London has agreed with my findings. They have given me provisional acceptance into the society because of my discovery of the comet." Her eyes shown with excitement.

"Excellent news." He set the letter on the squabbed bench next to him, for he'd much rather hear the rest from her. Later, he could read the missive for proof. "And?"

"They've allowed me to name the comet." A pretty blush stained her cheeks, and as her lips curved into a smile, he stared at her mouth. "I've decided on Comet Quill. I thought Ned sounded too pedestrian, as this has a nice ring to it."

"Your brother would adore that." Arthur was nearly beside himself with joy. "I'm so damned proud of you, sweeting."

"Thank you." She let out a whoop of joy that had him—as well as the driver—chuckling. "This is the greatest moment of my life." Then she gasped. "With the exception of marrying you, of course."

"Of course. But you're entitled to like this one better." He didn't care. She was his, and truly, he was merely along for the ride, going wherever she dictated.

Flushed with her success, she grinned. The black ostrich feather that had been placed in her upswept hair quivered with her excitement. "I never thought this day would come. I've worked so hard for it, and now it's finally here."

"I knew it would all along."

She dug her brother's pocket watch from her reticule, kissed the surface before putting it back and throwing the accessory to the bench beside her. "Finally, Ned's initial work and discovery has been acknowledged, and I've been accepted into the society." Her eyes shone. "Perhaps now the whole of London will be on notice that women are just as intelligent and as capable as men in the sciences."

"They will if they know what's good for them." Oh, his wife would continue to set London on its ear, and he couldn't be more pleased with that. "They won't know what to do with you.

Perhaps you'll set them straight."

"Do hush, Ettesmere." But she grinned and it was decidedly wicked and sent tiny fires into his blood.

He cleared his throat. "We need to hurry if we're to arrive at Ettesmere House in time for Mother's Christmas Eve dinner. She has some sort of musical entertainment planned for this evening, if I recall. I'd like for you to announce your good news tonight if you don't mind."

"I do not." She briefly touched her bottom lip with the tip of her tongue, and the way she looked at him had his member hardening. "Um, darling, would it seem incredibly improper if we arrived a bit late?"

"I suppose not. Mother does have other guests in attendance. She won't miss us right away." He arched an eyebrow. "What did you have in mind?" Since they married, Julianna had continued to lead him on a merry chase, and he was helpless to resist. She'd breathed new life into him, metaphorically speaking, had shown him what a second chance with love could mean to a man of advancing year.

"Hmm." Julianna came across the narrow aisle to join him on his bench. She straddled his lap in a cloud of skirting. The faint scent of apricots and vanilla wafted to his nose. In a barely audible whisper, she said, "Something I've always been curious about." She put her lips to his ear, lightly bit the lobe and chuckled when he groaned. "Intercourse while in a moving carriage."

"I think that can be arranged," he replied in the same soft voice as he fumbled at the clasp on her cloak. Would she ever cease to prove a delightful companion? Holding her gaze as the garment fell away, he rapped on the ceiling. "Drive through Hyde Park before we return to Ettesmere House, Farnsworth. I'm rather in the mood to enjoy Town for a bit as a celebration."

"Whatever you say, m'lord."

Julianna grinned as she removed his top hat and carefully set it on the bench beside them. "You've become decidedly improper since marrying me. I never thought I'd be such a bad influence."

"Such gammon. I've always had it in me; I merely needed someone to draw it out." Then he slipped his arms about his wife and set out to kiss her senseless. After all, this *was* his first Christmas with Julianna, and it should be a memorable one. And what was better for that than claiming her body minutes before they'd arrive at a dinner his mother hosted?

Improper indeed.

Grief and memories would always stay with him, but he'd learned during that memorable summer not to let them hold him prisoner. Never was he more grateful for deciding to live again, and though Julianna didn't know it, he wished on the North Star every night that she would remain in his for a long time.

Everything else was rather gilding on a lily.

The End

About the Author

Sandra Sookoo is a *USA Today* bestselling author who firmly believes every person deserves acceptance and a happy ending. Most days you can find her creating scandal and mischief in the Regency-era, serendipity and happenstance in Victorian America or snarky, sweet humor in the contemporary world. Most recently she's moved into infusing her books with mystery and intrigue. Reading is a lot like eating fine chocolates—you can't just have one. Good thing books don't have calories!

When she's not wearing out computer keyboards, Sandra spends time with her real-life Prince Charming in central Indiana where she's been known to goof off and make moments count because the key to life is laughter. A Disney fan since the age of ten, when her soul gets bogged down and her imagination flags, a trip to Walt Disney World is in order. Nothing fuels her dreams more than the land of eternal happy endings, hope and love stories.

Stay in Touch

Sign up for Sandra's bi-monthly newsletter and you'll be given exclusive excerpts, cover reveals before the general public as well as opportunities to enter contests you won't find anywhere else.

Just send an email to sandrasookoo@yahoo.com with SUB-SCRIBE in the subject line.

Or follow / friend her on social media:
Facebook: facebook.com / sandra.sookoo
Facebook Author Page: facebook.com / sandrasookooauthor
Pinterest: pinterest.com / sandrasookoo
Instagram: instagram.com / sandrasookoo
BookBub Page: bookbub.com / authors / sandra-sookoo

Lightning Source UK Ltd.
Milton Keynes UK
UKHW020646230622
404860UK00008B/550